Diary of a

Married

Call Girl

Also by Tracy Quan
Diary of a Manhattan Call Girl

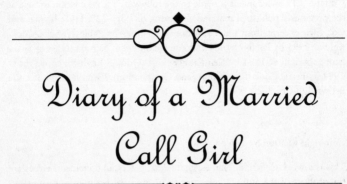

Diary of a Married Call Girl

A Nancy Chan Novel

TRACY QUAN

THREE RIVERS PRESS • NEW YORK

Grateful acknowledgment is made to the following for permission to reprint the previously published material appearing on page 229: **Little Brown and Co., Inc.**: excerpt from *Odes to Common Things* by Pablo Neruda. Copyright © 1994 by Pablo Neruda and Fundacion Pablo Neruda (Odes in Spanish); copyright © 1994 by Ken Krabbenhoft (Odes in English); copyright © 1994 by Ferris Cook (Illustrations and Compilation). By permission of Little Brown and Co., Inc.

Published in the United States by Three Rivers Press, an imprint of the Crown Publishing Group, a division of Random House, Inc., New York.
www.crownpublishing.com

Three Rivers Press and the Tugboat design are registered trademarks of Random House, Inc.

Library of Congress Cataloging-in-Publication Data
Quan, Tracy.
    Diary of a married call girl: a Nancy Chan novel/Tracy Quan. —1st ed.
    1. Manhattan (New York, N.Y.)—Fiction. 2. Married women—Fiction.
3. Prostitutes—Fiction. 4. Bankers—Fiction. I. Title.
    PS3617.U36D534 2005
    813'.6—dc22   2005006300

ISBN 1-4000-5354-4

Printed in the United States of America

Design by Nora Rosansky

10 9 8 7 6 5 4 3 2 1

First Edition

For Paulo Henrique Longo

Acknowledgments

I am deeply grateful to Charles Peck, a rigorous editor, wary first reader, and sharp-witted co-conspirator. His contributions are integral to the telling of this tale.

Caroline Sincerbeaux, my editor at Crown, has been relentless, thorough, and wonderfully supportive. Doug Pepper will always be Nancy Chan's Canadian godfather. Whitney Cookman, Andrea Peabbles, Selina Cicogna, Jennifer Hunt, Toisan Craigg, Juleyka Lantigua, Genoveva Llosa, Cathy Paine, Adrienne Phillips, Stephen Lee, Jason Gordon, Melissa Kaplan, Alex Lencicki, and Susan Schwartzman, thank you for making Nancy feel welcome in so many places.

My affectionate thanks to Will Crutchfield.

Katinka Matson, John Brockman, Louise Aibel, and Russell Weinberger of Brockman Inc; Peter Benedek, Craig Losben, and Howard Sanders at United Talent Agency; Dana Friedman and Vanessa Borcherding of Dragonfly Technologies: thank you for being in my corner. A special note of thanks to the New York Society Library and to Mark Piel.

Mike Godwin, Xaviera Hollander, James Wolcott, Ralph Martin, Bob Fogelnest, Juhu Thukral, Carole Murray, Andrew Sorfleet, Steve Richardson-Ross, Melodie Cantor, Robert Johnson at Maggie's in Toronto, Neke Carson, Lisa Napoli, Peter Hirshberg, Tim Noonan, Reagan Louie, Larissa MacFarquhar, Gerard S., David Sterry, Dana Tierney, Darren Star, Mari Aldin, Eugenia Zukerman, Gretchen Soderlund, Pico Iyer, Amy Kao, Howard Altman, Robyn Few, Robin Head, Dov Rueff, Rebecca Kaye,

Desmond Mervyn, Siena Wilcock, Lily, Lovemuffin, Adam J., Nomi Prins, Thessy Mehrain, John Dizard, Harley Spec, Joe Lavezzo, and Paul Shields; Kate Larkin, Jo Weldon, Veronica Vera, and Melissa Hope; Frances, David Andrew, Adrian, Andrea Piccolo, and Ronnie Lacerda: thank you for your support. For helpful advice. And for tickling my imagination.

To plot alone is to conspire with someone you trust.

—Simon Hoggart

Contents

Diary of a

Married

Call Girl

Roundheels and Caballeros

Dear Diary,

My two best friends are no longer at war: They invited *me* to brunch on Sunday. Do I want this unlikely alliance to succeed? Let's just say I'm ambivalent.

Yesterday, I was late for the brunch at Quatorze—which I had to embroider into a birthday celebration when my husband started asking too many questions about my day. Sliding into a banquette, I looked around furtively. Jasmine, sitting next to me, barely noticed my arrival.

"You can't fuck him on the first date!" she was telling Allison. "You're becoming a public figure!"

Across the table, Allie was sipping a mimosa.

"What do you mean, 'a public figure'? I'm just me," she protested.

"He met you at that crazy conference!"

"That was a panel discussion. For Lucho's course. Re-Writing the Extra-Colonial Body. He's fostering a dialogue with sex workers! And he wants to discuss his plans for a documentary. He was too shy to introduce himself at the harm-reduction conference. So we didn't really meet till last week. Tuesday will be our first chance to—"

"Discussion, conference. To him, you're a public figure. This isn't like turning a trick! This guy's a fan. Fuck him right away, and you'll destroy his illusions. Listen, those panties stay on if we have to glue them on." Jasmine paused. "You wouldn't want to disappoint a fan . . . would you?"

Amazing. Jasmine has gone from blanket rejection of Allison's "sex worker activism" to micromanaging all the details now that Allie's a budding spokesperson.

Allie blushed. "A fan? I never thought of it that way! But"— she began to looked worried—"I don't want Lucho to have illusions. I want him to really know me."

"For god's sake, he knows too much about you as it is. Now look at Nancy. I'll bet she didn't fuck Matt on the first date."

"Please," I warned Jasmine. "I am so not in the mood to dissect Matt!"

"What's wrong?" Allison was glad to change the subject from her latest crush to my new husband. "Is everything okay? With you and Matt?"

"Matt's fine," I said tersely. "I'd much rather hear about your professor friend. You met him at . . . a harm-reduction conference?"

Should I tell Allison about the birthday ruse?

Maybe not. There are things your single girlfriends just don't understand. Especially a friend like Allie, who seems to be grooming the man she just met for an illusion-free romance. Which sounds as appealing to me as a sugar-free meringue.

"When you became a spokesman," Jasmine told Allie. "You gave up your right to sleep with guys on the first date."

"I—what are you talking about?"

"He knows you're a working girl! If he doesn't, you can sleep with him anytime you want. Because he won't know he's getting free sex from a hooker! But he knows. And you're not just *any* working girl. You've got a reputation to maintain."

"A reputation. This isn't the 1950s," Allie objected.

"No kidding! If you sleep with him right away, he can go on Craig's List. Or yap about it on his website! You have to find out more about his past before you fuck him. And don't tell him anything about yours."

The waiter appeared at our booth. Jasmine ordered a martini and I, with genuine remorse, a businesslike Evian.

"No kir royale?" he asked.

"Not today," I said. "Medication," I added, as both girls were giving me owlish looks. "I have to leave early," I explained, when the waiter had drifted away. "Something at the Waldorf."

Alcohol and work don't mix. Or shouldn't.

Jasmine eyed my pale blue yoga pants with curiosity. Then my matching hoodie and my gnomish tote bag, larger than usual, chosen for its excellent zipper. The last thing you want, when carrying lots of dildos and a pair of fuzz-lined manacles (not to mention a serious change of shoes, underclothes, and a Donna Karan suit) is a clever bag with nifty magnets, Velcro flaps, or gimmicky pockets. A laptop case—my usual cover for a hotel call—is way too small for all this gear. And you don't want the zipper to jam!

"Smart move," Jasmine said, staring down at my new suede sneakers.

Faux sloppy is a look I've been cultivating since my marriage began. It's pulled together but says "no special plans." The goal here is to look vague, not mysterious.

Allison, who never has to think about married-girl mufti, was perturbed.

"It's a long story," I sighed. "Charmaine's using the apartment, so I have to change in the hotel bathroom!"

Or maybe here? But no, this restaurant's too intimate for that sort of thing. Why did I ever go in on this deal with Charmaine? *A married hooker has to downsize*—but I couldn't bear to part with my rent-stabilized lease. That would be like discarding your oldest friend. Charmaine is mostly a boon but sometimes I feel like my small sunny 1BR on East Seventy-ninth is being slowly colonized by a stranger whose ways I barely understand.

"You'll manage," Jasmine said. "Nancy always manages," she added, casting a meaningful look at Allie, who was gazing pensively into the distance.

"Nancy didn't sleep with Matt because she didn't know if she wanted to!" Allie began. "But Lucho and I are different. Besides, this doesn't feel like a *real* first date. We exchanged *at least* a hundred e-mails before I spoke at his class. Not *that* kind of e-mail," she added. "I had no idea who Lucho was. Someone gave him my e-mail address. *Then* I got something from his department, inviting me to speak on the panel. I know he didn't ask me out until *after* the panel but—don't you think this is more like a *third* date? Or even a fifth? We spent two hours IM-ing about the problems in his mother's homeland. His e-mails are totally articulate! And sensitive! And he wants me to be part of this documentary. That's the *real* reason for our lunch."

Jasmine was looking more Solomonic than usual in a subdued argyle V-neck. She pulled her dark hair behind her ears, and the eighteen-carat glow of her Bulgari knockoffs seemed to compete with her highlights.

"We'll make allowances for technology," she said. "Taking the obsessive e-mails into account, so long as you're not sending each other thinly disguised porn, you might be able to treat this like a *second* date. Hooking is like backgammon. Dating and marriage are like chess. This guy is a *knight*. Or, if you handle this right, a rook! Your strategy, as queen, is 'be enigmatic.' Don't be making these extravagant moves. At this point in the game, you and Lucho—"

Jasmine was cut off by a bouncy version of "Hungarian Dance #5," which caused Allison to fiddle nervously with her Prada bowling bag.

"Hello?" Allie whispered into the phone. "It's hard to talk here!" Extricating herself from the chess tutorial, she simpered incoherently. As I watched Allison heading for the front door, a tiny red cell phone pressed against her long blond hair, I realized she was thinner than usual in a pair of striped pants I've never seen before.

"Is this love? Or lipo?" I asked Jasmine. "She must have lost ten pounds! In less than *two weeks*."

"It's the Internet. How can you keep your pants on for a third date if you're falling in love before the first? Very dangerous. But great for your metabolism. I think she burns a pound of fat every time she gets an e-mail from this guy. Her hips are disappearing. That—or she's spiking her pomegranate juice with cocaine. Don't worry," Jasmine added, reading my mind, "better to be a size six, happily married to a banker, than a frazzled four throwing yourself at some nutty-sounding professor!"

Is hooking really like backgammon? What if it's *all* chess? And maybe our johns—so numerous yet essential—are the pawns? If, as Jasmine says, a devoted e-mailer is a knight with the ability to evolve into a castle, what is Matt? A king?

Allison's approach to the business reminds me more of *bingo*. As for Jasmine, she's good at backgammon and did well at chess in high school. But how much does she know about dating? Or marriage—never having lived with any man that I know of? Jasmine thinks real dating is a liability, cutting into the time she devotes to meeting her self-imposed quota of clients.

In fact, Jasmine doesn't feel right going out on a real date unless she tells herself that she's pretending to litehook. But here's the thing about being a litehook: you have to enjoy being "rescued" financially by a man. Even if he's only saving you from your Con Ed bills, you must feel victorious and grateful. This doesn't come naturally to Jasmine. It doesn't even come to her *un*naturally. That's why she'll never pass for a damsel in distress. Despite what Jasmine thinks, she can't fake being an amateur hooker.

Allison returned, just as the food was arriving. Jasmine had ordered her usual—"bacon chicory salad, hold the croutons"—followed by a dozen Fanny Bay oysters. With a righteous Atkins-powered smirk, she announced: "Looks like I'm the only chick at this table who knows how to order a real meal."

Picking at her salad, Allie giggled nervously. "I can't help it if I'm not hungry!"

Jasmine's got a point. Falling in love and sneaking around are the two most effective appetite suppressants known to woman. But Allie gets a metabolic boost—meriting low-slung pants—while I merely curb my intake to avoid discomfort.

On Seventy-ninth and Second, available taxis were so plentiful that I took it as a happy omen. What have I done to deserve such good fortune? Something in a former life, I'm thinking. Sitting in the back seat of a yellow SUV, I began my transformation, tucking my hair into a ponytail and slipping it beneath the collar of my hood. As we approached the Waldorf, I donned my sunglasses.

After years of coming here on a frequent basis, I'm still thrown off balance when I try to use the public areas. I'm hardwired to head straight for the elevator, keeping the time downstairs to a bare minimum. The Waldorf's not the worst offender when it comes to fanatical security but neither is it one of those cozy new boutique hotels where a single woman might be taken for a visiting dot-commer. At the Waldorf, you remember that once upon a time all unescorted females were inherently suspect. You can feel the ancient history when you pass through those revolving doors, and I'm always on the lookout for a snoopy security guard because, in fact, the ancient history is still with us.

My heart was beating a little too fast as I scanned the lobby for a ladies' room. In the privacy of my self-contained cubicle, I changed into high heels and stockings. Despite the luxury of my own sink and a good mirror, I felt a little too naked.

Jasmine's commentary—a happily married six, a frazzled size four—echoed in my head. Marriage *has* caused a few pounds to visit my hips, but it's nothing I can't reconfigure, damn it. I can get away with some fluctuation without alienating my regulars, but I might be approaching the limit.

As I hooked a smooth black garter belt around my waist, I felt like a superhero sprouting magical powers. In my high-heeled slingbacks and push-up bra, I was suddenly sleek yet curvy and my suit had not wrinkled: the finishing touch. I loosened my ponytail and played with my hair, stuffed my clothes into the tote, and hid my wedding ring in a change purse. Nobody would guess that the pastel-hued slacker in sneakers and sunglasses had just morphed into a womanly vision in crisp black-and-white houndstooth, hair falling around her shoulders, wearing just enough eye makeup. It occurred to me that lipstick would change my appearance even more. But lip color at three in the afternoon? Too . . . professional.

I took out my *Zagat*—essential camouflage when posing as an out-of-town guest—and checked the clock on my cell phone. Transformation accomplished. In less than ten minutes. I'm definitely getting better at this!

Then, spotting a run in my left stocking, I felt a pang of remorse. I forgot to bring spares! Suddenly I felt less like a superhero and more like a refugee, yearning bitterly for the lost comforts of home. Not to mention my supply of stockings. It is maddening to have all the right stuff when it's totally out of reach.

I've been turning tricks since my teens. Never, until I married an investment banker in my thirties, was I reduced to changing my underwear and brushing my teeth in a public bathroom.

Is this what "going straight" is really about?

In the lobby, a tall man with a walkie-talkie was dangerously close to the elevators. Adopting a matronly scowl, I walked right by, hoping the ladder in my stocking was not reaching my knee. On the twenty-fifth floor, I glanced around quickly to make sure I wasn't being followed. Not until I was in the room, with the door securely bolted, did I feel truly safe.

Trisha's weekend regular was put out by my solo arrival but did his best to couch things in submissive terms.

"Thank you for coming, Mistress." He paused and looked

around. "Mistress Thalia was planning to arrive at two-thirty. Would you like me to wait for her?"

Colin was wearing gold-rimmed glasses, silk boxer shorts, and nothing else. Despite a round, childlike face, he looked rather virile. It was that salt-and-pepper chest hair, much thicker than the hair on his head. I could feel steam from the shower seeping out of the bathroom.

"Of course," I said sharply. "Thalia is definitely on her way."

"May I offer you a drink, Mistress . . . ?"

"Sabrina," I reminded him. "You may."

I nodded at a row of bottles on the dresser. Five bottles of mineral water! This guy is more than prepared.

"Some coffee or soda perhaps?"

"Just the water," I replied.

I could hear my cell phone chiming in my pocket. "Mistress Thalia" stuck in traffic, no doubt.

"It's me! I've been trying to get some privacy so I can call. What a disaster! You're gonna kill me! Let me talk to him, then I'll talk to you."

What? Why didn't she talk to me first? I was doing my best to look imperious while feeling somewhat unnerved when I summoned Colin to the phone.

"Yes. Yes, I will," I heard him saying in that flat monotone that slaves like to use. "Yes, Mistress. Of course, Mistress. No, I promise. One moment, Mistress. Right away."

Slinking off to the bathroom, he looked both dejected and turned on.

Trisha was apologetic and panicky. "I told him to wait in the bathroom. My daughter's playdate was canceled! At the very last minute! Do you have a ball gag?"

"Um, no."

"You'll have to improvise. Put some of your underwear in his mouth. Okay? Later on. Don't do it right away."

"What time can you get here? He's in the bathroom."

"I CAN'T. I have simply got to stay and deal. I told him this was my secret plan to test his loyalty. He doesn't come out until you tell him."

"Oh?"

"Yes." Trisha was recovering some of her composure. "If he can please you, he's allowed to see us together next time. But he has to follow all my instructions—and yours—in my absence. You report back to me and give him, like, a grade. Then I decide if he deserves—"

"I get the idea." But I was also getting irritated. I've never been good at domination—and what about the ball gag? Colin's used to all this fancy equipment, and I brought only a few props to supplement Trisha's arsenal. "Do you think it's *safe* to stuff my underpants in his mouth?"

"Oh, please. It's fine. Just use your common sense. If he starts choking, you pull them out. But he won't."

"Are you sure you can't just come later? Take over when I leave?"

"No! You don't understand! I can't find a babysitter."

"But I can't do it all myself! You *promised*."

"What do you mean?" She paused. "Oh. Just drink a lot of water! What's the big deal?"

This was hardly the moment to be discussing why a golden shower's a big deal to me and not to her. How do you explain your spic-and-span prohibitions without making it sound like you're judging the other girl as unsavory? It's a conversation no sensible hooker gets into. I took a deep breath and gazed at the bottled water on the dresser. People with kids seem to be a lot less squeamish about some things.

"Look, I told you upfront!" I said, moving toward the window.

I didn't want Colin to overhear. Our lack of cohesion must be finessed. Like two parents dealing with a wayward child, Mistresses Thalia and Sabrina must present a united front.

"I'm sorry! My day's been a disaster! I'll work something out on the cut if you want. I have to go but—call if you have to. I'm alone this weekend."

How can the mother of a five-year-old *sans* babysitter say she's "alone"? I guess she means her husband's out of town so the coast is clear for phone calls. I've never asked Trisha what he does but he travels a lot more than Matt—and she, in turn, is never inquisitive about *my* husband.

Standing in front of the bathroom door, I wondered if my normal instinct—a quiet knock—would be too submissive a gesture. What should I say? I had really been expecting to play second fiddle to Mistress Thalia. *You can come out now* sounds kind of lame! More like a sidekick than a sole proprietress.

In a cold dignified voice, I advised Colin to stay on his hands and knees.

"Yes, Mistress."

"Is the door unlocked?"

"Yes, Mistress."

Do they say this just to get on your nerves?

"Reach up and open it with your right hand. I will be waiting in the bedroom."

Colin crept out of the bathroom hardly daring to look up. His eyes were trained on the carpet as he crawled toward my feet. Suddenly, I had a brainstorm.

"You will adjust my garters."

"Yes, Mistress," he paused, ". . . Sabrina. You have beautiful legs," he added shyly.

"I know. Come here. Start with my back garter." I turned around slightly so he could reach it. I couldn't let on how good it felt to hear about my legs when I'm starting to angst about my weight. "Slowly. Not like that. You have to loosen it first, then pull—very softly." I turned again. "Now the front." I could see a bulge in Colin's shorts. "Good. Now the right garter. Carefully." I leapt back. "You clumsy idiot! You ripped my stocking!"

"I'm sorry, Mistress! I didn't meant to!"

"This will be taken into account," I told him. "Mistress Thalia will not be pleased."

"Yes, Mistress. Will you allow me to make it up to you?"

"We'll see."

Stumped for a response, I decided to go the implacable route.

"Go to my bag and unzip it. Slowly."

I ordered him to remove a few instruments. Unfortunately, Mistress Thalia wasn't here to wield her whip, but I did have a small black leather paddle.

"Come here," I told him. "Not like that. Stay on your knees. Put the paddle between your teeth. Hold it between your teeth and don't drop it. Do you understand?"

He nodded, and I ordered him to crawl slowly toward the bed. Removing the paddle from his clenched teeth, I told him to rest his head against the bedspread and pull down his silk shorts.

"Slowly!"

I needed to prolong our session because, after all, I was trying to make up for Trisha's absence. Snapping the leather cuffs around his wrists, I peeked at his erection, then walked over to the clock radio while he enjoyed a moment of suspense. I hunted around for WQXR.

"Thank you," he said.

We both know that a genteel-sounding concerto can muffle a telltale spanking. He stays here often and needs to be careful. Was Colin's "thank you" acknowledging my thoughtful discretion? Or was he just praying for a nice loud whack?

I was so nervous and irate—about Charmaine hijacking my apartment, about the lobby bathroom and my ripped stocking, Trisha standing me up—that I obliged him with a *very* harsh smack. So harsh that my wrist felt it. I had to sit down for a moment and order him to worship my feet with his mouth. After a few minutes, I rose, giving him a gentle kick.

"If you're very good for the rest of the afternoon, I'll recommend a golden shower as your reward," I told him.

The toe of my shoe caressed his groin.

"I was hoping . . ."

I leaned over and silenced him by inserting my crumpled thong panties in his mouth.

"Mistress Thalia and I will discuss it. After I leave. And you will be punished or rewarded on our next visit. It all depends on Thalia's verdict."

The skin on his cock was firm and very pink. When I brushed the toe of my shoe against his erection, he flinched. Colin was closer to coming than I had realized. I withdrew my toe by tracing a line down his thigh, carefully eyeing the clock to make sure he wasn't being rushed. Trisha, the absentee dominatrix, was very specific about his time allotment. I walked over to the chair and picked up the paddle.

His wrists were still bound together behind his back, encased in the fuzz-lined leather. I was tempted to reach down and finish him with my hand. But no, that would knock me right off the bitch-goddess pedestal. Instead, I removed the manacles.

"You may place your hands in front." It was a routine he'd been through before. "Two inches apart, no more and no less."

I refastened the manacles, then picked up the paddle and used it to caress the back of each thigh. Remembering the impact to my wrist, I tapped his skin lightly. His hands were playing near his erection, getting closer. When I began to smack his buttocks, the panties fell out of his mouth. He grabbed his cock as best he could and came on the carpet.

"I'll clean that up," he said meekly. "If you take these off."

I brought my phone into the bathroom. Charmaine wasn't answering the landline or cell. But the deal we struck at noon was very clear: at five PM, I return to the apartment, stash my work toys and clothes, change back into what I was wearing when I last saw my husband, and fly so she can prepare for her six-thirty. We've had a few close shaves, but Charmaine has always been prompt about answering the phone.

And this time, I really needed to get back into my apartment. The laddered stocking was a serious liability. Changing in the lobby bathroom again would be pushing my luck. If noticed, I'd be earmarked for future visits and singled out by security. But putting on your sneakers in the hotel room is just out of the question.

Fortunately, dommes are supposed to be aloof, not warm and friendly like normal hookers, so I didn't have to overcompensate—much—for my disturbed attitude.

In the elevator, I was having mixed feelings about the session. It's exciting to rise to the challenge of being something you're not, but domination is a chore. I never feel convincing and it's

not really what I do. I hate having to worry ab[...]
slave is happy while pretending not to give a dam[...]

Avoiding the Park Avenue entrance—where the [...]
vie for taxis—I waved anxiously at a cab on Fiftie[...]
in, still clutching my cell phone optimistically. But when it rang, it
was not Charmaine.

Why, when somebody owes you a phone call, do you get
called by the one person in your life whose call must be dodged?
I watched my husband's cell phone number flashing on my display screen and waited for him to go into voice mail.

"I've changed my mind," I told the cab driver. "Can you take
me to Starbucks on Seventy-fifth and First?"

Nursing a small decaf and a large bottle of water, I dialed
Charmaine obsessively. What was she doing? Trying to squeeze
in a quickie before her six-thirty? In voice mail, I could hear Matt
urging me to meet him at the Gap. "Hey, babe. If you get this by
six, come on over, you can help me pick out some underwear."
God, what part of the city is he in? Matt has a tendency to treat
his own whereabouts as an afterthought. "I'm almost there.
Oh . . . hey, it's the one at Citicorp."

I *should* be the kind of wife who can turn a trick at three PM
and help her man decide between boxers and briefs a few hours
later without raising a hint of suspicion. So why is Charmaine
screwing this up for me? It's almost five-thirty and I want to be
there for him!

I left a tense message for Jasmine, another for Allie. Among
the blue-jeaned, stroller-pushing couples, I felt ridiculously overdressed. I was in the right place in the wrong outfit, dying to look
like a pseudo-slacker again.

Suddenly my cell phone was chiming, flashing "Private."
That's either Jasmine calling from anywhere—she's a fanatic

out that—or Charmaine, calling from the landline. I've got everybody's relationship to Caller ID completely mapped.

Or so I thought.

"Nancy!" said a female voice. "How and where *are* you?"

"Where—?" I couldn't believe it. My sister-in-law never calls from a blocked number—and she had twins two weeks ago! Isn't she better off at home? Recovering?

"Gotcha!" said Elspeth. "How's it going?"

"Where are *you*?" I asked back.

"Oh, I'm leaving Karen's baby shower."

I froze. Her friend, Karen, lives eight blocks from here.

"I have an appointment with this amazing cake designer. Her birthday cakes are gorgeous! And so original! She designed one for the mayor's son—listen, is it true you're allergic to chocolate? Did Matt tell you I'm planning a surprise dinner party for Jason?"

Who knew that there was such a thing as postpartum *mania*. Elspeth, talking at breakneck speed, was hard to keep up with.

"Ummm. Not yet," I mumbled nervously. "How many guests?"

How can she be planning a dinner bash for her husband when she just started nursing twins?

"Twenty *max*. My brother says you never eat chocolate. Well, it's Jason's birthday, not yours, but still! I wanted to ask. Should we go for the praline? Or the genoise? Or maybe—do you want to come with me? Meet me at her loft. I need some female input. And you need to check out these cakes!"

"I can't! I'm in a cab—I'll call you right back!"

A man at the next table looked up from his laptop and gave me a long thoughtful stare. I pretended not to notice and called Charmaine again. As her voice mail began to chatter, another call was coming in—Matt, causing a twinge of guilt as I imagined him pacing the floor of the Gap, confounded by too many choices. I was praying that Elspeth wouldn't call *him* in the next few.

I took another swig of bottled water and fumed. Okay, Plan B: shall I duck into the bathroom here and change? What the hell. Take a cab to Allison's and leave my tote bag with her doorman. Then meet my husband at Citicorp in my vague, woman-without-a-plan costume.

As I got up, drawing more stares from the laptop user, my phone chimed. When I saw Charmaine's long-awaited phone number, I wanted to scream with gratitude.

"I thought he would never come," she whispered. "Can you get here soon? He's dressing."

The apartment was dim when I let myself in, the door to the bathroom wide open. Charmaine was standing in front of the sink in a pair of lace bicycle-shorts. Her wavy hair was piled high, held in place with a plastic clip. I know the look well: she was wiping her shoulder carefully with a damp cloth, dabbing her neck and cleavage.

"He came on my chest but he took for freaking *ever*. And he kept losing his hard-on." She frowned at herself in the mirror, grabbed another washcloth, and patted her hair. "I guess I should be grateful! He could be one of those young guys who fucks for an hour and stays hard the whole time. . . . I know things have been crazy but I *had* to see some extra people before my trip to Florida." She paused, knowing full well that I won't mind having the place to myself while she's gone. "I picked up two boxes of Trojan Extra Large. They're in my closet."

As the cab sped down York Avenue, I closed my eyes and waited for Matt to answer his cell phone.

"So I have it narrowed down," he said. "Message in a bottle? Dalmatians? Or sliced fruit?"

Matt was still at the Gap.

"What . . . kind of fruit?" I inquired, trying not to express too much emotion.

"Huh. They look like oranges but they're bright turquoise."

"Are you sure they're not supposed to be limes? Don't do anything until I get there!"

"I knew I could count on you," he said cheerfully.

The Meaning of Wife

This morning, while Matt was dressing for work, I was pretending to sleep.

Marital possum is a newly acquired habit, more puzzling to the player than the played. Why am I doing this? Do other women pretend to be asleep for no apparent reason? What about their husbands? And why do I compare myself to other marrieds? Is it all just a normal side effect of matrimony?

As a kid, I faked sleep to trick my mother after Lights Out, but I never asked myself if the other kids were doing it. The scam was all instinct, my approach zenlike. I did not second-guess myself; I simply *became* the sleeping daughter. Now, as sleeping wife, I'm beset with self-doubt.

Fortunately, I have therapy later.

Late last night when Matt drowsily remembered that he had a breakfast meeting, I tiptoed out of bed. Muffling the coffee grinder with a batik teapot cosy—wedding gift from Mother—I felt like the very model of a modern wife. After filling the coffee maker with Aged Sumatra and filtered water, I placed a packet of sweetener on a saucer, then took stock of my domestic achievement. With one flick of a switch, my husband has access to caffeine when he will most need it *and least expect it*. How cool is that? When I returned to our bed, he was snoring. I fell asleep with the aroma of tomorrow's coffee lingering in my nostrils.

When I woke, he was quietly selecting a shirt from his side of the closet. I quickly closed my eyes and sniffed the air for signs of coffee. And now he was leaning over my pillow, kissing my forehead tenderly to wake me from a phony but convincing slumber.

"Thanks for the java," he murmured "You're a genius!"

As I stroked his smooth, shaved cheek, he added, "I like that purring sound you make when you're happy."

How often do I touch a man's cheek?

No matter how many clients I've seen, days can go by when my hands do not venture above the chest. I might blow lightly into a customer's ear while straddling his body—or ruffle his hair while he's going down on me. I might kiss a john's cheek or his neck to evade his mouth. But Matt is probably the only guy whose face I touch with my fingertips. How long has he occupied this exclusive slot? It's funny how I work to avoid some things— like kissing—with my clients, while others just don't happen. Why is it so personal and sweet to touch a man's face? As we kissed good-bye, I realized that my hands have been accidentally faithful for more than a year. For a brief second, I felt like a stranger to myself.

I heard the apartment door close and got up quickly. My cell phone, snug in the bottom of my tote bag, had three messages on it—one from Allison (eager to dissect her first date with Lucho) and another from Steven, the typical voice mail of a disappointed impulse buyer: "I'm in the neighborhood, try you again next week."

If you don't grab Steven while he's hot, you simply have to wait for the next urge to strike, and this is the third time we've struck out in a month. What with Charmaine's timeshare and my new responsibilities as a wife, I'm starting to lose my impulsive quickies. It's hard to connect these days if a guy can't make his appointment in advance.

Too bad: Steven's the easiest guy in my client book and I miss his *pret-a-porter* erections. So reliable. Too big and fast to fail. Even when you know better than to take it personally, a dependable hard-on makes you feel more successful, more attractive. A three-quarter erection backed by regular visits might yield more profit in the long run—and I know how to keep a man from going soft because it's my job. (I've been doing this since Ronald Reagan was in office!) But I like it when desire's a bit more obvious.

Lately, I'm working harder to retain those regulars who find it easier to make appointments way ahead of time. It's better for my marriage but not so good for my ego: a man suddenly hot to see you has a more straightforward erection than one who plans ahead. A long-winded way of saying, will Steven really call next week? His hard-ons are more reliable than his projections.

The last message in my system was the most promising. I called Trisha back pronto on her cell.

"Yes," I said.

"Yes?"

"What time?"

"One second," she said. "The dinosaur cape? It's upstairs. Don't forget your juice. We have three minutes. . . . Next Tuesday at two, he likes boots," she mumbled quickly. "Can you find an extra girl? What about Allison? We're getting ready for school here. That sounds perfect!" she disconcertingly chirped. Suddenly, her voice was clear as a bell. "For sure! We have to talk. The picnic is a great idea!"

Picnic? These sudden non sequiturs—second nature to Trish—always precede a hang-up. Her husband must have popped back into sight. Of course, you don't end a conversation too abruptly when you want things to sound normal.

I can't believe Trish has the nerve to take all these calls from girls and clients when he's around! But I'm learning not to make judgments about other people's marriages. Every girl must decide for herself when it's safe to answer the phone.

•◆• LATER •◆•

My shrink has moved her office from Riverside Drive to Central Park West—and wants to know how I feel about it. Of course, you can say things to a shrink that you wouldn't say to others but there are some things I don't get into. Not because I'm ashamed or anything—it's just that she would regard my feelings about hair as Material for an entire session and I don't want to go there. My hair is a little too delicate for this world and tends to lose its shape when exposed to the elements, but I can't explain this to Dr. Kessel, who always looks like she needs a haircut even when she's just had one.

I used to dread visiting her windy corner. Last month, to prevent my hair from being whipped out of shape, I wore a pleated Hermès scarf—and almost lost it. My head scarf, viciously attacked by a sudden gust, went flying toward the river. When I arrived at my session, having chased the scarf for half a block, a layer of perspiration was threatening my hair. If I never have to brave Riverside Drive again, I'll be a happier camper than most.

On Central Park West, the air was calm today. Upstairs, a small plaque identified Dr. Wendy Kessel's new whereabouts. In the waiting room, I found myself staring at a collection of black-and-white portraits: Eleanor Roosevelt and Josephine Baker on one wall. A young Doris Lessing on another. Where has all the ethnic pottery gone?

"How do you feel about the new look?" Dr. Wendy asked.

"It's a little *in your face*."

"Somebody else made the same observation."

She seemed to take pleasure in the disturbance her new decor was causing. A nerdlike pleasure, not malicious. But still.

"Maybe I'll get used to it," I said. "It's a trade-off because your location's more central. Not that there's anything *wrong* with the pictures," I added.

Am I a lab rat under scrutiny? Or a valued emotional stakeholder? I couldn't quite tell.

"Change is always a challenge," Dr. Wendy pointed out. "Even when we expect it."

Her therapy room is more soothing than her new waiting room: plants everywhere, peachy hues, a harmless quilt on the largest wall.

"But Josephine Baker seems out of place in there."

"Really?" As Dr. Wendy leaned forward, some light bounced off her glasses. "In what sense?"

"Not for racial reasons," I added. Wendy looked relieved. "She's the only one showing any flesh."

"That's a good place to start," Wendy replied. *"Nu?"*

"Yiddish?"

"Just keeping my hand in. I'm not that invested. Or proficient."

"Well, speaking of . . . proficient, I did some business on Sunday."

Dr. Wendy's reaction to this short-term achievement report was hard to read.

"I know it's risky to work on Sundays—it's safer when Matt's at the office. But I took the call and guess what? I almost made my quota." I told her about my visit to the Waldorf and the ensuing muddle. "Matt was so happy when I finally showed up at the Gap, he didn't suspect a thing. But the situation almost turned against me. His sister could have called him, said something incriminating. Or he could have spotted me leaving the hotel. But I got a fairytale ending. For now."

"*For now* is not an ending," she said. "How do you feel about the outcome?"

"Well, I didn't get caught—which is good. But I still have this nagging guilt."

"Because you kept Matt waiting?"

"Because I fell short of my quota for the third week running! When I got married, I had this policy—never on Sunday—but it's totally clashing with my quota. And my quota is much older than this policy. Or this marriage. It's too important." I felt my face growing warm. "I can't just abandon it."

"Many things are older than your marriage. But some women in your position would adjust their expectations. Is it realistic to set the same goals when you have a new living arrangement which might impact your energy level?"

I blinked at Dr. Wendy. So I'm like a working mom who should be on halftime? But I have no kids, and Trisha (who *does*) is just as driven as any unmarried hooker. Okay, she no longer has a place where she can see guys, so her expectations may have changed—but now she has a stable of outcalls, really good ones, who stay at hotels.

What's *my* excuse?

"Are you telling me I should reduce my quota?"

"No," Dr. Wendy said firmly. "That"—her tone grew softer—"is not my role. I'm asking how you feel about that idea."

"When we were engaged it was easier to hide my business. Now I have to sneak out, find some place to get ready for a date, do the date, get unready, hide the money. It's like working two jobs and getting paid for one! And I'm sharing my old apartment with a New Girl—she's only been working for a year or two. Matt doesn't know about that, of course. He thinks I gave up my apartment because I moved all my best furniture into the new place."

When I moved my art moderne bedroom set into our newly-wed nest on East Thirty-fourth Street, Matt never asked what I was doing with my queen-size bed. Or my 310-count sheets. The upheaval, the unpacking, a different neighborhood—if you can call this cluster of generic dwellings a neighborhood—made it easy to forget things. Besides, when leaving his bachelor apartment, he thought nothing of leaving his own bed for the landlord to dispose of. We never questioned the purchase of a completely inexperienced mattress and box spring for our new life together.

"It's a lot to keep track of," Wendy said. "But you're not alone. Some women call it 'the second shift.' Taking care of a household and a personal relationship while maintaining your professional foothold."

"In secret?" Well, I suppose keeping secrets might qualify as relationship upkeep.

"Most people have secrets. But if the secrets are too numerous, keeping them becomes a full-time job. In today's world, it's common to have more than one part-time job. But most people would find it impossible to hold down two or three full-time jobs." Dr. Wendy paused. "I want to call the management of your secrets 'the third shift.' Is this a useful concept?"

"So the first shift is what you do for money. The second shift is what you do for love. And the third shift?"

"Maybe it's what brings you here."

I told Dr. Wendy about my discovery, how this morning it suddenly occurred to me that I've been almost faithful in a roundabout way for more than a year.

"In my own fashion," I added ruefully. "I don't think my husband would understand, though."

"The arithmetic of emotional fidelity is extremely private," Wendy assured me.

"Are you sure it's arithmetic? And not geometry?"

Dr. Wendy wasn't sure.

"But you do have a system for making sense of your actions. I'm pretty sure of that." She paused and gave me a quizzical smile. "Were you good at geometry?"

•◆• FRIDAY, 3/16/01. EAST SEVENTY-NINTH STREET •◆•

The last few days have been profitable and peaceful. Charmaine, true to her word, has gone to Florida, leaving our shared one-bedroom spotless and orderly. Dust-free. Charmaine's even more of a clean freak than I am: buys her lubricant in those disposable one-use packets, has an air purifier in the living room, and keeps a box of surgical gloves next to the kitchen sink. On the twenty-fifth day of each month, she hands me a neatly arranged pile of hundreds and fifties, her share of the rent and utilities. I couldn't ask for a more desirable roommate.

All her things are stashed in the hall closet as agreed, and I have the run of this place until she returns. It's like being single again—when I'm here, that is—and my phone has decided to co-operate. It rings often, making me realize that I still have what it takes: an active client list and a safe place to work from.

This apartment's safe because the neighborhood's safe. I've taken steps to ensure that Matt has no excuse to be strolling past my apartment when I'm here, and no reason to be uptown on a casual basis. That's why we moved to Thirty-fourth Street, to a neighborhood I don't even like. I nixed every place we looked at that wasn't safely south of Seventy-ninth, even when I found my dream condo with the perfect balcony on East Eighty-fourth. It was too close to my stomping grounds, so I made a huge sacrifice and chose, instead, the impersonal two-bedroom with the twenty-ninth-floor view, in a part of town that feels like a giant parking lot. When people ask how Matt and I can live so close to the heliport, so far from all the great food shops, I cite the FDR and limitless views. I sometimes think about the apartment on Eighty-fourth Street that I fell in love with and walked away from, but never with regret.

Today, I saw Howard at noon, followed by a surprise visit from Steven. After Steven left, I examined my naked body in the mirror and liked what I saw.

My breasts look perky and my stomach somewhat flatter. (I don't eat as much when I have all these consecutive dates.) My face looks smoother because I'm more relaxed when I see my customers here: less chance of being spotted by my husband—or someone who knows him. Better working conditions make a girl instantly better looking.

Woman with a past has a warped new meaning this week because I feel like I'm playing a trick on time itself. When Charmaine returns, things revert to the married present. For now, my afternoons are spent in a place that belongs to my single years. But my next customer's due in twenty minutes and the sheets need changing! So much for outwitting the notorious arrow of time.

•—•· LATER ·—•·

Just before Milt arrived, Charmaine called with surprising news.

"I'm changing my flight," she said. "I need five more days. But I'm seeing someone the morning after I get back," she reminded me. "I'm booked solid that week."

"Of course. I'll stay out of your way. But don't get too much sun!" I warned her.

"Oh, I'm not—it just *looks* like a vacation." She giggled. "I'm as careful about the sun as you are. It's really a doctor's visit. Didn't I tell you?"

Charmaine's having . . . surgery?

"But you're only twenty-two!" I exclaimed. "Aren't you kind of young for that?"

"It's never too early," she told me. "This is like using birth control so you won't have to have an abortion—or end up looking like one! Anyway, I've been using Botox on my forehead for two years. And I've already had my nose done. I'm not exactly a virgin."

"But you have to know when to stop. If you keep modifying . . . You've done Botox? I had no idea!"

"Because it's very natural. And this will be too."

" 'This'? Do you mind if I ask what you're having done? There's nothing wrong with you!"

"You'll see. Nothing dramatic. Don't worry, I know what I'm doing. It's *my* face and *my* future. And the biggest mistake is waiting too long to get the work done. I'm not going to let that happen to me!"

So. Charmaine thinks cosmetic surgery is wasted on the elderly.

I decided not to argue with her, but, while I was giving my four o'clock a long slow blow job, I found myself thinking about my roommate—wrinkle-proofing her brow at twenty-two! I didn't start worrying about such things until *twenty-six*.

My lips were sliding toward the base of Milt's erection but my mind was elsewhere: *Is Charmaine tempting fate by starting too early with her face? What if something goes wrong in the operating room?* For me, surgery's a last resort rather than a lifestyle. So it's her money, her body, and her future. I should mind my own business, but other people's body parts *are* my business. And therein lies the problem. I'm so accustomed to making decisions about other people's bodies that I'm ready to tell Charmaine what not to do with hers. Meanwhile, I'm the one who has gained six pounds—and when you're 5'1" it shows. Shouldn't I focus on that instead? As I removed my mouth from Milt's cock, I was turning over a new leaf.

I reached for a glass of water on my bedside table to cleanse the taste of latex from my palate. There is nothing more icky than condom-breath—a hazard of the profession because you get so used to having rubber in your mouth that you might not notice.

My favorite customer was lying on his back, eyes blissfully shut, stroking my thigh. As I poured some Astroglide onto my palm, he became more alert.

"Before you do that," he suggested, "why don't you bring that luscious pussy over here and let me return the favor?"

"You lazy beast. All right. Don't move."

I turned around and sat over his face with my buttocks in the air. My hands now had access to his cock, which was threatening to grow soft. But he was getting hard again, thanks to the nearness of my pussy. I decided to let him lick me until he was properly erect. I never come with Milton but I allow him to do more with my body than, perhaps, I should because he's the client I like best. When I wriggled away, my ass was still facing him and he sighed happily.

"What a gorgeous view!"

I mounted his cock with that in mind, bending forward as much as possible to enhance his view. His climax was louder than usual and I made a mental note not to fuck him in this position for the next two sessions. Despite his cuddly personality, Milt gets jaded rather easily. It might soon be time to suggest a threeway with Allison. Or Jasmine. I never call a client to promote *myself* but it's okay to call a guy if you're making a sales pitch involving another girl.

While dressing, he gave me an affectionate pat.

"You've lost weight, kiddo."

"You're every woman's dream," I laughed.

He slid an envelope under the tissue box on my bedside table.

"Don't exaggerate. Now . . . where did I put my briefcase?"

Five minutes later my cell phone was chiming at me. Liane, trying to locate Charmaine. Or someone like her. Or, in the absence of someone like her, someone who's available. After five decades in this business, first a call girl but mostly a madam, she knows that you can't always get what they want.

"I need somebody fresh and wholesome. A Charmaine *type*. For Bernie. Remember Bernie? I told him about Charmaine but she hasn't called me back!"

Bernie wants to meet a college girl (or someone who looks like one) who is supposedly getting paid for the first time. After "corrupting" the alleged newbie, he likes to cultivate her. As a result, I've seen him at Liane's apartment five or six times.

Liane provides as many professional innocents as she can for the harem in Bernie's mind.

"Charmaine would be perfect," I agreed, "if she weren't . . . still in Florida."

Though somewhat tempted to share the truth with Liane, I held back. A trustworthy timeshare is hard to find and I don't want to alienate Charmaine by gossiping about her new implants—or whatever the mystery process of the week happens to be.

"I wonder if Bernie would like to see a naughty little *married* girl," Liane said. "I could tell him that you graduated and met—"

"I don't want Bernie to know I'm married! Nobody's supposed to know!"

"Well, not if you feel so strongly about it, dear. But it might pique his interest. A restless wife can be titillating. And it makes you respectable. You know how important that is. And it gives me an entree. I can't just say, 'How about Nancy instead of the New Girl?' I've got to have a nice story to tell! A way to make you sound *new*."

"Maybe another time," I said. "I have to hit the cheese counter at Agata Valentina before they close. I'm making something special tonight."

"Of course, dear. What are you preparing for dinner?"

"Baked pecorino cheese with toasted pine nuts and truffle honey. Followed by a whole trout. Steamed with bay leaves. And an arugula salad. With a very light pinot noir."

"I think it's wonderful that you're taking this marriage so seriously! I've always said that women like us make the best wives."

But I still prefer to keep my marital status under deep cover. Even Milt isn't sure I've actually tied the knot—he thinks I'm still engaged. If the customers find out I'm actually married, it might spook them. They might fear a spying, curious husband or an enraged, jealous one. Worse yet, they might think he knows what I'm up to, that he *lets* me hook. Not the sort of image I want to be promoting at all.

What if they think I married a guy who can't support me or mistreats me, that I turn tricks in order to make ends meet? Maybe they'll think I have to support *him*? I don't want my customers to think I'm that kind of hooker—that I married purely for love. Rich girls can sometimes marry for love, but girls like me, we're supposed to marry *smart*. Not get taken advantage of. You can be in love, sure. But use your head. If you seem to be the kind of call girl who marries a ne'er-do-well or behaves foolishly with men, the clients lose respect.

It's sexy to let on that you're a lady when you're not working, a hooker who feels equally at home on a pedestal. But it's not just *my* vanity kicking in—I also want to protect Matt's image. What if I run into one of these clients when I'm at the theater with my husband?

Do I want them looking at Matt and thinking he's a bum? Not!

And yet, if they know I'm married to a banker, they'll think I don't really need the money. When it's time to raise my prices, I invoke the high cost of living in Manhattan. There are times when I must appeal to a client's desire to help a brave, defenseless single girl. If a john finds out that I'm married to a guy with a good income, he's got a ready-made excuse to keep the price "stable." You're just doing this for extras, pin money, or cheap thrills.

I made that mistake only once, with Etienne, who now lives in Paris. When I tried to hit him up for something extra on his last visit to New York, my marital status worked against me. Never again!

Trish doesn't tell her clients she's married—or that she has a kid. It's understood that we can trust each other not to blab. Jasmine and Allie are both under strict orders to keep mum. Charmaine I *have* to trust—in the hope that she values the great deal she has here, enough to keep her promise of silence.

Liane might be right—married women can be alluring—but I don't want to go there with her clients.

·•·• SUNDAY MORNING, 3/18/01. EAST THIRTY-FOURTH STREET ·•·•

This morning, while cleaning out my in box, I almost deleted two e-mails from Allie. Thrown off by her new address, I took m.power@trollops.org for just another spammer.

Subject: Come to the NYCOT Cabaret!

A benefit for the New York Council of Trollops at The Pussycat Lounge . . . featuring punk soprano Wiltrud Mars . . . Miss Chelsea Jane at the piano . . . the Triple-X Cheerleaders . . . stand-up comedy's Domina Blue. Doors open 7:30 pm.

Members of the Media: Please contact our fabulous EmCee, ALLISON m.power@trollops.org for ticketing, interview requests and more.

The Pussycat Lounge? Is Allie planning to appear *on stage*? And what's all this about the media?

This was followed by another e-mail with a more personal subject header:

Re: urgent lunch need yr advice

Hey! Lucho is taking me to a special party next weekend. Lots of people from his faculty! Do you think it's too soon to meet his friends? What should I wear? It's all the way uptown near Columbia. Can you meet for lunch? It has to be soon because I need your advice!

PS: He used the L word last night! Twice! But he's making some really strange demands and I'm not sure what to do. Don't tell Jasmine but . . . I couldn't hold out til third date. And now there's this THING that he wants me to do. I'm crazy about him too but—not ready for this!

Strange demands? Thing that he wants her to do? I wrote back immediately.

What is this THING? Let's discuss in person.

The Ballad of East and West

This afternoon, a pilgrimage to my sister-in-law's shrinking Carnegie Hill condo. Her once-spacious two-bedroom has been completely transformed. As we entered, there was a whiff of baby powder in the air but no sign of the twins themselves. Or their father.

Elspeth held a finger to her lips, and told Matt, "Your niece and nephew are finally asleep. And so is Jason!"

She, however, was showing no signs of fatigue. She placed our present—still in its shopping bag—next to a box of disposable diapers.

"You went to Bambini! I love their clothes! But I'll wait till Jason gets up before we open it."

Two high chairs with gingham-covered seat pads stood next to the foyer closet. A Peg Pérego stroller built for two was blocking Matt's access to the living room couch. I pushed the crowded vehicle cautiously to one side. The front unit was harboring a blanket covered with appliquéd ducks and daisies. In the backseat, more baby presents, decorated with pink and white ribbon, were jumbled together, waiting to be opened. In the storage area below, I spotted a large diaper bag designed to match the gingham seat pads.

"This carriage is huge! How do you manage?" I asked.

"Oh, I had the mommy biceps before I was even pregnant," Elspeth said. "I call it the baby Hummer," she added proudly. "Want some herbal tea? Or"—she gestured toward the kitchen—"I could fix you a cappuccino with steamed breast milk." Snickering at her younger brother's discomfort, she changed the subject, sort of. "Yams are the culprit! Everybody's eating yams twice a week for the betacarotene but you end up having twins because of all the plant estrogen. Well, Jason and I were planning on having two, anyway. Nancy, I want to show you something. This is right up your alley!"

She returned seconds later with a square box.

"I want Bridget and Berrigan to learn Spanish; Jason thinks they should be learning Japanese." The box was decorated with words and numbers in various languages. "How's your schoolwork going?"

I flinched inside. I haven't actually attended a class yet, but I've been carrying around my French textbooks just to get Matt accustomed to my new alibi.

"Oh . . . kind of rusty," I said hesitantly. "But I'm determined to make a go of it."

"Nancy plays these tapes at night. I can't understand a word." I felt Matt's arm on my waist. "She's studying for the . . . DALF?"

"DELF. Eventually. Not yet. I have to get up to speed conversationally."

"Well, they say that learning a language will increase a baby's

IQ. What are you working on these days?" Elspeth asked. "I'm still waiting to see the acupuncture book!"

"Oh that"—my voice trailed off—"was nothing but problems! I'm waiting, too."

Elspeth thinks—or I hope she thinks—that I do some freelance copyediting. Last year, I convinced Matt, Elspeth, and my own family that I was toiling over an illustrated guide to acupuncture. Since there's no hope of the book actually materializing, I've decided that the author is having a personal crisis that prevents him from finishing the final chapter.

"Well, my part of the project is done," I told Elspeth. "And," I said, with more conviction, "I feel like that part of *my life* is done. I'm ready to focus on something else. So I'm just working on my French. No distractions."

When Matt and I met, he assumed—quite wrongly—that my family was paying my rent. I concocted a few slacker gigs to generate income for those extras that a moderately supported adult would have to buy for herself. It wouldn't make sense to pretend I'm *rich*. (What if he tried to marry me for my money? The complications would be embarrassing for both of us. Not that Matt is the type who marries a girl for money. But still.)

Now that we're married, I can't fall back on freelance editing. He would surely expect to see me carrying around a manuscript from time to time. Poring over a stack of papers. So I announced a career transition and became, instead, a student at the French Institute on East Sixtieth Street, a student who aspires—one day in the future—to pass the DELF and become a translator.

Matt finds my fuzzy career plan quite plausible. For some reason, when Elspeth starts asking questions about it, I can feel the moisture rising on my skin.

"Matt and I were thinking . . ." Elspeth began.

Before I could stop myself, I flashed a nervous glance at my husband. I wish he would stop "conferencing" with Elspeth behind my back!

"Christopher's coming to dinner next week—you know, the surprise I'm throwing for Jason." Her voice dropped and she made a warning gesture in the direction of the master bedroom. "Let's invite your friend Allison!"

"Allison?" I squeaked. "Why—um—why Allison?"

Matt and Elspeth looked surprised.

"Why not?" Matt said.

"Matt keeps telling me she's single and great looking! And Chris is a catch," Elspeth added. "Didn't you meet him?"

I felt my throat drying up as I recalled my brief encounter with Chris at one of Elspeth's parties. Before taking maternity leave, Elspeth was a prosecutor. When I met Chris, he had just started working with her in the Special Prosecutions Unit of the Manhattan DA's office.

"Tall? Dirty blond hair?" Elspeth was saying. "He just bought a sailboat. Does Allison like to sail?"

Allison is indeed single—and better looking than most—but her eligibility for mating with Chris ends right there. Inviting her to Jason's surprise birthday event would certainly have an impact—a disastrous one. For all kinds of reasons, I am determined that Allison must never come within five hundred feet of Elspeth and Jason's apartment. And now that Allie has been promoted to media czar by the Council of Trollops, one thousand feet sounds even better.

"Allie," I said, casting my inner net for answers, "is seeing someone."

"Are they engaged?" Elspeth asked

"They just started dating but she—"

"That settles it. Don't tell her about Chris. We'll invite her and see what happens! There's no pressure. If she's not engaged to this guy and they just met?"

"Let the best man win," Matt suggested. "I think we should invite her. What if they hit it off?"

"What does Allie do, anyway?"

"Do?" I repeated numbly.

Elspeth sat on the love seat, quizzing me with one eye trained on the passageway to her bedroom.

"She's—uh—temping," I said. "And thinking about getting a social work degree."

Elspeth cocked her head to one side and gave me a wide-eyed look. Jason had appeared in the living room doorway, short-circuiting any further discussion of the guest list. Or my best friend's occupational history.

I've never been happier to see a man in my life!

•◆• MONDAY, 3/19/01 •◆•

This morning, as he dressed for work, Matt tried to reopen the possibility of inviting Allie.

"I wish you would let me decide what's best," I replied petulantly. "Elspeth doesn't know Allie the way I do. And I wish you wouldn't discuss it with her."

"Why does it bother you so much?" He was standing in front of the mirror, straightening his tie.

"Aren't there any single women in your office? Chris is *not* Allison's type."

"How does this look? And how do you know?"

"I just *know*. It looks, hmmm. Even better than I expected." I got out of bed in just my panties and embraced my fully clothed husband. *He's wearing the tie that I gave him the other day, purchased with my illicit earnings.* I could feel my nipples responding as I pressed my bare skin against a crisp cotton shirt, a silk tie. I was surprised to feel so aroused just seconds after being annoyed with him. Matt pushed me away gently. Holding my shoulders, he kissed the side of my neck.

"Not now," he said. "But later . . ."

I began sliding to my knees, but he blocked my descent. "Honey, I know this seems counterintuitive but I have to ask you to stop." He pulled me closer. "I have a meeting with a very important client. Try to understand."

One of his clients is interfering with our sex life? I guess there's a first time for everything.

I gave him a tender smile—and accepted my raincheck obediently, determined to save my pleasure for Matt.

But, this afternoon, during a session at Jasmine's apartment, my body misbehaved.

Jasmine, under pressure to deliver some "real" action with a girl, had lowered my bra to expose my breasts. Harry, her favorite client, was rubbing his erection against my thigh, urging Jasmine to "get Suzy" (that's me) "nice and wet." Her fingertips caressed my nipples and she closed her eyes. Jasmine hates getting too close to another girl's body, but she'd rather do the hated thing with a girl she likes. An excited-sounding moan (hers) was followed by a wet flicker—Jasmine's tongue reluctantly touching my breast. I couldn't hide the fact that my nipples were hard. This fresh tingle, spreading quietly through my flesh, reminded me of my early-morning encounter with Matt.

My nipples are a little too independent. They can't be told what to do and they don't want to hide. The pleasures of my pussy are more discreet: they can be obscured by my outer lips. But I can't tame the visual evidence of a tingling nipple.

As the pleasure grew more intense, I grew more quiet and didn't mind listening to Jasmine's fake sound effects. Harry was removing my panties, convinced that Jasmine's mouth was on its way to the place where I now had my finger. But she stayed firmly on my left nipple. As I touched myself, I kept hoping she wouldn't suspect me of enjoying her tongue. I wondered if I might even get away with coming, but Jasmine was just too near. She would be horrified if she figured it out!

I turned toward Harry—he was already wearing his condom— and got into a sluttish kneeling pose. Jasmine's hand was at the base of his cock, guiding the head into my mouth.

"She's ready for your cock," Jasmine told him. "She's wetter than she's ever been."

When Harry was finished, he offered a half-baked apology for being premature. As he always is!

"I didn't give you girls enough time," he said. "You were just getting warmed up."

"But I think *Jasmine* got off."

"Sure did," he said. "You have quite an effect on that gal. You're dangerous together!" Jasmine, now out of earshot, was listening to her telephone messages while Harry dressed. A Town Car was waiting downstairs to take him to his office. When she had closed the door behind him, she apologized for the girl-on-girl action: "These guys get spoiled by other girls and there's only so much you can do. Or not do."

Jasmine looked vaguely disgusted, not with herself but with the sorry state of the sexual marketplace. But I was impressed by how little she had gotten away with.

"It's okay," I assured her. "It's just business. And he's still an easy date."

"And I raised him!" she said happily. "I got him up to five. This is yours." She handed me a thick stack of new-looking twenties. "But"—her tone grew darker—"the girls today have no control over their customers! Our guys are *trained*. These New Girls don't even know what that means. Harry's never been a runner," Jasmine mused.

A runner rarely sees a girl twice—until he's forgotten her, at which point he can be talked into seeing her under a new name. That's not Harry.

"But they all stray now," she said. "Even a regular like Harry. Have you seen what some of these *websites* are like?"

"No." I shuddered. "I don't think Harry would go online. Do you? He's so . . . old school, you know?"

He looks like one of those semiwired senior execs who gets a young assistant to open his e-mail, print it, and type a response! Would a guy like that go shopping for lesbian sex *online*?

"Well, if he's gonna pull that stuff, I'm glad you're here. You, I can count on. Once I did a date with Eileen, and she practically had her tongue up my snatch! That girl's a degenerate at the best of times."

"I'm sure Eileen was just trying to be helpful—"

"Gratuitous muff-diving is not helpful! Why does any girl do that when it's not being requested?"

Jasmine's cell phone interrupted, giving her the last word.

What can you learn about a girl from the way her phone rings? Not, um, how often it rings—I mean the ring she has chosen to announce her callers. Allison's phone is playing a lot of Brahms lately, because she read on some website that he practically lived in a brothel. (Well, his name *was* Johannes.) Jasmine's phone goes off like a smoke detector.

"Allison's postponing our lunch," she told me. "She has a customer."

"You're kidding. She was so . . ."

". . . psyched about our meeting!" Jasmine agreed. "But she's practicing some fiscal responsibility for a change. Putting business before boyfriend was never Allison's default setting."

It's Jasmine's, though. And I sometimes wonder, *What's it like to be Jasmine's boyfriend?* She must have had more than one. She positions herself as such an authority on relationships, but I know very little about her love life. And she claims she has never "shacked up" with a man for longer than a weekend.

"So what about this guy?" Jasmine was saying. "This boyfriend of hers. Sounds like he might be trouble."

"She says they're in love."

"The L-Word. On the second date? Whatever! As long as the guy goes first."

"God. Allie wouldn't use the L-Word first—would she?"

"It's possible," Jasmine said. "If she did, we'll find out. Look, is this guy some kind of bedroom freak? Did she tell you anything?"

"Just—there's something she's not ready to do! I'm kind of worried."

The thing that has no name!

Is Lucho pressuring Allie to quit the business? Even though she's a spokesperson for the Trollops' Council? Or maybe he's going to the other extreme and trying to have a threesome with one of *us*? Does he want to hide in the closet while she turns tricks? That's the problem with telling a guy you're in this business. If he doesn't want you to quit, he thinks you're a one-woman fantasy fulfillment center. In fact, if a boyfriend knows you're hooking, it doesn't matter whether he accepts or rejects it. Either way, he'll cause trouble and make impossible demands.

It's the wrinkle, not the war, of the sexes. Allie joined the hookers' movement thinking she could eradicate this wrinkle, but you can't reconfigure the male animal with a manifesto.

•➤• THURSDAY, 3/22/01 •➤•

Well!

I don't know if Lucho qualifies as a bedroom freak, but he's making some very unsettling requests. Creating a bit of a lifestyle crisis for Allison.

Today, over thin-crust pizzas at Petaluma—veal salad for Jasmine—Allie came clean about the source of their first quarrel. Which made no sense at all to Jasmine.

"Isn't he *from* Brazil?" she asked. "Personally, I thank the Brazilians for teaching us how to wax! As far as I'm concerned, less is more! He should be glad you're taking an interest in his cultural heritage."

I had to agree. When I think back to how things were before pubic hair got Brazilianized! It was like being *preliterate*. Memories of underdevelopment can be elusive—especially in matters of style. I can hardly believe we were once so naive about our lower parts. These days, even if you let your hair grow, it won't look simple and carefree—instead, it's like you're taking a stand, refusing to wax. It now seems quite natural to be hairless.

But Lucho has other opinions.

"He's from Colombia, not Brazil," Allie explained. "Bikini

waxing isn't part of Lucho's heritage! He lived in Paris for ten years—"

"Paris!" Jasmine interjected. "No fucking wonder! I bet they're still doing the 'natural' look. Well, now he's in Manhattan. This is Brazilian territory!"

"—and his mom's Lebanese. She met his dad when they were studying in Geneva, and they moved to Bogotá before he was born. His dad is a fifth-generation Colombian. There is nothing . . . Brazilian about Lucho, but he does speak some Portuguese," Allie added. A dreamy expression took over. "I've never known a man like Lucho. He makes love to me in five different languages and he's totally supportive of everything I want to do!" She paused. "Well, everything but the waxing. Would *you* grow your pubic hair back for a man?"

I was at a loss for words. Matt would never take the liberty of tampering with my pubic hair. He might make suggestions about redecorating the *apartment,* but redecorating my pussy would be out of the question. Like trying to redesign my essence.

"Not a chance," Jasmine said. "My clients like it this way. And it's cleaner. This guy has some nerve!"

"He says I'm the love of his life! Why does he want me to change?"

"Maybe he's just experiencing culture shock," I suggested.

"This is what happens when you start messing around with someone from the Upper West Side." Jasmine stabbed a piece of pink veal with her fork. "If he prefers going down on some un-waxed bohemian, let him stay on the West Side! He *knew* you were an Upper East Sider before you even met. What does he expect? Of course you're gonna wax!"

Allie began nibbling the pointy end of a pizza slice. Her eyes widened with dismay as Jasmine continued.

"This is not *culture* shock. It's the ultimate clash of civilizations!"

"But I want this relationship to work!" said Allie. "And you're being totally divisive. Escalation is not the way to resolve—"

"You're from two different worlds," Jasmine insisted. "And he's trying to impose his values on you. *I* did not invent these divisions."

"I don't think this has *anything* to do with him living on the Upper West Side." Allie flashed a worried look at me. "Does it?"

"Actually," I told her, "Jasmine's got a point. The only client who ever complained about my waxing was that divorced rabbi. What's his name? On West End Avenue. He looks like a guitar-strumming priest from the sixties . . ."

"I met him last year," said Jasmine. "Melvin. I call him the day before I get my pussy waxed and he's, like, *in a cab* before the call ends."

"Well, I can't see Lucho only on the days before I wax!" Allie pointed out. "He's not a client! Isn't compromise essential to intimacy? Maybe I should try to meet him halfway."

"But you're already halfway," I said.

Allie retains, at all times, a small fuzzy triangle above her labia . . . I prefer a complete waxing, so I can watch my hair growing back to a uniform softness. I relish the dark silky hairs that emerge every six weeks. It's a psychic treat to feel like a proud little twelve-year-old, surveying her womanly evidence. Further proof that being a teenager is way more fun when you're a grown-up. . . . By comparison, Allie's blond topiary is not extreme. More of a hedge than a bush, perhaps, but still. Why isn't that enough?

"Lucho says"—Allie took a nervous sip of Chardonnay—"he says I should stop removing it from my inner thighs and let it peek out of my panties. I'm just not ready for that! I've been waxing since I was sixteen!"

"Does he want to take pictures?" I wondered.

"Of course not!" She blushed. "He says it's about oral sex. And my lower lips 'were meant to be like a wild forest, not a suburban lawn.' Removing too much pubic hair makes it hard for him to 'experience my scent.' Well, that's what he said last night."

"Well," Jasmine conceded. "He's telling you something very important."

"He is?"

"And he's paying tribute! That's a good thing."

"Paying tribute?"

"When a man isn't paying, he'd *better* be paying tribute. This guy"—Jasmine, looking inspired, raised an index finger—"this guy is paying tribute to your pheromones. Love is the grand total sum of all the brain chemicals and pheromones and whatever else coming together in the great big ledger book of human experience. The sense of smell is connected to the tastebuds," she continued. "So it's all one package."

"You mean . . ." Allie was unconvinced. "The way to a man's heart is through . . . ?"

"His nostrils? Maybe! He can't get enough of your natural scent. But here's the thing. When you're dating a guy, you go out with him just twice a week—to keep things fresh. Men always want what they can't have. Well, the same thing applies! This guy already knows he likes your natural scent, and he wants more. From your point of view, that's all that's needed. You've won the first round! You don't have to satisfy his appetite, you just have to recognize it. It's like The Rules for Sweat Glands. Always leave them wanting more!"

Jasmine's biology lecture was interrupted by my chiming phone. Trish, calling from her gym to confirm a repeat performance with Colin. He's coming into town with his wife! For his next session, he's booking a room at the Mayflower on Central Park West—a safe distance from the Waldorf, where they'll be staying.

And way off the beaten path where Matt's concerned. Thank god! When I entered this business, I never thought I'd see the day when a three-star hotel trumps a five-star.

Marriage changes everything.

Lingerie Liberal

This morning my fingers were engaged in a painstaking task—removing tiny green rosemary leaves from a stalk containing too many black ones—when both phones started ringing at once. The domestic landline I share with Matt and my cell phone (shared with no one), vying for attention. I grabbed the phone on my kitchen wall.

"Nancy! What's up? Those bibs are adorable! I can't wait to break them in."

One of Elspeth's newborns could be heard wailing in the background.

"My au pair started yesterday. She's a *god*send. *Fab*ulous. And I finally had a chance to open all the presents! What are you doing?" she inquired.

"Making a rosemary marinade. And I have garlic all over my hands!"

It was nice, for once, to have an easy answer for my sister-in-law.

"We have to talk about your friend Allison."

"We—um—we do?"

"You're obviously uncomfortable about inviting her to Jason's birthday party."

"I don't think—"

"Nancy, it's the kiss of death. You can't let this happen."

"What are you talking about?"

The garlic on my hands was now overwhelming.

"During the first year of my marriage, I made the same mistake. You're alienating yourself from your single girlfriends. It's a normal feeling. But you have a great relationship with Matt and there's no reason for you to act so insecure! Besides, I'd like to meet Allison."

"I don't think any of this is relevant," I said, rather stiffly.

"I think it *is*. And I've been there. I know what you're going through."

Been there? Elspeth has no idea where I've been!

"I am not going through what you think I'm going through."

I instantly regretted the coldness in my voice. Then realized there was nothing to regret. Elspeth was barreling ahead, determined to liberate and reform.

"I know *exactly* what you're going through. Matt already told me how uptight you're getting about Allison. I just want you to know—this is a phase and it's not a healthy one! Single women are not the enemy! They can make married life more interesting. And acting paranoid about single women makes you less attractive to your husband. I found that out on my own, and I'm giving you the benefit of my experience." After a heavy silence, she continued. "You missed out on having a sister."

She's trying to be . . . my big sister?

I *am* a big sister. With two brothers! As an eldest sister herself, she should know that this is just not done.

"I always wanted a sister," said Elspeth. "We need to communicate more! Besides," she added, "all my girlfriends are married or engaged, and Chris is such a catch! I hate to see a guy like Chris at loose ends."

The distant wailing resumed. Would Elspeth's maternal instinct please override the sisterly one? But her fabulous new au pair wasn't going to let that happen.

"What about . . ." I hate to do this to my twenty-something cousin, but she doesn't have to know it was *my* idea. "What about Miranda?" I suggested. "I know she isn't dating anyone special."

"Your cousin? Isn't she a little immature for Chris?"

"Chris would be perfect for her! She needs to start dating above Fourteenth Street."

"Good point. . . . Hey," she said, "aren't you—? Don't you have a French class on Friday mornings?"

Elspeth has an unnerving habit of starting a new topic just when I think I'm getting a handle on the previous one.

"I—um—I don't always go at the same time. My instructor switched days this week."

"Oh. I thought it was a *class*. It's one-on-one?"

"I have to go!" I gasped. Riffing desperately, I added, "Someone's at my door—I'll call you back."

I hung up fast and counted to ten. Gazing in horror at the kitchen wall, I discovered that I had a bad case of garlic phone. You can't tell your phone to chew a handful of raw parsley, so I attacked the handset with a succession of cleaning potions and hoped for the best.

As I returned to my marinade, I could feel the mantle of frumpiness enveloping my deltoids. Settling upon my shoulders like a ghost. Elspeth has no idea what my life is really about, but something she said managed to hit home: couple-centric paranoia isn't pretty. And makes single women look soooo much more attractive to a guy. Especially your own!

Of course, there are plenty of other good solid reasons to keep Allie far away from Elspeth and Jason. I'm doing the right thing.

But still. I *don't* trust my best friend the way I used to. Because she's not married! And I trust Trisha—whom I've known for just a few months—because she *is*.

Married hookers instinctively trust each other. We speak the same code, tell the same lies, fear a common peril. I can't help feeling that an unmarried hooker—especially one like Allie—hasn't got enough to lose.

Does that make her the enemy of my marriage?

·◆· SATURDAY, 3/24/01 ·◆·

Matt told Elspeth how uptight I'm getting? Paranoia "makes you less attractive" to your husband?

It's all starting to get to me!

Last night, sitting across the table from Matt, while he gazed at my candle-lit presence, I felt betrayed.

How dare he discuss his lurking disenchantment with his sister?

Did he discuss disenchantment with his sister? Or did he merely hint at it, in the way men sometimes do—before they're even aware of their own feelings? In which case, the betrayal is unconscious, as so many masculine betrayals are. For some reason, that doesn't make the loss of face any easier to digest.

"These tomatoes are great!" he enthused. "What's in this dressing?"

I threw him a flirtatious, secretive smile. If you admit to a loss of face, then you've *really* lost it.

"I think you're a better cook than . . ." he paused. "Don't tell Elspeth I said this, honey, but you're a better cook than my mother."

I tried to look pleased, but this wasn't what I needed to hear.

A good marinade is no replacement for that mysterious allure which pulled him toward me when we first met. I was smart enough, while dating, to save something for marriage. Matt didn't know I could cook until we moved in together.

Okay, so I know how to date, which is no mean accomplishment. Too many hookers are good at their job yet abysmal at the dating game. But am I smart enough for marriage? It's a lot to keep track of. Provocative single girlfriends. Keeping my career a secret while keeping it afloat. An extra six pounds. And now, this stain upon my self-image that I'm too proud to discuss with him. Being cast as an insecure member of the Couples Brigade makes me feel *officially* overweight.

As Matt cleared the table, I made a decision. After he disappeared from the kitchen, I gathered up every bread stick and new potato, and all the crackers, then threw them into a bag. I started to remove a sliced loaf of Eli's sourdough from the freezer. But Matt will freak if I do that! He's so impressed with our constant supply of distinctive, ready-for-toasting bread. I spared the sourdough and trashed the frozen wholewheat waffles.

After I disposed of the starch-filled bag, I discovered a box of hazelnut biscotti in a cupboard.

"What are you doing?"

Matt's voice startled me as I approached the apartment door.

"Throwing these out!" I said petulantly. "I thought you were online! Why are you spying on me?"

"Why are you throwing out the biscotti?"

"They're stale! Can't I clean up my own kitchen without being questioned about it?"

He gave me a puzzled look and disappeared again. Perhaps I should have said something else, but I refuse to admit to a man that I'm thinking about my weight. I learned many years ago that if you don't mention the first five pounds, most men don't see them. This means I am only one pound overweight in the context of our relationship—even if I'm six pounds heavier in real time. Math is more like a language than people realize. With many dialects.

Later, as I tried to sleep, Matt placed an affectionate hand under my camisole. The memory of his curious compliment came back to me. Cooking. Mother. *Maybe the six pounds is taking its toll after all.*

"I am not the one who confides in your *sister* about the details of this relationship!"

His hand stopped moving.

"What are you talking about?"

"What do you *think* I'm talking about?"

Sitting up, he put his hand on my hair and stroked it gently.

"Something's bothering you," he said. "I knew it when you threw out the biscotti."

Why doesn't he remember comparing my cooking with his mother's less than three hours ago? Or what he said about not telling Elspeth? If I don't remind him, I run the risk of being seen as an irrational harpy, possessed by mental demons! And if I *do* remind him? He just might decide that I *am* his mother.

God.

What's happening to me?

Matt has replaced the biscotti. A loving gesture, but I wish he wouldn't.

After a weekend of moody reflection, make-up sex, and a Pilates class (to take my mind off the mood that the sex didn't dissolve), I've got an emergency session with my shrink—to discuss the mood that Pilates could not vanquish.

Yesterday, while we made up, I imagined that Matt was degrading me in all sorts of unspeakable, systematic ways. I sometimes wonder about the orderly nature of my fantasies. Of the lurid underworld I've invented where I only have to fall into my correct place for everything to go according to plan.

Is this a hooker thing? In the business, there are too many days when sex doesn't go the way you hope it will, and the body (his, yours) miscalculates. A hard-on falters, a dollop of K-Y is just not as much as you need, or another girl is in bed with you, misreading your cues. Sometimes a customer is late, or *you* get stuck in traffic, which throws off your whole routine. A perfectly choreographed day with the sex just so and everybody coming (or showing up) on time is a dream I've been chasing since I started hooking. In my erotic fantasies, it is somebody else who plans and organizes the sex. Within seconds of envisioning such efficient depravity, I find it hard to stop myself from coming.

And making up with Matt is always good. He's got that instinctive knowledge about how to touch me. As I held on to Matt after an explosive climax, he had no idea what I was thinking.

Matt has a certain way of coming that satisfies and possesses. Because I'm not the first or second girl in a list of favorite phone numbers. And there is no chance that I may have been the third number called, in the hope of fitting in a quickie before the Metroliner. When he comes, it's with *me*, and the sensation can't be replicated—for either of us—because it's too intense.

In the physical afterglow, our bodies were at peace. But my mind was still warring—with itself.

•◆• LATER •◆•

This afternoon, I put it to Dr. Wendy: "I have every right to protect my marriage from my best friend!"

Dr. Wendy leaned back in her chair, clasping her hands in her lap. I could see her biceps peeping out of her polo shirt.

"Say more," she urged.

"Allie would be hurt if she knew this but lately I trust Trisha more than I trust *her*. I could introduce Trish to anyone in Matt's circle. Even my nosy sister-in-law."

While I've met Allison's parents—a trusting gesture on *her* part—I keep her as far from my husband as possible.

"I can't trust Allison to keep our story straight. I feel close to her—because of what we've been through—but that's not the same thing as trust."

Trish is just a girl I work with but there is so much I don't have to explain to her. Our priorities are the same: preserving a husband's innocence without losing too many clients.

"Matt and Elspeth are asking me all these questions. They can't figure Allison out. And I don't want them to," I said. "Straight people always want to know how you spend your time. They have no idea how nosy they are! Nobody would ask me what Trish 'does.' Trish doesn't have to explain herself because she's a mom. I feel safe around her. I hardly know her but I know we belong to the same tribe."

"And yet, this tribe is a faction of a much larger tribe," Wendy said.

"Marital Nation," I suggested.

"Do you and Trish belong to a special branch of the marital tribe? Or do you feel like the married branch of the sex worker tribe?"

"Nobody I work with—except for Allie—calls herself a *sex worker*," I said.

Wendy looked thoughtful.

"Is there a preferred term?"

"Oh, it all depends. Allison likes this word Trollop, actually. She's got a new e-mail sig: 'Trollop-at-Large!' She's putting together a benefit for the . . . Council of Trollops. And she's dating this guy who's making a documentary about hookers! She went and spoke to his class at the New School because he wanted to make sure there would be an actual working prostitute to answer all his students' questions! And now they're going out together!"

"What does he teach?"

"Something to do with American Studies. He wants her to be in his documentary—and she hasn't said no, which worries me sometimes. I don't dare look at my e-mail when Matt's around. What if he sees Trollop-at-Large swimming around in my in box? Allie's turning into a liability."

But my shrink was looking impressed rather than horrified.

"Your friend sounds rather brave."

"Brave! Allie's not—I was hustling in hotel bars when I was fifteen! That was brave!"

"Yes," Wendy said "Perhaps—"

"But if I continued to do the things I did when I was a teenager, I wouldn't be brave, I'd be out of my mind!"

"But what do you think Allison was doing? When *she* was a teenager."

"I know *exactly* what. She was a cheerleader! At some high school in Ridgefield, Connecticut! Allison didn't have to clean her own room until she went to college! I had to clean my room, do the dishes every night, AND rake the leaves. Her *mother* picked up after her."

I had to nip my shrink's budding admiration in the bud ASAP.

"You have different parents and you've led different lives," she said in a more neutral tone. "But you're very close to her. Or you have been. Is friendship always about sharing the same values and experiences? Sometimes—"

"It's not about her!" I blurted out. "It's me! I found out the other day that everybody thinks I'm some kind of overweight paranoid housewife who hates single women!"

"Everybody? How did you find this out?"

"My sister-in-law! She's—she's conspiring with my husband—"

Wendy was staring at me intently.

"—to invite Allison to a dinner party. There's only one way to deflect Elspeth from hunting down Allison. I have to let her think I'm one of these, you know, hardcore wives who just wants to hang with other couples. I know how to keep Matt and Elspeth off the scent—but I hate myself!"

"For betraying Allison?"

"For being the victim of my own frumpy game! I guess I should feel like I'm winning. They have no idea what I'm really hiding. But my sister-in-law thinks I'm a clingy wife, shunning my single friends. And my husband is starting to compare me with his mother! I'm turning into . . ."

I couldn't say it.

"What are you afraid you might become? Marriage can play havoc with a woman's particular sense of her own identity," said Dr. Wendy. "In your case, there are multiple identity issues—"

"I don't have multiple personality disorder!"

"I didn't say that." Dr. Wendy was gentle but firm. "It's clear that you've chosen your various identities. But what are you trying to say or not say about being a wife?"

"Could I have become, in less than a year of marriage, the total embodiment of everything that causes men to see hookers in the first place? That's so not fair!"

I was getting shrill and looking around for the box of tissues.

"That's probably not how I would describe it," she said. "But that's how it feels to you. Today."

"Not just today—all weekend! But if I seem to be that and I'm not really, then I guess I'm doing a good job at being a wife?" I grabbed a few tissues. "In fact, I'd be doing a *great* job."

"Because you're still in control of your identity."

"But if I'm really becoming what I was pretending . . ." I was fighting back tears of anger. "I don't know how to do this—this married thing. And all these questions she was asking—my sister-in-law started pestering me about my French lessons. It was awful. Remember the plan I came up with, to become a translator?"

"Yes. I remember that."

"It's a lot more stressful than I thought it would be."

"Career transitions are emotionally demanding," said Wendy. "I went through one myself when I decided to be a psychotherapist—after six years of teaching phys ed."

That explains the biceps! I've been to three different female shrinks, all on the West Side, and Dr. Wendy's the only one who takes responsibility for her upper arms. I'm not saying that's why

I stuck with her, but it certainly didn't hurt. It's hard to take advice from a therapist who doesn't take care of herself—like my first shrink, Dr. Anita Samson, who was very overweight and chain-smoked. During sessions! There's nothing more discouraging than a shrink who looks physically unhappy. Dr. Wendy hasn't got a clue about hair and she doesn't bother with her nails, but she takes good care of her body. She has the cheerful yet earnest look you want in a shrink. Or a phys ed instructor.

"But this is a fake transition," I said. "I'm just transitioning from one cover story—one fake job to another!"

"You aren't the only person I've encountered who is juggling additional career narratives," Wendy pointed out. "An imaginary transition is quite challenging."

Put that way, my situation sounds *almost genteel*.

"From a therapeutic perspective"—Dr. Wendy adjusted her glasses and leaned forward—"the imagined career is as meaningful as a remunerative job. Perhaps even more so. Every career is an exercise of the imagination, if you think about it. Your transition is not unique," she told me. "In the world of work, it's common to exaggerate or invent. I knew a man who was unemployed for months. His family had no idea. He got up every day, put on his suit, and went out of the house, without ever missing a beat. The human imagination is pretty resilient."

"Oh my god. Like that middle-aged guy in *The Full Monty*? Are you saying I'm in the same boat as *him*?"

The out-of-work factory manager with the bad lawn decorations? Who can't tell his wife that he lost his job?? My self-image doesn't really see itself that way.

"That's a good example of what I'm talking about." Wendy looked pleased, as if she might be on the verge of handing out a gold star. "The boat is very full."

When Allie called last night to set up something for this morning, I couldn't say no. Matt was in the shower, and when my phone started vibrating, I answered cautiously. Despite misgivings about her lifestyle, I still trade customers with Allie. Besides, turning down business from another girl is rude when she owes you a date.

Allie has never specialized in early-morning business. Today was a lucky exception. Ten AM on a weekday is the married call girl's favorite time slot. I don't feel guilty about returning home by six if I'm starting to make money before noon.

Ideally, I'm preparing dinner when Matt returns from the office. If I show up later than he does, I'm on the defensive, and he's more likely to ask about my day. While it's not always possible to keep a low profile in your own home, it's something to aim for, and early-morning clients contribute to my effort.

Getting from Thirty-fourth Street to Eighty-fifth should be a cinch—a straight line up First—but my cabdriver was forced to take a detour near the UN. When I arrived at Allie's building, flustered and late, the doorman waved me through without asking for my destination.

Allie was half-dressed, in a transparent polka-dot camisole with matching panties. In her bare feet, showing off pearly white toenails, she looked like somebody's very willing dessert. A low-fat Dean & Deluca blondie, perhaps.

"Leave your skirt and blouse on," she whispered. "I'll undress you in there."

I followed her to the bedroom, where a familiar-looking client was waiting, relaxed and ready, on his back. I couldn't remember his name. Lanky, pale, with a birthmark on his thigh. Where did I meet this guy? And when? More than five years ago, I think, but I'm supposed to be a New Girl. Or so I was told when Allie called last night.

Happily, he didn't seem to recall our brief encounter at Liane's apartment. In those days, I was Suzy, wearing my hair in a wavy perm. Now, my hair is long and smooth, long enough to confuse any man who isn't prepared for a condom—unrolled with expert lips onto his cock—and long enough for other reasons. Allison began to unbutton my blouse. She played with my skirt, exposing my thighs, then—gradually—more. When I was reduced to bra and panties, I became the aggressor, pushing Allison toward the bed. Her own panties slid to her knees and, with my help, to the carpet.

My face was pressed against her pussy while my hair, falling around her thighs, formed a gentle curtain. I felt Allison pulling my head closer, a signal that he might be in the mood for a "work inspection." Neither of us wanted him peeking behind my hair, to see if I was really eating her pussy or just playing at it.

"You wait your turn," she told him. "Nancy's not finished. . . . If you do that, she'll stop!"

Nancy's the name I now use when I want to be taken for a New Girl. I've used lots of names on the job, but never my own. In this case, Nancy's a newbie who prefers girls to men—or so I was told, last night. I unhooked my bra and began stroking Allie's clitoris with my nipple while she made all the right sounds and movements. My panties were staying put, to discourage any masculine exploration of the contents. Something a girl-who's-only-into-girls would surely insist upon, even if she's getting paid.

But Allie's customer was excited about getting those panties *off*. If a guy thinks he's having sex with someone who's not into men, I suppose there are two ways to play it. Grit your teeth like you hate every second of it (that's awfully dark and edgy but there's probably a market). Or act like you're in the throes of being converted to cock. I chose the latter. A sensible move. Allie's client was trying not to come too fast—but the whole idea of Nancy, enthusiastic lesbian about town, losing her cool while getting fucked on her hands and knees, was too much for him.

He departed in a good mood, never hinting that he recognized me as Suzy.

While I stood in Allison's bathtub, rinsing Astroglide from my inner thighs, she wandered in, to give me a boyfriend bulletin.

"I just got a text from Lucho!" she announced. "I've been accepted by the Colloquium Committee. He nominated me last week because one of the members had to resign. They all voted for me because I'm a sex worker. And a member of NYCOT."

"That's nice," I said, but my mind was really on other things. Like checking to see if the lube was really gone from my inner lips. If you don't remove it all, it's a magnet for germs and you can get a UTI. At the same time, I was trying not to rinse all the moisturizer off my legs! A tricky balancing act: avoiding cystitis and maintaining silky skin are both crucial to a call girl's survival.

"So! I'm helping to plan the Colloquium on Informal Economies and Human Rights! It's going to be at Cornell," Allie was saying. "And my job is to represent NYCOT on the Colloquium Committee. I spoke to Roxana about it. We're going to need your help."

I turned off the water.

"*My* help? Roxana knows I don't want to be involved with NYCOT," I told Allie. "Much less this new committee you're joining."

Roxana Blair is the founder of the New York Council of Trollops which is—in theory—leaderless. But she's also chief spokeswoman, keeper of the e-mail list, and, for almost ten years, the engine that runs NYCOT. All their meetings are held at her apartment in the East Village. I wish Roxana weren't so keen on grooming my best friend for a leadership role but there's nothing I can do to stop her. Why, oh why, doesn't *she* want to sit on that Colloquium Committee? Roxana must be getting burned out.

"I understand that you do worthwhile things," I said, "but this—all this activism isn't for me. This is a job, not a cause."

"It's a job *and* a cause. We have to get people to recognize it as a job. *That's* a cause."

"Each to her own," I said as Allie handed me a towel. "As long as *I* know it's a job, I don't care what people think."

And the less people are thinking about my job, the better!

"Tell Roxana to forget she ever met me and to stop talking about me. Did she bring this up at one of your meetings? I don't want all those NYCOT members to have me on their radar," I added.

"Don't worry!" Allie said in a tense voice. "Roxana doesn't have your number. Or your e-mail."

"She'd better not."

In the living room, a pot of ginger tea was brewing and Allison had organized a plate of odd-looking munchies.

"No cookies," I insisted. "I'm trying to lose six pounds."

Allison was wearing just her camisole and panties again—with a pair of huge white terry cloth slippers that no client has ever seen.

"Try these! They're made with soya protein and sugar alcohols. I made them myself! From a recipe on the low-carb vegan site."

They were like dried sweetened glue.

"Very nice," I said, midnibble. I washed the cookie down with some ginger tea. "And they're so filling," I said strategically.

"Now," she said, counting our money out. "I have to explain. We aren't asking you to come to any NYCOT meetings. Roxana knows you can't come to meetings."

"Good. But I don't want her to know *why*. I want you to promise you won't discuss my marriage with her."

Allie looked hurt. "I already promised. Why don't you trust me?"

"Of course I trust you!" I lied. "I'm just reminding you."

Bits of soya cookie were lodged in my molars. It was maddening.

"We want you to help us find a lawyer," she told me. "Roxana—"

"After all these years of running a hookers' union, Roxana doesn't have her own lawyer?"

"Her contacts are with Legal Aid. And there's Reverend Moody at Judson Church—he knows a few people at the Urban Justice Center. But this is different. And it might cost money."

"I can donate. Anonymously."

"That's not it. I have to find a lawyer who can help me get a visa."

Uh-oh. What is Allie getting into now? She was standing near the window, bent over the computer station. Her camisole slid north and a patch of smooth, fat-free midriff peeked out above her panties.

"Noi is going to be the keynote speaker at the Colloquium on Informal Economies. She's the Bangkok coordinator of Bad Girls Without Borders." Allie fiddled with her trackball on a mouse pad that proclaimed SAFE SEX SLUT in white block letters. "We need a visa so she can attend the conference and we need to find a place for her to stay. If she really has to, she can stay here. But she needs a lawyer. The Legal Aid people can't help because she's in Bangkok. They don't do visas . . . and *this* is the BGWB website!"

Against a pistachio-colored background, a series of magenta greetings—*Hola . . . Bonjour . . . $awadee Kha*—wiggled slowly across the screen. When Allie clicked on the dollar sign, hot pink condoms tumbled forth, followed by a montage of dancing girls with long black hair and light brown skin in bikinis and heels. In another picture, a banner was held high on a crowded street: EN-TERTAINMENT WORKERS SANS FRONTIERES. I could see two slim black-haired girls in sunglasses, T-shirts, and jeans carrying the banner.

"That's Noi at the International Women's Day march. And her friend Ying. The bar girls had their own banner!" she explained. "They have a branch in Phuket. And a sister group in Cambodia. But anyway, Noi lives in Bangkok. And I need to find a lawyer who can help her apply for a visa."

"Can't Lucho help?"

Allie blushed.

"I can't ask Lucho."

"But he must know somebody. These exotic college professors deal with visas and forms all the time."

"Maybe, but"—Allie's voice was getting a little squeaky, she looked away from me—"he nominated me for the Colloquium Committee because he thinks I can locate a lawyer. He thinks NYCOT has more resources than we really do and he . . . he sort of thinks I've done this before. When the girls from Ecuador came to that conference in Berkeley."

"You lied to him? About your activist credentials?"

"No." Allie looked down at her Safe Sex mouse pad. She tugged nervously on a strand of her long blond hair. "I just— when I realized what he was thinking, I didn't, you know, say anything different."

"Allie, it's good to let a guy think what he needs to think but you're taking it to extremes. Why don't you let him help you? Instead of acting so accomplished, let him be the rescuer! Guys love that!"

"It's too late! And if I did that, I wouldn't be on all these committees and panels! I'd just be—I want to be on the Colloquium Committee. I don't want him to save me or have to do things for me. Or feel sorry for me! I'm an activist now and I think Lucho and I could be a power couple. But I have to get more, you know, successful at my activism."

"A power couple?"

"I told him I would raise the money for Noi's legal fees and he thinks I'm already interviewing lawyers."

"How much do you need? I can afford—"

"I want you to help me find a lawyer. What about Jason? Your brother-in-law? *He's* a lawyer."

Allison's passive-aggressive idealism tries my patience. Is she out of her mind?

"We cannot go there," I said. "And you know it."

As I glared at her, she bit her lip, averting her eyes.

"You could say you have a friend from Thailand who—"

"There's no way! I don't want my in-laws to start wondering how I know someone who's in this business."

"But this isn't business. It's about social justice. And it's my chance to make a difference. For a Bangkok bar girl to be a keynote speaker at an Ivy League school? Do you realize how huge this is?"

Allie was staring at a close-up of Noi. Then she clicked on something and brought up a street scene: working girls in long colorful saris, carrying yellow placards. Three dark brown girls in their twenties appeared to be dancing in the street, in front of a purple banner. The letters, in gold, were in a language I don't recognize.

"These are the girls in Bangladesh. Last year, a judge ruled they couldn't be evicted from the red-light district and they had a huge celebration."

Allie looked radiant. As if she herself had been threatened with eviction. From a red-light district in South Asia rather than a doorman building on the Upper East Side.

She moved on to a chubby pink-skinned redhead in a leopard-print bustier holding up a sign: U.S. OUT OF OUR UNDERWEAR . . . FREE THE NEVADA THREE! A group of protestors in leopard T-shirts, nighties, shorts, and much less were gathered around the redhead.

"This is Leopard-Look Solidarity in Vegas! When the Nevada Three got arrested they were at a bachelor party wearing leopard-print thongs. . . . Everyone went to the courthouse to protest the sentencing. In leopard print. To show solidarity. Oops. Except for David—he's wearing a zebra hat. He might be coming to the Cornell colloquium."

So these are Allie's new friends! A global in-crowd of sign-waving, sari-clad, zebra-hatted card-carrying "sex workers."

"Well, I don't think Jason can help you with this. And *I* certainly can't ask him," I said.

As she clicked and surfed, Allie didn't seem to be listening. She returned to some snapshots of Noi. Lithe and gutsy, in a pair of capri-style jeans, platforms, and a tank top, holding a bullhorn on a busy street corner. *"From Soi Cowboy with love and con-*

doms, Noi." Standing at a podium in front of yet another banner in yet another language. I noticed a poster decorating the podium: a sewing machine in a big red circle with a diagonal line crossing out the machine.

Allie turned to face me. In a quiet voice, she asked, "Are you absolutely sure?"

Something had changed. The expression on her face—I'd never seen it before—made me realize, *If I ignore this, it's not going away.*

But what does a girl like Allie know about visas? Her determination and ignorance could get a lot of people in trouble. Including me, perhaps. The safest course is to placate her for now. Even if I have no intention of asking Jason for anything.

"I have to think about it," I said carefully. "He's not the only lawyer in this town . . . maybe I can ask him for a referral. But you need to give me a few days. It's a bad time to ask Jason for a favor. And I have to figure out how—without, you know, saying what it's for."

Indeed, I'm not quite sure what it is for. To help a righteous bar girl? Or to save Allie from looking like a silly East Side princess in the eyes of her West Side intellectual boyfriend? Maybe Jasmine's right, and never the twain should date. But now it's too late.

Fluff and Aft

Today, while picking up the rent, I got my first glimpse of Charmaine post-Florida.

"It's . . . rather natural," I said. "Like you went to a spa."

"You see?" Looking pleased with herself, she tilted her face slightly. "More fluff and loft. Dr. Fielding is the best. Actually I did go to a spa. Just—a really *good* spa."

There's something different about her cheeks. And what about her mouth? Is it the shape of her lips? Or the color?

"I did some A.F.T. And I'm all recovered from the liposuction."

"A.F.T.?"

"Autologous Fat Transplantation. I'm not waiting for God to give me cheekbones."

With a pang of guilt, I suddenly realized that I've always taken my cheekbones for granted. But Charmaine's already used to the way she looks now, even if I'm not, and what she really wanted to show off was our new thigh-high state-of-the-art . . . shredder.

"You're gonna thank me for *this*!" she enthused. "I had it delivered this morning."

A sleek gray object with a black switch and a small green light stood in the corner of the living room.

"It matches the carpet," I said. "But why do we need such a powerful shredder? It's not like we generate a lot of paperwork!"

"That's what *you* think."

Charmaine disappeared into the bedroom and returned with a small stack of cardboard. She's been hoarding the condom boxes, storing them flat, and waiting for a chance to get rid of them. We both want to make sure the landlord doesn't find anything incriminating in our trash.

"How many of these things have you got?" I asked.

"No idea. Better safe than sorry." She held the stack of red, white, and black boxes. "The problem is . . ."

Our eyes met.

"I know. The different sizes. It's a total tip-off," I agreed.

"Totally."

It's not safe to take them outside to the corner where a neighbor might see you. Charmaine flipped a switch and started feeding condom boxes into the shredder.

"It's built for volume. Turns everything into confetti. Even a Trojan Magnum box."

She tipped open the receiving bin and showed me a small pile of black confetti. The answer to our nightmares.

"Oh—and if we really need to," she added, "you can destroy the video boxes. But some guys like to look at those. What do you think?"

"The Bells of Saint Clemens" started chiming madly in my handbag, and I scrambled to answer.

"What a happy occasion," said the voice of Barry Horowitz. "I tried to call you back twice, but I didn't leave a message."

"I think we should talk in person," I told him. "Do you remember my friend Allison?"

"How could I forget?"

Barry's the kind of lawyer who takes a perverse delight in solving the personal problems of hookers.

"I promised Allie—" I glanced sideways at Charmaine, now sitting on the couch doing rehab on some chipped toenail polish. "I'll call you later when I know more."

I flipped my phone shut and tried to take my time leaving the apartment. It wouldn't be right to discuss Allison's predicament in earshot of someone who's been working for two years. Older girls shouldn't hang their laundry out to dry in front of the New Girls. And Charmaine looks up to Allison, despite being more serious about her work than Allie has ever been. She has no idea what the real deal is because Allie, after all these years, still looks great and has her own clients. I would be the worst kind of traitor if I don't let Charmaine believe that the girl who introduced us has her act together. (And a traitor to myself! Charmaine might question *my* credibility.)

When I got to the corner of Seventy-ninth and York, I tried to call Barry but found myself in voice mail.

"You have reached the law office of Barry M. Horowitz. Press one if your message is urgent. . . ."

Then I called Allie.

"I should have some news for you soon. About your friend's visa."

"Omigosh. Really?"

"Don't get TOO excited," I said. "One step at a time."

"I got an e-mail today from Noi. I told her not to worry. She was warned by someone in Australia not to plan on coming to the colloquium! Can you believe it? The Australians are telling her I'm unreliable and arrogant. I have to put a stop to these rumors."

"Making extravagant promises won't—"

"It's Molly, the webmistress. She's been posting mean remarks on the list-serve about the girls in New York. As if *Melbourne's* the center of the universe?"

"Well, it's closer to Bangkok than we are."

"And she's trying to destroy my friendship with Noi!"

After promising to report back very soon, I hung up.

•◆• THURSDAY, 3/29/01 •◆•

This morning, Barry greeted me in the waiting room of his office. I was surprised to find him sitting at his assistant's desk, bent over a pile of envelopes and magazines. He was wearing suspenders that almost matched his bow tie—an offhand yet well-planned marriage of wavy yellow stripes.

"Leonard is attending the birth of his first child," he announced. "I am my own receptionist."

He ushered me into his office. "But it's kind of fun, working for yourself. I might adopt this as a lifestyle," he added.

A collection of Troll Dolls from the 1960s decorated a glass-encased cabinet behind his desk. I complimented him on the renovation of his office space—finally complete—then tried to summarize Allie's situation. He steepled his fingers and assumed one of his most enigmatic expressions.

Finally, he said, "Allison's in a romantic pickle with global overtones. But I prefer that to a global pickle with romantic overtones. It's not so easy for a Thai national to obtain a visa from the United States. Especially for a Patpong bar girl."

"But that's what she told her boyfriend she would do."

"The boyfriend . . ." Barry narrowed his eyes. "Did *he* suggest that she import this lady? How did this whole thing come about?"

"He's a professor," I assured him. "It's a conference at a university. What are you implying?"

"Not implying. Asking. What does Allison's new boyfriend look like? How old is he? And where did they meet?"

"I have no idea—she says he's really handsome."

"No doubt."

"He teaches at the New School. And he met her at a harm-reduction conference. He's a fan," I added.

I left Barry's office under a nerve-wracking cloud of apprehension, having promised to give Allie his cell phone number. He followed me to the elevator, speaking in a low voice.

"She might want to avoid discussing the matter with her paramour until we meet. Nothing should be said about this in e-mail. And you can tell her it's a pro bono project."

"We're both willing to pay for your time," I protested. "I can give you a retainer."

"Don't worry," he said. "I know what you're thinking, but I'm too jaded to seduce a damsel in distress, and there's no danger of Allison seducing me."

"I wasn't thinking any such thing!"

I stepped into the empty elevator and Barry blocked the door for a moment with his arm.

"I would hate to see the New York Council of Trollops entangled in visa fraud. Or a possible INS sting. The world is more dangerous than Allison will ever realize." He sighed. "That's part of her charm."

•◆• LATER •◆•

Dare I tell Allison that Barry suspects her "paramour" of being a possible security threat? She might freak out and say something to Lucho. Allie gets so talkative when she falls in love. *My policy is to censor 25 percent of all pillow talk. That means putting every fourth revelation, no matter how trivial, harmful, or sincere, on hold. I can always say it later if it was really a good idea. And half the time it really isn't.

•◆• FRIDAY MORNING, 3/30/01 •◆•

Jasmine was a Barry Horowitz client when she was a ticket scalper, long before she started hooking. And later on, during her drug-dealing phase. Hooking was Jasmine's way of settling down after a few narrow escapes, and Barry's the reason she could enter her newest profession without a criminal record.

I called her from the nail salon while waiting for my toes to dry.

"Barry seems to think this professor might be up to something. And I don't know how to break the news to Allie. She's so, you know, *smitten*."

"Let her discuss it with Barry," Jasmine advised. "He's more persuasive."

"Thanks a lot!"

"For all her stupid ranting about hooker solidarity, you know she'll pay more attention to something her lawyer tells her. Because he charges for his advice, and you don't."

"I guess you have a point there."

"You *know* I do. If anyone should listen to my advice, it's Allison, but she never does. I ordered a baby present for Barry's assistant. Your share's seventy-five. I'll get Allison to chip in. That brings it down to fifty."

"May I ask what 'we' have picked out?"

"A Tiffany piggy bank. Every child should be learning how to save before he can talk."

"Leonard had a boy?"

"That's right! One less piece of jail bait for us to worry about—before you know it, these little girls are leaping out of their playpens, hitting the hotel bars, and they're big enough to be stealing your dates. I swear to god, some of the New Girls look like they were born when I was in college! Our economy needs some extra men. And Leonard has been good enough to provide us with one."

I just hope Leonard's *co-parent* never has to encounter Jasmine.

"Why don't you drop by and sign the card?"

It's a form of feminine machismo to brave Manhattan sidewalks in paper slippers while your toenails are still drying. (Exposing your feet in deepest winter takes it right up to the next level.) All the staff at Pinky's are accustomed to the paint-and-run syndrome, so they keep a special supply of used shopping bags for customers' shoes. With my Prada sneakers stuffed into a Duane Reade bag, I made my way—carefully—to Jasmine's apartment.

As I crossed Eighty-fourth Street, Matt was ringing from his office. I love it when it's actually safe to take a call from my husband! Though it's not considered "safe" by most people to answer the phone while barefoot in a crosswalk. Safety's a relative concept.

"Hi, babe." He sounded so happy to hear my voice that my heart skipped a beat, as if we were still dating. "I got us a table for seven o'clock at Verbena."

"Is there any way to move it forward?" I pleaded. "Just a little? I'm way uptown and there might be traffic."

Matt respects the fact that I have all these preexisting Upper East Side relationships—places where I go for my nails, hair, Pilates, and skin care—making it quite natural to be hanging out uptown, even if there are five Korean nail salons I could walk to from Thirty-fourth Street.

I dare not disclose that I'm on my way to Jasmine's to sign a baby card for Barry's assistant! Matt would wonder how such a well-known criminal lawyer—Barry's exploits are too often in the news—became a fixture in *my* life. And I don't want to give Matt any more ideas about babies than he already has. The other day, he walked right up to a Bugaboo stroller in our building lobby, ostensibly to examine the wheels, and *waved at its occupant* while making small talk with the baby's father. This isn't something I want to encourage.

I stepped out of my tattered paper slippers onto Jasmine's pristine carpet just as they were giving out. Jasmine was eager to show me a picture of the sterling piggy bank. And the baby card we're all signing.

"I'm having the pig monogrammed. Here's a pen."

"I don't know if this card is in good taste," I objected.

On the front: "Thank You" in gothic script. Inside, in Jasmine's handwriting: ". . . for having a boy!"

"I think it's in *very* good taste," Jasmine told me. "Anyway,

Leonard just spent the best part of a night watching his girlfriend give birth. You think *that's* in good taste? And Barry says it was *not* one of those 'north end' delivery jobs."

Are deliveries now defined by . . . where the father happens to be situated??

•◆• FRIDAY NIGHT •◆•

A strange but rewarding session with Trish, this afternoon, at the Stanhope. I arrived at three-thirty sharp to find Trish strutting around the hotel room in extravagantly high boots, a skimpy black push-up bra that shows off her nipples, and a tight black leather skirt. Our customer stood quietly in a corner, hands behind his back. He was wearing a jockstrap and, on his face, a rather apprehensive expression. He stared at his feet, and barely looked up when I entered, but his posture was excellent, showing off his elderly but toned muscles.

"And now," Trish was telling him, "the apprentice has arrived."

As a "junior interrogator," I don't have to dress in such a pointed or obvious fashion—just a girlish sweater, skirt, and normal heels. I'm supposed to be the teacher's pet at a pornysounding institution, a cross between *Private School for Girls* and a prison camp.

"Now, Sabrina, listen carefully." Trish adopted a low sinister voice. "When a male prisoner has ejaculated a hundred times, his greatest fear is that he'll be forced to come for the hundred and *first* time. Tommy's been having nightmares about you."

"He has?"

I stood closer and made an effort to touch Trisha's nipples.

"Not now," she said, pulling back. "Do you know *why* Tommy has these nightmares?"

"No," I quivered.

"His greatest fear is a young, tempting interrogator. She makes him come on his own boots, while he's standing up."

She picked up a long thin stick, which she pointed at his groin. "*This* is the most vulnerable part of your prisoner," she continued.

Tom emitted a dramatic gasp that couldn't possibly have anything to do with the pressure from the stick.

"Not there! Please," he said in a hoarse voice. "You'll ruin me. No! Not in my boots! Standing up . . . no!"

I've never seen anything quite like it. He was pretending to be in pain. For me, that's a new spin on the concept of customer satisfaction. Masochists usually try to *provoke* pain—real pain. Is he more interested in the drama? Or just too jaded to go through with it? At his age, it's anyone's guess.

Trish waved her pointer in the general direction of my pussy.

"Now this," she explained to me, "is the interrogator's liability. As a female you must be in total control of your weakest body parts at all times. Does the sight of a man, erect in his jockstrap, make you damp?"

I nodded shyly and looked away, like a blushing schoolgirl.

"I'm going to show you how to interrogate, humiliate, and arouse a man without losing control of your own desires. No matter how damp your panties get."

Tom was staring at the floor again. His erection was protruding and I reached out to touch the head of his cock with my fingertip. Trish held my wrist while I teased him.

"When his jockstrap grows full, it's a sign of your power as a female but you *must not let him turn the tables on you.* Do you understand?"

"Yes," I said, feigning nervous excitement. "I think I do."

I continued to stroke him lightly, while taunting him with my lips, parted and only hinting at what he wanted.

"Now go back to your seat, Sabrina, and don't return until I decide it's safe for you to interrogate our prisoner. And stop looking at his jockstrap."

After the session had ended, I sat waiting for Trish to change out of her spy-from-hell costume into her day-in-town pantsuit. Tom was pottering around the room, still in his jockstrap and nothing else. He poured a glass of spring water for each of us, and settled into an armchair. He's clearly proud of his taut physique—with good reason.

"Thalia tells me you're a student at NYU," he said. "What are you majoring in?"

"Well, just part-time," I allowed, not wanting to get in too deep. "I dropped out for a few years and then I decided to go back part-time."

"It's the best way," he told me. "See a bit of life while you're getting your degree."

"Do you row?" I asked. "Or do you swim a lot?"

"How did you know?" he replied with a cocky grin. "Used to be on a rowing team. But that was years ago. Swimming! There's nothing like it."

Trish came out of the bathroom carrying a tote bag very similar to the one I sometimes use. In a black pantsuit and ankle boots, she now looked like a benign bank manager. On the way to her favorite garage, where she stashes her SUV, Trish decided to follow me into Agata & Valentina.

"I really miss this place," she sighed. "There's nothing like it near my house."

She paused in front of some cannoli.

"Not for me," I said.

"You look great, by the way. I don't know what this is all about. You keep telling me you gained weight but you still look like a New Girl! Tommy really thinks you're twenty-five."

"Well, after sixty, they all think we look like kids."

"Not this one! If a girl's not young or pretty? I never hear the end of it. Tommy's picky. And he was happy with you."

"Thanks. I need some salad greens."

But there was a tense moment when Trisha picked up a container of dressing for *hers*.

"No thanks," I said, as she offered me a container, "I always make my own."

"You do?" She looked amused. "This is good stuff! You should try it!"

"No, really. I never serve a dressing I haven't made myself."

"It's so much easier to get it here. And it's better than Paul Newman's. This is balsamic, you know."

"I've never . . ." *been near a store-bought salad dressing,* I started to say, ". . . tried that," I replied. "I've, um, moved on from balsamic, actually. I've been using aged red wine vinegar and walnut oil."

"I don't have time for all that. Do you really think guys know the difference? They're like kids."

What is she talking about? I preferred homemade dressing as a *child*. I remember watching my mother tossing salad in a big wooden bowl in her first bachelor apartment, a month after my parents broke up. The stove and fridge were separated from the dining area by a wall she constructed with cinderblocks. Her kitchen table was fifties Formica, rescued from a garage sale. Except that, having no fondness for anything of the fifties, she hid the table under a flowery sheet that worked quite well as a tablecloth.

"My husband can't tell whether I'm serving Paul Newman's or balsamic from Zabar's. Men are visual. If it looks good, they think it tastes good. Anyway," Trish said, grabbing a box of steamed shrimp, "if I can fake an orgasm, why not salad dressing?"

"You fake orgasms at home?"

"Oh, sure." But Trish looked quite cheerful. "What's the big deal?"

"My husband would *know* if I was faking."

"An orgasm? Or the salad dressing?"

"Both! He likes my cooking. And I *want* him to like it."

Trish was pushing her cart toward the coffee section.

"You sound like Betty Crocker," she mused. "Don't tell me. I'll bet you grind your own beans, too."

She seems to regard my way of life—which I *thought* was a lot like hers—as a quaint, irrational museum exhibit. Real sex, homemade salad dressing, and freshly ground coffee. But I can't think of anything sadder than eating dressing out of a bottle—and having sex with a guy who's neither paying nor getting me off! What kind of home life has Trish settled for?

"Did you ever have good sex? What happened?" I wanted to know.

"With Jake? Oh, sort of. It's not really about that. He's a great father. . . . I've had better and I've had worse. Coming isn't that important to me."

But she has such a great business! Does having a low sex drive give her an edge??

Five spams entitled "The Mother Of Your Children Caught You Looking @ Free Pussy?!" Gosh. How many buttons can you push in one subject header?

Special instructions from Elspeth Re: "Dinner Bash 2nite, Kids! Shhhh!" How does she find the energy to orchestrate a surprise for Jason involving twenty people? I still can't get over the fact that the twins are barely one month old.

A *New York Times* article from Charmaine, about Rentocrats who pay $326 for rent-controlled palaces that they actually inherit:

> *Should we be concerned? It's the first of a series!*
> *Worried. C.K.*

According to this crusader at the *Times,* rent-control tenants are as lazy as landed gentry—they never have to work very hard because the monthly nut is so small. Could this be the start of a crackdown? He's making a list of the ten worst Rent Stabilization abusers—and naming them! I guess I'm a rent offender—though hardly a 'crat since I paid key money to get my lease. That's illegal, of course, while inheriting a lease from your parents is within the law. But surely the person who pays key money is morally ahead of the person who inherits! Besides, I use my apartment to keep my work a secret—not to *avoid* work.

It's hard to give up a rent-stabilized apartment once you have your name on that lease. No matter what happens with Matt, I know I'll always have a roof over my head. But if I told him that, he'd be insulted. Matt wants me to believe he'll always protect and support me. I want Matt to believe I believe him. And what would this crusading *Times* reporter say if I ended up in his column? That rent stabilization promotes infidelity?

A rather blunt e-mail from Miranda, my very single, very downtown cousin who, strangely enough, is responsible for my marriage.

> *I have to leave Elspeth's before dessert—think she'll mind? I want to arrive early but not spoil her surprise. There's a book party for my boss at The Gershwin and I MUST be there. Elspeth keeps talking about that rightwingpreppy who was chasing me at her last party. Why is he still available if he's so great? Call me! Cousin M.*

Uh-oh. Hopefully she won't find out that I'm to blame for Elspeth's match-making efforts.

Miranda introduced me to Matt on the grounds that "two conservatives might be able to start a fire." Just because I don't pierce my navel, she thinks I'm a total fogey—an assumption I've never challenged—and just because she *does* pierce hers, she considers herself a cultural exile. Well, Miranda hides her piercing from her parents, but if I wore a navel ring, my parents would be quite unfazed. Not that I would!

While cleaning up spam, I spotted a bulletin from "Trollop-at-Large." Instinctively, I turned around to see if Matt was nearby. But I could hear him doing something in the kitchen.

> *Wow! Guess what? Two NYCOT members have been invited to speak @ the Open Society Institute by George Soros himself! And *I* am one of them! I*

*have to prepare a 20 minute speech and they're
paying an honorarium.*

*I'm on the panel with Gretchen who wants to
compare the street outreach programs in the Bronx
with the harm reduction agenda in Glasgow. Anyway,
Roxana says Gretchen's talk will be ALL ABOUT
THE INEQUITIES. So I should be more upbeat.*

*I've never been PAID for this before—it's a great
honor! I'll put it towards the legal fees for Noi. I
know, Barry H. says he won't charge us but I feel like
I should give him SOMETHING. Don't you?*

I just wrote to Lucho. Want to see his reply?

*>>darling allison, having you in my life is a delight. I
>>love being in love with the goddess of social change
>>who happens to reside in 5H. See you very soon
>>but not soon enough. 8 oclock? L.*

*And I met with Barry this morning. Thank you
BIGTIME! I'm learning about the obstacles to getting
Noi her visa. He's got some ideas about how we can
get around the rules. Something about a waiver? I
showed him the website and he was very impressed
with the sewing machine logo.*

*Hugs!
Allie*

Followed by an e-mail afterthought.

PS: I'm not sure about Roxana's advice. If I'm TOO upbeat, Gretchen will hate me. Don't you agree?

Gretchen, who was a streetwalker at fifteen, now has a masters in public health. Not only has she got more street cred than Allie, she has an extra degree—from Columbia. In Gretchen's view, call girls are just pampered lightweights. And Allison, who went to Marymount, hasn't been able to change Gretchen's mind about that.

NYCOT's an alternative universe for hookers, with its own laws. No wonder Allie's intimidated.

But Lucho's saying all the right things now. That little dispute about Allie's pubic hair seems to be on hold. And Barry has completely distracted her from wanting to consult Jason. "Thank Goddess" for Barry Horowitz!

Almost two-thirty. MUST sort out my Dinnerwear. Something that won't look eager or dressy. As a married guest, I don't want to look like I'm trying to outdo the single females. I always feel safer around Elspeth when I'm wearing flats—the unconscious trademark of sexual virtue! Of course, they have to be *good* flats—I don't want to look *frumpy* around my sister-in-law. Casual Saturdays are such a minefield.

•❖• SUNDAY MORNING, 4/01/01 •❖•

When in doubt, wear black. Last night I wore my Bottega slipper-mules: black satin with subdued beading. And a black tailored blouse over black Gucci jeans.

Casual black's coherent. And a dressy black outfit is the essence of simplicity. In any case, black looks self-confident no matter the format, like you almost don't give a damn. As long as you're not wearing too much jewelry.

Miranda arrived, wearing the single, downtown version of my all-black outfit: tighter pants with a sassy fringe around the hem, smaller top, chunky heels. She was carrying a canvas messenger bag and wearing . . . a rasta hat. She's been listening to a lot of reggae lately, and preaching about how we, "the children of Trinidadian Diaspora," need to make common cause with Jamaicans—a concept I'm just not sure about. She kissed me on both cheeks, hugged Matt, and bestowed upon Chris—standing across the room—a perky but distancing wave.

So far, so cordial. She pulled out a bottle of champagne from her messenger sack and disappeared into the kitchen, where Elspeth was convening with her caterer.

Chris, hoping to play it cool, stayed out of the kitchen and attached himself to Matt and Jason. But Miranda wandered over to the drinks table, casting a beckoning glance in my direction.

"What is Elspeth thinking?" Miranda hissed. "She says Chris has been asking all these questions."

"No idea," I lied. "What kind of questions?"

"About V.S. Naipaul! He wants to chat with *me* about that reactionary coolie?"

Miranda, who spent her childhood in Trinidad, occasionally says things like "coolie," which I find a bit shocking. I left when I was a baby so never learned to use these expressions. My mother never spoke to me in the local slang of her birthplace, and my father waited until I was an adult to fully indulge his verbal peccadillos.

"He wants to discuss *The Enigma of Arrival*," Miranda continued. She looked like she was ready to spit.

"Relax," I counseled her. "He's trying to be well read. And multicultural."

"The new socially acceptable code for covert exoticization!" Miranda said. "Every suit is reading *The Enigma*."

"Well, have you read it?"

"No."

"Then tell him that. And tell him why. Talk to him about what you *like* to read."

"Why must I talk to him at all?"

"Would you at least smile at him? He's looking so forlorn."

Brokering a friendly impulse from my twenty-something cousin was not an easy task. I wonder if this is how a madam feels when business is going badly.

Ten minutes later, I wandered past a corner of the room, where Chris had managed—after much effort—to engage Miranda.

"The tragedy," I could hear her saying, "is that Jamaica succeeds in exporting all this wonderful revolutionary pop music to the rest of the known world while Trinidad's cultural export is this"—I prayed that she would not say "coolie" to this well-meaning WASP who was leaning toward her angular brown cheeks, lapping up every word—"self-hating, colonized racist despised by his own people and embraced by . . ."

I decided to rescue Miranda from the intensity of her admirer's gaze: "Is it possible that steel band music isn't as universal or as good to dance to as reggae music?" I asked. "Or maybe calypso's too local."

"But it's as relevant as rap," Chris said. "Isn't The Mighty Sparrow still a contender? Trinidad exports words and Jamaica exports music. And what about Byron Lee? He's Jamaican but he plays Trinidadian music."

Miranda was not prepared for this.

"Trinidadian music has a following throughout the Caricom region," Chris added. "Maybe that's more important. And soca's big in Britain."

It seemed like a good time to leave them alone. Isn't that what a madam would do?

How did this sandy-haired, slightly freckled lawyer from Darien become so familiar with The Mighty Sparrow? I'm almost sure he had no idea where Trinidad *was* a year ago. But Miranda inspires him in some way. He's been doing his homework, the sort of thing girls were once instructed to do when dating an eligible man. When I looked back, Miranda was actually sitting down on a large ottoman next to Chris. There was a tentative, softer look in her eyes as she listened to Elspeth's pet bachelor waxing multicultural about Caricom and the global reach of calypso.

I found myself drawn into a small circle of wives—two of whom had adopted, like me, the all-black strategy. My hostess linked her arm through mine and said, "Nancy's gonna be finding that out for herself!"

A birdlike blonde began to enlighten me: "Elspeth was just saying that finding the right ob-gyn is as tricky as—"

". . . nailing down Mr. Right!" Elspeth explained. "I had a hell of a time finding a doctor who would let me deliver Bridget and Berrigan vaginally. But I knew I could do it. You have to hold out for the right guy *and* the right doctor. I should start a matchmaking service for mothers and obstetricians—I interviewed twelve in two weeks! I know each one's MO and each one's specialty."

"You do?" someone asked. "How about Dr. Wallace. My sister went to her for—"

"Fertility," Elspeth told her.

"Yes! She's supposed to be one of the best."

"She is but only for getting pregnant. She won't deliver twins unless you agree to a C-section. And I knew I could do it myself."

"How did you, um, know this?" I dared to ask.

"A Woman Just Knows."

The birdlike blonde looked as faint as I felt. I stared with sympathy at her slim hips.

"Well," she sighed. "More power to you. I myself wasn't ready for—"

"I'm not saying it's better," Elspeth assured her. "Just because *I* chose vaginal!"

Nobody was buying *that* but it would have seemed rude to say so. A tall pale redhead broke the awkward silence. "I'm sure your babies will be *beautiful,*" she told me. "My nephew's half-Korean, by the way."

"And half-Irish," Elspeth added. "He must be adorable! But Nancy keeps telling me she isn't 'pure Chinese.'"

"I'm partly Indian," I explained. "On my father's side. Like Miranda—but she gets it from her mother."

Miranda's mother, Kasturi, grew up as a nonobservant Hindu in Port of Spain. Aunt Kas went to a convent school and converted at sixteen. As a hyper-Catholic Indian, she was able to marry Uncle Gregory, my mother's eldest brother, without too much opposition from my grandmother, also a devout Catholic. Grandmummy would have preferred a Chinese wife for her first son. In Trinidad, people don't make adoring remarks about the mixing of the races. They either take it for granted or disapprove. My Chinese grandparents disapproved *and* took it for granted.

"Nancy's adding some melanin to the lineage," my sister-in-law said. "Her kids will have suntanning capacities that Matt and I could only dream about."

Thank goodness Miranda was safely out of hearing. She would probably start in about Matt's genes diluting the suntan capacity of *our* line.

"Time for a refreshment break!" Elspeth was looking at her watch. "And after this feeding I can have my glass of champagne. Yay!"

When Elspeth emerged from the bedroom area, Miranda was already en route to her next party.

"What happened to Chris?" she asked hopefully.

"He went downstairs to help her into a cab," I told her. "Even though she believes in hailing her own."

"Good move!" Elspeth rejoiced. "How did you pull that off?"

Later, Matt and I stood by the elevators on Elspeth's floor. We were the last guests to leave. After too many hours of circulating, drinking, and socializing, we were finally alone. He kissed the top of my head while I leaned against his shoulder. Then he placed a gentle hand on my cheek. I moved my right hip a little closer to his body and, feeling some hardness under his pants, made a quiet purring demand. With both hands on my waist, he made me face him and started kissing my mouth with real authority.

Suddenly, a door opened. I turned around. Elspeth's voice filled the hallway.

"ASK ME ABOUT cryogenic cord blood storage! *Don't forget.*"

"Yet" Means "Now"

"If we want things to stay as they
are, things will have to change."
—*Giuseppe di Lampedusa*

This afternoon, I returned from Pilates to find Matt barefoot and pottering in the kitchen.

Wearing dalmatian-covered boxers and a black T-shirt, he stood before a random collection of bottles, cans, and jars. The sight of his sturdy limbs and rumpled hair made me want to undress him. Something about Matt, available in the kitchen, felt novel, intimate, and just right.

"What's this?" I asked, setting down my gym bag.

Leaning against his muscular arms, I felt more like a girl than a woman. Despite an hour of upper-body rigors, designed to pump me up, I was intrigued by his relative strength. Ready to be overwhelmed.

A dozen tins of imported tuna were neatly stacked on the counter. "I'm sending the tuna to a homeless shelter," he said. "I'm not sure about the anchovies. And we should talk about these," he added, holding up a bottle of cod liver oil capsules. "Why do you take this stuff anyway?"

To keep my pubic hair from getting dry when it grows back! But that's kind of personal, isn't it?

"For the vitamin A," I said.

"There have to be other sources. What about carrots?"

"Where I get my vitamin A is really up to me, I think. And why are you throwing out a whole case of tuna fish? We don't have niçoise salad THAT often. If you don't like it, I'll just make it for myself when you're working late!"

A cloud was settling around my heart, smothering my libido—and he didn't even care!

"Nancy . . ." Matt followed me to the master bathroom. "Don't close the door! Let me explain."

While I showered, I applied a mint mask to my pubic region—and pondered Matt's insensitivity. First of all, and he obviously doesn't appreciate it, I carefully sprayed each one of those tins with Clorox and rinsed them clean—just in case he decides to open one in my absence.

I guess that's not insensitivity. It's just typical male ingratitude based on a lack of information. He thinks those tins are just sitting there, doing nothing. He doesn't understand—

But you have to know when to retreat from domestic tension if you want to keep the romance alive. I *must not* argue with my husband about whether he appreciates my preemptive house-keeping strategies.

Secondly, and he obviously doesn't care, Salade Niçoise is a treasured souvenir—which I share with *him*—from my French

Immersion summer. When I returned to Ottawa, after six weeks *en famille* with the Ducharnes, I knew way too many nouns and adjectives—and nothing about verbs. But I had learned to prepare a balanced, nutritious meal—thanks to Mme. Ducharne's tutelage. For an eleven-year old of the latchkey genus, Salade Niçoise was an ideal intro to the domestic art of multitasking. You must learn how to cook an egg (a more delicate task than Matt realizes) while you remember not to overcook the new potatoes. And, of course, there's the dressing that you make first, so the flavors have a chance to know each other.

I emerged from my shower, wrapped in a huge towel, and gave Matt a wary look. It was hard to suppress my disappointment.

"It's the mercury," he told me. "And I love your salad. Can't we have it without the tuna?"

"That's Madame Ducharne's recipe. And you're the first man I ever made it for," I added. "I'm faithful to the way she taught me, right down to the dressing. The only thing I changed is steaming the potatoes instead of boiling."

I also add whole peppercorns and a slice of lemon to the water, but he doesn't have to know all that.

"I have never heard of a vegetarian niçoise," I lied. "I refuse to even discuss it."

As I picked up a bottle of lotion, Matt drew nearer. He kissed a bare shoulder and began playing with my towel.

"Let me help," he said.

Then he pushed me gently toward the bed, where he made me lie on my stomach. He opened the towel slowly, gaining access to my upper back.

I closed my eyes while he rubbed the lotion into my shoulder blades.

"I thought you liked my cooking, but if you don't like something, you should say so, and I won't make it for you. Instead of depriving me—"

"But you're the one I'm concerned about," he insisted. "I love the way you make that. You can make it three times a week for me!"

His hands were massaging the small of my back.

"The mercury levels in tuna fish are toxic for the fetus," he said. "And the risk of you poisoning yourself with fish oils—"

"But there's no fetus!" I protested. "And I just bought a whole case of tuna fish!"

"But there will be, honey." His palms were now on my buttocks. "And you have to start being more careful."

He was working on my thighs now, and my skin was appreciating the treat. But my mind was buzzing with anxiety. What is *up* with the men of today? Allie's boyfriend—interfering with her pubic rituals! And Matt. Planning my pregnancy right down to my vitamin intake! Does he have any idea how invasive this feels?

"We're talking about *me* becoming a mother. Not you!" I told him. "You're my husband, not my doctor. And I'm not even pregnant." I turned to look at him. "Yet."

•◆• MONDAY, 4/2/01 •◆•

A phone message from Roland, calling from the transatlantic sky: "I'm landing at JFK in about two hours. How does breakfast tomorrow sound? I'll call you in the morning."

Why does living overseas make a customer ten times more attractive, no matter what he actually looks like?

You have to catch him while he's in town. And make him feel lucky that he caught *you*. For some reason, a game of ping-pong between his vanity and your ego makes the man himself more intriguing. And then there's that sterling-dollar exchange rate—ping-pong of another sort. Whatever trauma New Yorkers feel when visiting London these days, Roland's Manhattan experience is the opposite of Sticker Shock. At home, he's just a normal customer paying the normal rate, but he's a generous date in New York.

Now, Roland is also one of those old world "punters" who likes to seduce a girl. He doesn't just lie there—which, technically, I would approve of. Nor does he try to devour my tender body parts like some kind of misguided wannabe. But he does try to coax my body into wanting or doing more than it has to.

Which would annoy me, if he weren't a big spender. When the dollar grows weak, is the flesh more willing?

•◆• TUESDAY, 4/3/01 •◆•

With some clients, there's a flirtatious encounter with my bra—removal's a challenge but they like to try. Still, I'm primarily responsible for disrobing. Roland is the exception.

Today, he began by unbuttoning my dress—a nostalgic shirtwaist with a pretty belt that I had to stop wearing three months ago. But my Body Mass Index has returned to premarital levels and my favorite outfits are back in business.

As he opened my dress, I turned my head away and let his kiss land on my neck. I never let a client kiss my mouth. I'm also not keen on having my neck kissed, but when Roland lingers there, I'm relaxed. Today, I even permitted a playful tongue at my earlobe and felt no dismay when my skin shivered.

If the wrong tongue caresses the side of my neck, a nipple, an ear—it's like chalk on a blackboard. My skin seems to crawl, to recoil. When it's the right man, my body tingles with approval.

My pussy is less discriminating: a man who's not permitted to kiss my neck can still take liberties if he knows where to go.

Above the waist, I'm at the mercy of my senses, unable to control my likes and dislikes. A million goose bumps into my career, I now appreciate the effect Roland has on me. Even if I hated the sensation, I would keep him as a customer—there's no good reason not to—so I'm glad my body likes him. And to think there was once a time when I tried to resist!

Soon I was completely naked, lightly pressing my bare pussy against his trouser-covered leg. I pulled away, and fell onto the bed, one hand instinctively moving toward the smooth skin below my navel. Roland removed his tie and began to open his shirt. He gazed at my hand and said, "Go on. Let me watch."

If I continue, I'll come too quickly. And if I come now, my nerve endings will be too sensitive for him.

I stroked myself gently, stopped, then spread the outer lips with two fingers to show him the results. Yes, it's just business but his attentive eyes were making me rather swollen. I slid a finger inside—things I might do with any other client to keep him away from my body while keeping his engine humming. It's a nice way to pass the time while a man's undressing. But in Roland's case, I have to admit a conflict of interest. My clitoris tingled discreetly as I opened my pussy. I wasn't doing it for entirely professional reasons.

His lips, kissing me lightly on each knee cap, approached my inner thighs. His mouth teased the intersection at the top of my pussy lips. When he began to kiss my stomach very softly—this flat, girlish stomach that I work to maintain, which my husband has designs on . . . never mind!—my knees felt lighter than air.

I opened my legs wider and gave him what I'd been waiting

for, as quietly as I could. When I came, I felt my stomach contracting—because I was trying not to make the telltale sounds. Yes, he did seduce me. Successfully. But I still don't want Roland to know what I'm "really" like. It's a sneaky, surreptitious climax—not a wild noisy release. Noise is reserved for those times when I'm faking it. What a strange little game, orgasmic cat-n-mouse—he wants me to come; I don't want him to know for sure that I did, but I never leave his hotel room without getting off.

First.

Once inside of me, Roland did his best to hold back.

"Damn it," he gasped. "Lie still."

I complied but gripped his buttocks so he couldn't get away.

"And the trouble," he muttered urgently, "is that I am fucking coming, god damn it. Much too soon." He fucked me harder for a few seconds, unable to stop. "I'm sorry, my dear. You were just too delectable."

He must say that to everyone but it feels uniquely true each time I hear it. He collapsed against me, making the removal of condom and cock somewhat awkward, but I managed to slide my hand between our limbs.

In the upstairs corridors of the Parker Meridien, there's a permanent midnight effect—hip-looking blue lights made me forget it was almost noon. On the sidewalk, I noticed all the people—shoppers and office workers rushing around, macho messengers in bicycle shorts—and felt out of place. Too relaxed for a crowded sidewalk. I stopped at a deli for a caffeine fix, then floated down Fifty-seventh Street, pretending not to hear the catcalls from a group of Con Ed workers clustered around a manhole. I thought of Roland's lips caressing and worshiping my small, hard-working waist. The combination of gentle and rowdy admiration—all in one morning—made me smile.

As I neared Bergdorf's, I found myself eyeball to grommet with a brilliant, textured handbag sitting in a display window, its toffee-colored surface suggesting miniature cobblestones.

In the nick of time, I hailed a cab and got my existing handbag out of the beckoning handbag's radius. A narrow escape. With my earnings still intact, I felt like one of those men who suddenly remembers that he has a very good "steak" waiting at home. Except that my particular steak—a tenured Kelly bag—was sitting on my lap. And that handbag was no mere hamburger.

Anyway, the real problems in life aren't hamburger-driven. The temptation to splurge on that extra filet has been the downfall of too many people in this steak-ridden town.

•❖• FRIDAY, 4/6/01 •❖•

The week has been good to me. So good that I just *might* venture back to Fifty-seventh Street for another look at the microcobblestones . . . also available in brick red, off-black, and igloo-evoking white, according to *Daily Candy*.

Today, a lunch-hour quickie at Jasmine's brought me within $200 of my weekly quota. While she changed the sheets for her next date, I mused about my prospective purchase.

"If you can hold out for nine more weeks, it'll go on sale."

"How do you know?"

Jasmine was standing in her bedroom doorway, naked, partly covered by the used sheet that was bundled up in her arms. Sunlight was streaming through the gauze curtains behind her bed, causing her to squint.

"I've been studying the handbag market for years," she said.

"I have an excellent collection and not one was a retail purchase. Hey," she added. "I think you're losing weight!"

Long-waisted and lean, Jasmine is that rare girlfriend who never lies about another woman's appearance. If you have a chin that doesn't go with your blouse or an extra five pounds you don't need, she'll tell you.

"My BMI's down to 20.9," I boasted. "I'd like it to be 20.3."

"Well, mine's deceptive. Muscle weighs more than fat," she said, patting one of her well-formed buttocks.

Jasmine has a porn star's rump, ballerina legs, a tiny waist— and a Body Mass Index approaching 25. A gloomy feeling reasserted itself as I contemplated Matt's new plan for increasing *my* BMI.

"There's a conspiracy against my waistline," I told her. "And I have to do something about it before things get out of hand." Jasmine glanced at the clock next to her bed. "Matt's talking about babies! I didn't think he'd want them so soon."

"But that's good! He wants you to be the mother of his child! His dynastic partner-in-crime." As she disappeared into the hall-way to deal with her laundry, her voice grew much louder. "He wants to make you the CEO of his DNA!" Now she was back in the bedroom straightening out the pillows. "Maybe it's a little too Me-Tarzan-You-Jane for your taste?"

"It's a little too soon," I said. "We've been married for less than a year! And I just spent eight weeks getting rid of six pounds. The minute I start wearing my size-four dresses again, he's talking about putting me in maternity clothes? It's totally unreasonable!"

"Is he actually talking about maternity dresses?" Jasmine looked stunned. "I don't know if that's a good thing. He's a banker, not a clothing designer. Shouldn't he be talking about trust funds? Or tuition fees?"

"Oh for god's sake. Not literally. But he goes online and reads up on Bugaboo strollers! Then he tries to throw away my cod liver oil. And he's a registered user at Urban Baby. What is happening to this generation of bankers?"

I can't imagine Milt—who had kids with all his wives—getting so involved with the minutiae of pregnancy. Or any of the other bankers I see.

Have I spent so much time around men old enough to be my father that I've lost touch with my own age group?

"Well, it just goes to show you." Jasmine was rummaging through her dildo drawer. "The smaller your waistline gets, the more he's inspired to plant his seed there. It's one of nature's sweet ironies." She tossed a black leather device and a matching rubber penis onto her half-made bed. "Well, I have to throw you out in five minutes. This guy's so horny he's liable to show up early." She followed me to the living room where I retrieved my skirt, shoes, and raincoat. Jasmine was fastening the dildo harness around her pelvis. "What are you gonna do? Tell him you need time. You're a young married couple, for god's sake. If you're still having good sex, he shouldn't mess with that."

"Last night, he tried to fuck me without a condom! He's never done that before."

"Never?"

Jasmine slipped into a pair of black marabou slippers. There was something incongruous about the fluff around her toes and the fake veins on her bulging strap-on.

"I told him, 'We can't do that until I've seen my doctor.' He put it on but . . ."

"Did he stay hard?"

"Of course!"

"Then your disagreement's only superficial. He'll forget all about it. Hot sex gives you a rhetorical advantage."

"Hot sex just makes him want to look at baby furniture! This morning, he got to the office at eight-fifteen and he sent me a link to this Norwegian high chair. It's a baby chair that 'grows' with your baby! You can use it until your kid's in high school! I don't think he's forgetting a *thing*." I stared at Jasmine's outfit. "Aren't you going to wear a bra with that?"

"It's in the other room—." We both heard the intercom. "Damn it. There he is."

I left quickly, to avoid bumping into her two o'clock, and took the stairs to the next floor while he was in the elevator.

Less than two hours later, my phone chimed. "Where are you?" Jasmine asked.

"The bagel section."

I was standing in front of Vinegar Factory's plentiful selection of rolls, savoring the aroma.

"Get your ass *out* of there and meet me at Pinky's. Carbohydrates are not your friend."

"They're for Matt, not for me," I tried to explain, but she hung up quickly.

When I got to the nail salon, Jasmine was absorbed in a current issue of W magazine.

A shy, chubby girl with a jet black ponytail applied Quick-Dry to Jasmine's red toenails. She gave me a polite nod, picked up her plastic tool basket, then wandered off to her next customer. I peeked over Jasmine's shoulder.

"Look at this!" she exclaimed. "Anna Nicole Smith! She's a total grillionairess now. Four hundred and fifty. Million. She met him in a topless club."

Four pages of snide but cheerful advice—"plus-size financial planning for the Merry Widow"—from the likes of Blaine Trump, Frederic Fekkai, and Bill Blass: "Don't try so hard. How about a breast reduction? Now that you're a lady, lunch."

When lunch becomes an imperative verb, you've crossed over, I guess. Had I taken Anna Nicole's route and married a ninety-something billionaire with middle-aged kids—and made a living displaying my breasts, rather than taking off my panties—I probably wouldn't be fielding e-mails about Scandinavian high chairs.

But that's the difference between the topless and bottomless sectors. Dancers and call girls have completely different priorities. For one thing, we're more concerned about appearances. See an elderly billionaire in private? By the hour? No problem. Becoming his thirty-something child bride—now *that* I would have to explain to my family. What people can see is what's really at stake. As a hooker, you can have sex with multitudes and still be respectable, as long as people don't know. Topless dancers have no privacy. The topless definitions of success, respectability, what's okay, what's not—it's a language I'll never understand.

But who am I kidding? My C-cup breasts are natural and firm, but they have more in common with a girlish B-cup than a voluptuous D. These days, you'd have to be a *Double*-D like Anna Nicole to be taken seriously on the topless circuit. What I have, in fact, are call girl breasts, not dancer breasts. Anna Nicole's destiny was never mine to reject in the first place.

"So look," Jasmine said, in a low voice. "This is what I think you have to do." She closed the magazine and leaned closer. "Make an appointment with your gyno. Get her to put you on the Pill."

I thought I had outgrown the Pill. Condoms have been in vogue for so long that using one is second nature. . . . But the Pill was the answer to my prayers at thirteen when it cleared up my acne. And now?

"I'll never hear the end of it if I go back on the Pill," I sighed.

I just want some time. To get used to the idea. To save some money. I can't keep working if I get pregnant! I've heard that some johns are turned on by pregnant women but this is the stuff of myth and legend if you work on the Upper East Side. It certainly doesn't correspond to the co-ed call girl image. When you're thirty-five going on twenty-five, you have to look the part.

"If you go on the Pill, he can't impregnate you and you don't have to argue about condoms. You're buying time. Just don't tell him."

I glanced around the room to make sure nobody was listening.

"Can I really get away with that?"

"Think of all the women who pretend they're *on* the Pill and they're not! You're gonna do the same thing—backwards and in high heels. If they can get away with it, why can't you? You're already getting away with plenty," she said. "You have a proven track record."

"But that's what I mean. I don't want to push my luck."

How much can—or should—one person get away with?

"You won't be struck down by a thunderbolt for delaying motherhood. It's your evolutionary prerogative!" she said. "Like holding out till the fifth date. And you shouldn't be confrontational with this guy. That'll just wreck the mood. You don't need that."

" 'This guy'? You're talking about my husband! Sometimes I wonder if you've ever had a normal relationship with a man!"

"Would you get a grip?" Jasmine said. "I'm not the one who sneaks around on your darling husband. You are. So don't get all sacred with me about the institution of holy matrimony."

Jasmine picked up her magazine. "Forget I said anything. I was just trying to help a friend out of a jam."

She gave me a tight, cold smile and resumed her investigation of Anna Nicole Smith's social makeover.

•→• SATURDAY MORNING, 4/7/01 •←•

I spent yesterday evening in a sheepish snit—simmering with resentment, biting my tongue in self-reproach. Why did I say that? Why did she say *that*?

In bed, Matt tried to unbutton my pajama top, but I turned away from him.

"Honey . . ." He was kissing the back of my neck. "I'm sorry about last night. I'll use a condom until we're ready. Why are you crying? Talk to me."

"I—it's not about that." I curled up into a ball and hid my face in the pillow. I knew in my heart that I was depriving him of sex to pay him back for causing, indirectly, that exchange of caustic words in the nail salon with my best friend. "I just want you to hold me," I said. And he did.

The Schoolgirls Come and Go

Trish is in a tense mood about our upcoming date with Tommy. This morning, when she called, I was negotiating light starch and quick turnaround on two of Matt's favorite shirts.

"Please," I begged the sphinxlike assistant handling my order—but she was oblivious to my panic. "I promised my husband they'd be ready *tonight*."

I answered my phone while she went to the back of the shop for a consultation.

"Jasmine confirmed, but she's giving me a hard time about the cut. And Charmaine hasn't called back. Is she reliable?" Trish asked.

I felt a twinge of dismay. Is this Jasmine's way of letting me know she's still pissed off? She knows I'm the one who gave Trish her number.

This week, Tom wants an entire schoolroom—well, a quartet of torturers-in-training, under the guidance of "Thalia" (Trish), who continues to play chief inquisitor. Though still a trainee, I've been promoted to "teaching assistant." And I'm also helping Trish—IRL—with recruitment. My quota, this week, depends in part on picking up half of Trisha's commission from two "New Girls"—Jasmine and Charmaine. New to Trisha, that is.

"I'll talk to her," I promised.

"To Charmaine? Or Jasmine?"

"Both. And I'll make sure it's okay with Jasmine."

"Well, she wants to send me return business. She doesn't like taking a cut. Or paying one, I guess."

Jasmine, ever the builder, prefers to exchange clients. That's how a business continues to grow. Taking a commission is a good way to pick up some quick money but it's not always the best long-term strategy.

I looked around to make sure I was alone, then lowered my voice.

"Jasmine has good dates. They're easy." In fact, her dates are a lot easier than any I've seen through Trish. "You won't regret it."

"But I can't split the cut with you unless I have the cash," Trish objected.

The assistant returned with a ticket on which the magic words SAME DAY had been stamped.

"Anyway, I need to do the cut," Trish went on. "I can't wait for people to send me business. There's a crisis here. My husband . . ." She lowered her voice. "My husband's having a crisis at work and I need to start covering our monthly payments." As I left the shop, Trish said, "Don't call this afternoon, he might be home. I'll call you. Don't worry, I will *be there,* everything's fine. I mean, it will be when things get back to normal. I have to figure out how to get the mortgage paid without him finding out where the money came from."

Minutes later, Jasmine called.

"So," she said. "Trish doesn't trust me to reciprocate? Why is she giving me such a hard time? I've had the same phone number for ten years. I'm not some fly-by-night—"

"Don't be ridiculous!" I protested. "I totally vouched for you. She knows you're good for the date *or* the cut. Listen, she's under a lot of pressure." I didn't want to tell Jasmine something that Trish could barely bring herself to tell *me*—but it sounds like her husband lost his job. "Trish has a daughter and she's embarrassed about having to ask you for the cut. It's not about you."

To my relief, Jasmine didn't argue.

"And what about this torture academy? That girl's notorious. I've been hearing about her freaky guys for years," Jasmine said. "I hope I'm not expected to, like, draw blood. I mean, I'll do it if he insists but it's not my thing, you know? How much of a freak *is* he?"

People really exaggerate about Trish!

"Strictly torture lite," I assured her. "He's not really a pain-seeker."

"Thank god for that!" she said. "Masochism's so exhausting."

·•· WEDNESDAY. 4/11/01 ·•·

When I arrived at the Michelangelo, Jasmine was in the bedroom of the suite with Tom and Trisha.

Charmaine, waiting her turn in the living room, answered the door. Like me, she was dressed in a simple skirt and a pretty blouse, but hers was more unbuttoned. To show off her recent acquisitions. The supersizing of Charmaine was, technically speaking, a success, but her breasts are a little larger than they need to be. In fact, they're too big for her frame.

"Debbie's here," she said. "And Jasmine's keeping him busy."

A tall, slender girl with heavy bangs, wearing small, rectangular glasses, was curled up in a chair, playing with her cell phone. She wore her hair in two thick auburn braids that reached her shoulders. When she looked up and smiled, I realized she was also wearing braces.

"I'm next," Debbie said, with a giggle.

How did Trish manage to locate a twenty-something with braces for the torture academy? She's perfect for playing the part of a schoolgirl, especially with Tommy who requires no oral sex but . . . it would be rude to ask how she, um, normally deals with that.

"Debbie's not my real name," she volunteered. "That was Trisha's idea. I like my real name but Trish thinks Emily sounds too plain. We're cousins. She's always been opinionated."

"I'm Sabrina," I told her. Something about her chirpy disclosures made me want to keep my own name under wraps.

Charmaine looked uneasy. Debbie's about the same age as Charmaine, but only chronologically. In hooker years, they're almost a generation apart. Charmaine wouldn't dream of letting some "older chick" tell her what name to work under!

"Is this your . . ." The possibility was beginning to dawn on me, too. ". . . your first time?" Charmaine asked.

"Not exactly," Emily/Debbie said. She went back to fiddling with her phone, then looked up. "Do you both live in New York?"

Jasmine, wearing just her bra, skirt, and high heels, slipped out of the bedroom, closed the door behind her, and said in a loud whisper, "Debbie to the rescue! But she wants you to wait for, like, a minute so she can talk to him."

Debbie/Emily was already on her feet, drawing attention to her eagerness and her long legs. She's almost willowy, almost gangly. She was wearing a pleated miniskirt that would look wrong on most of us. On her, it was just right.

"Don't forget your purse," Charmaine told her. "And your phone."

Debbie's handbag sat on the carpet, half open, and she was about to leave her phone on the chair.

"But I'm coming right back," she said.

Still, she bent down to retrieve her belongings, inadvertently flashing her red lace panties before she disappeared into the "torture chamber."

A few moments later, I joined her. Debbie's naïveté in the living room—an experienced girl doesn't leave her phone lying around, much less her pocketbook—was duplicated in the bedroom. More than once, Trish had to stop Debbie from getting too close to our "prisoner."

And braces turned out to be no impediment after all. Debbie has a natural tendency to use her mouth, and she wasn't interested in tormenting Tom. She wanted to please him, instead—which is touching, I suppose. But that would cut our afternoon short and totally upset the erotic apple cart. The implicit deal is that Tom enjoys a few hours of torture/suspense/variety before coming, finally, through his own efforts. (Self-service is a recurring theme with Mistress Thalia's clientele.) And how can Charmaine participate if Debbie finishes him off now?

These calculations were lost on Debbie, who—typical newbie—is selfish in all the wrong places. New Girls can be annoying, and this one got on my nerves. Creating extra work. For me, and for Trish. Every hint, every gesture, went right over Debbie's head. But Trish was determined to make lemonade out of this lemon.

"Now this," she announced, in her Thalia voice, "is a good

example of yesterday's lesson. When your prisoner is aroused and vulnerable, he becomes more attractive. Come here, Sabrina. I need your help. Debbie, turn around and lift up your skirt. We have to check your panties. As you can see, Debbie is in danger of giving in to our prisoner. Yes, you can use your hand, Sabrina."

I slipped my hand between Debbie's thighs and patted her panties. She wouldn't even be here if she weren't related to Trish!

"Very moist," I said, in a stern voice. This was a wild exaggeration. Though Debbie was eager, her panties weren't sloppy. Thank god! But I could smell perfume on the back of her neck—another no-no that Trish should have warned her about. "I don't think Debbie's been doing her homework," I added.

Debbie's hips made a wriggling motion.

"This is a very important lesson, girls. When this happens—" Thalia addressed an imaginary assembly. "When you become aroused by the prisoner's responses, you must allow one of your classmates to bring you off."

Tommy, standing at attention in his jockstrap, gasped.

"This will have an effect on your prisoner, if you make him watch. Debbie will demonstrate this technique for the benefit of our prisoner and her classmates." She gave Debbie's thigh a gentle prod with her pointer. "That will teach you to make overtures to the prisoners!" she said. "It's easier if you kneel."

Debbie got on her knees in front of my skirt. I lifted the hem, expecting her to flirt with my pussy through my panties. Instead, she pulled my panties down to my ankles and buried the tip of her tongue between my outer lips. Tom was staring at Debbie, who—it cannot be denied—gives an excellent impression of a schoolgirl from behind. Wearing just her bra, skirt and heels, she tossed her hair backward, and her smooth braids were now lying against her delicate shoulder blades.

Thalia, concerned with keeping Debbie away from the customer, gave an approving nod. She stood close to the prisoner and continued talking to the imaginary schoolroom.

"Our captive, as you can see, is massive when he's erect."

I parted my thighs a little more while concentrating on Thalia's pointer, like a fascinated scholar of all things hard and throbbing.

Debbie's tongue was surprisingly graceful. She was applying just enough pressure to the outside of my clitoris, stroking the side with her tongue. For one long moment, she reduced the pressure. I closed my eyes and waited for her to continue. Then I remembered that I had a job to do. When I opened my eyes, Thalia was still stroking Tom's erection through his jockstrap with the end of her pointer.

"Don't make me watch!" he moaned. "Don't make me come in my boots! You'll ruin me!"

Tom's melodramatic contributions weren't as distracting as they should have been. I placed a hand, politely, on the back of Debbie's head. She didn't resist. Instead, she began to lick very slowly, with a greater sense of purpose. I shuddered hard when I came, and pulled away, slightly ashamed of this orgasm. It's one thing to come with Roland—I control my reactions, and it's my secret. But coming like that? In front of three people? It seems really inappropriate. Thalia might assume it was faked, Tom might wonder. But Debbie—despite her amateur antics—knows it was real. As for Tom, his routine is sheer camp! Did I get off in spite of that? Or because of it? The whole thing makes me queasy.

Well, Debbie would be a menace to the enterprise if she weren't kept busy. I'll just try to think of that orgasm as a professional sacrifice.

"Class is dismissed," Trish announced. "Sabrina, you may leave, but Debbie stays behind. I have some questions about your performance this afternoon."

I picked up my panties and stuffed them into my pocket. Tom was gazing at the carpet like a trapped man, but he gave me a furtive look that Thalia didn't fail to notice.

"Do not attempt communication with the students," she scolded. "When Debbie's detention is over," she told me, "I'll have a word with Charmaine."

Debbie was half-kneeling, half-sitting, on the floor, looking pleased with her situation. They wanted me out of there, but I was dying to stay and watch. What's going on with those two? Was Debbie about to get a spanking? It seems like a game they've played before.

In the living room, Jasmine was still half-dressed in her push-up bra, pacing the room while she talked on her cell phone.

"Friday the twentieth," she was saying. "Well, how about Thursday? Eyebrow wax and Brazilian. And a full arm. There *has* to be a way! She can't just leave me like that!" She frowned. "Well, if she only has time for the eyebrows and bikini, I'll take it. Thanks. I'll be waiting." She flipped her phone shut. "Well," she said, brightly. "My eyebrows and pussy are handled. I just found out my beautician is going on her honeymoon. For *three fucking weeks*. I'm wait-listed for an arm wax! I can't believe this! But my pussy, at least, will be flawless. There's nobody else I can go to at this point."

I know how that feels. My pussy, never faithful to one man, has been unfailingly loyal to the same beautician, and I've never been tempted to stray in the twelve years that I've been going to her.

"I don't know why you bother with waxing," Charmaine

said. "I got mine lasered at the place where they did my eyebrows. I never worry about penciling my brows or waxing my pussy. Why don't you just have everything lasered? And get some permanent eyebrow color?"

"No way," Jasmine said, "would I go for permanent markings up there or permanent removals *down*stairs."

Charmaine rolled her eyes and flashed a polite smile. "Each to her own," she said. "I had *all* my pubic hair removed. Maybe it's, you know, generational. Are you afraid of the technology?"

Jasmine was sitting on the couch, arms folded across her chest. She glared at Charmaine.

"*I* am not afraid of the technology," she said. "I have been around long enough to see a few style cycles. Aren't you worried that your pussy will have 2001 written all over it in 2010? I hate to say this but certain things can really date a bitch. Permanent cosmetics are just ladylike tattoos. In a few years you might be walking around with eyebrows that are *over*. And when the Botox starts to get old, those permanent eyebrows will be swimming all over your *chin*."

Charmaine sat up straight. She tossed her hair, and her nostrils flared. But it was hard to judge her mood because her forehead was as smooth as marble.

"Cosmetic surgery is evolving," Charmaine said, "unlike some *people* I could name." Hard to believe she used to be intimidated by Jasmine! "I'm a very experienced Botox user. If I start having problems, I'll consult my doctor. And *I* think a hairless pussy is classic. If I had a permanent landing strip, *that* would date me. Or a Hitler mustache. But I don't."

I was trying to look bored but found this oddly thrilling. Charmaine, standing up to my best friend! And Jasmine—ready to defend the honor of her pubic mustache.

The bedroom door opened. Holding her shoes in one hand, her skirt in the other, Debbie—in just her bra, panties, and glasses—looked radiant. The quibbling ended abruptly.

Another *Times* article from Charmaine, sent at 3:07 AM with a discreet note:

> *Thanx 4 that biiiig day @ the races. Can't sleep. Made mistake of reading NYT after drinking green tea! CK*

This week, the Metro section crusader pursues a rent-stabilized spinster who spends no more than three days per month in her East Seventy-eighth Street 1BR. She says she's on the road pursuing her "true calling" as a cabaret singer. But here's the catch. Each time she's about to audition, she has a minibreakdown. She's working on her "chronic fear of success." The reporter maintains that rent stabilization is enabling her dysfunctional noncareer because her rent is so low—$536!—that she'll never have to succeed at anything. Her little scam is giving rent stabilization a bad name. And she's one of my neighbors. A remnant of the Girl Ghetto.

That's what they used to call this part of the Upper East Side when single women filled the tenements and highrise apartments. Now I see them on the sidewalks: former girls who never left, walking their Yorkies, ignoring the baby carriages and the kids streaming out of P.S. 158. I see them in the nail salons and, occasionally, picking up their Paxil at the York Avenue Duane Reade, dressed like somebody's fantasy of a 1970s call girl in a bad dream. The hair is brilliant and blond or jet black and huge, but never gray. Sometimes I want to ask, "What were you? A lite-hook? A suburban daughter with an allowance?" Or perhaps an aspiring cabaret singer with a deficient work ethic.

When will the conscience of the Metro section figure out that some rent offenders—like Charmaine—actively embrace the spirit of enterprise? Are—like yours truly—*in bed with* said spirit!

I sent a quick e to Charmaine—

> *This is material for ten headaches. Wish he'd go back to the West Side where hardcore offenders have ten rooms and a balcony! Best time for reading the *Times* is the morning. It's good to stay informed but beauty sleep is THE priority for girls like us.*

—then discovered a strange-looking e-mail, which I almost deleted.

<BEAVER query—How's this for an opening?>

Allie's subject headers are beginning to sound like the worst kind of spam!

> *Hi Nancy! I'm working on my speech for the Open Society Institute:*

> *The San Francisco prostitutes' movement was conceived in a hot tub by Margo St. James. She called her group COYOTE—Call Off Your Old Tired Ethics. At first, the other prostitutes adopted animal names to show their solidarity. The Prostitutes Union of Massachusetts was called PUMA. In the 1970s, an*

English sex worker made history with . . . Prostitutes
United for Social and Sexual Integration. Some sex
workers have chosen to express their national pride.
Like the Canadian prostitutes who came up with:
Better End All Vicious Erotic Repression. (BEAVER!!)
THIS IS BECAUSE. . . . ???

I need your help filling in the blanks here! Do you
have any thoughts about why Canadian sex workers
are so patriotic? You're the only Canadian I know!
Roxana says I should project a global perspective,
make our movement sound politically relevant in
UNEXPECTED WAYS. Coz—get this!—somebody
from the BBC will be TAPING THE PANEL
DISCUSSION. Sooo I might be on British television
if I play my cards right! NY1 is sending a reporter,
well they're thinking about it. Also NPR. And
Roxana's talking to someone at C-SPAN! Is the CBC
part of the BBC? Or the other way around? What can
you tell me about the role of the beaver in Canadian
life? I hope you don't mind all these questions. I have
to sound knowledgeable.

Yikes. Allie on TV? As the New York alphatrollop? Why is
she asking me about the CBC? If we're lucky, this won't air in the
States but—I sent back a hasty reply.

Have you considered the implications of being on
TV??? Anyone could end up seeing you, including
*your **parents.** How will you explain to your*
mom that you're a member of this Trollops'
Association! Please think it through before you
proceed. Video is forever! It could be used against

you. And against your FRIENDS. Hello??? Your
FRIEND, N. C.

After collecting my thoughts, I tried to say something helpful about "the beaver in Canadian life." Well, the beaver is a monetary symbol because it's on the tail side of the nickel. But I'm sure the members of BEAVER don't want to be associated with a coin that's currently worth about three American cents! I decided not to mention the Canadian nickel. Instead I wrote back:

re: castor canadensis & the BBC

Believe it or not, the Beaver is the symbol of national sovereignty. Beavers were prized for their warm pelts and megaprofits generated by the fur trade. THAT is how the beaver came to be such an important symbol, by making money for the trappers and traders who sent the pelts to European hat-designers. Beavers were so profitable they almost became extinct. When Europeans started wearing silk hats instead of fur, the existing beavers were spared. The Canadian beaver survived because it was no longer in fashion. I know that's hard for a New Yorker to believe but it's true. Fortunately, Canada has other ways of making a living.

BBC is NOT part of CBC and vice versa. Will explain when I have more time.

PS: Your subject headers are confusing my spam filter. Please put your name in the subject line or Beaver in Latin (see my example above)

*You should NOT allow TV cameras at this event.
NY1 is a very bad idea. Too many people around here
watch that. NPR sounds safe. It's just radio! And
radio is where you shine. If they have to concentrate
on your voice, people will really LISTEN TO YOUR
IDEAS.*

Why does she want to be on television? Is it the novelty of having all those cameras pointing at her? I suppose she wants to keep up with Roxana. Whenever there's a hooker scandal in the air, you can be sure that Roxana will be on Fox News or NY1 pontificating about sex workers' rights. But Roxana can afford to do that! She's a has-been where hooking is concerned and was never a success, so what does she have to lose? These TV shows generate interest in her Tantric sex tutorials and her sex-positive vibrator workshops—that's how she really supports herself. And I'm sure she makes a better living running these Clitoral Consciousness groups than she ever did working two days a week in a massage parlor! You have to simultaneously throw up your hands in despair—she was a hopeless hooker—and congratulate her, for finding a way to make money from sex anyway.

But successful hookers can't afford to imitate Roxana. Allison has a lot to lose. No reputable madam will work with Allie if she does this. A lot of the girls who send her dates will avoid her. And her clients?

When I called Jasmine, her voice mail kicked in. "We have to talk about Allison," I told her. "She's in danger of ruining her life. I'm convinced of it."

Dr. Peele's office just called, to see if I would come earlier due to a change in her schedule. Today's appointment with her is totally urgent. If I plan to follow Jasmine's advice, I must get myself looked at NOW.

I insist on a female gynecologist but not (like Allison and her activist pals) for airy-fairy feminist reasons. It's more like a business decision. If a male doctor examines my pussy, he's getting a free peek. Jasmine, who swears by her own guy-necologist, disagrees: "It's all demystified. A male gyno's just like a bank teller, handling money all day. He's not copping a freebie when he examines your breasts. He's working."

When I'm naked with a man, I don't care if it's my husband or a john or my doctor, I don't want to relinquish my feminine mystery. That's even worse than giving someone a free look!

And it's not just about my naked body or my lower parts. When I was twenty-two, I decided to try a male shrink. I thought he'd be a good alternative to the chain-smoking weirdness of Dr. Anita Samson. For our first consultation, I spent an hour figuring out what to wear, putting on my makeup just so. I wanted to leave no doubt in Dr. Botstein's mind that any problems I had in connection with men were a consequence of being attractive. Of course, I was ridiculously late, incapable of doing therapy with Dr. Botstein. I just wanted to impress him.

•◆• FRIDAY NIGHT •◆•

In deference to the soft feet of her patients, the stirrups in Dr. Peele's office are covered with chintz, pastel booties. Today's booties were pink and white. As I reclined on the examining table, I noticed a large padded model of a spermatozoon hanging from the ceiling. Suspended above two microscopes, it was covered in silver fabric—a kind of sperm-shaped cushion.

"Wow," I said. "That sperm . . ." Dr. Peele was gently touching my breasts with both hands. Not wanting to break her concentration, I waited for her to finish. "Normal?"

"So far so good. You had a question about sperm?"

"I was looking at, um, the new sperm sculpture."

"New? There's nothing new about sperm and nothing new about that one. It's been there for about five years." Now she was applying a condom to a wandlike device that peers at the layout of your womb. It's amazing what they can do these days without being truly invasive. "Breathe through your mouth. Good girl."

"That sperm was always there?"

"Always," she said, inserting the probe. "You just didn't care. A dangling spermatozoa. Now you see it, then you didn't."

"I'd like to start my pills as soon as possible."

"Are you no longer using condoms?"

"Oh, I still do. I have been. But I got married, you know. Don't worry! I wouldn't ask you for the pill AFTER I need it. I'm not that kind of girl." Dr. Peele doesn't really know what kind of girl I am. She thinks I'm a freelance copy editor. Since most of her married patients don't have to work, she doesn't ask a lot of questions about my pseudocareer. "Listen, I've never been pregnant. How do I know I'm really fertile?" I asked her. "Is there a way to test for that? To be sure?"

"We can look at your FSH—" She paused, frowning at the screen next to my head.

"What? Is something wrong? It's okay, you can tell me. What's going on down there?"

"Nancy. You worry too much. Nothing is wrong. You're about to ovulate. See that?"

Turning my face toward the black-and-white monitor, I saw my ovaries in real time. She twisted the probe in one direction, then the other. It's like having a hidden camera in the stockroom of a department store. If I stayed on this table for another forty-eight hours, hooked up to the machine, would I spot the escaping egg?

"So we don't need to test your FSH," she explained. "You can see both ovaries. They like taking turns." She pointed to the right ovary on the screen. "You are definitely about to ovulate. So you're in business," she added. "And you look healthy. Cynthia will take your blood and then we'll talk about your pills."

"When I—if I become pregnant, what are my chances of conceiving twins?"

"Twins? Well, it depends. We'll discuss that in my office."

Moments later, I was sitting in front of Dr. Peele's desk, surrounded by autographed pictures of newborn babies and adult celebrities. The models and actresses are easy to recognize, familiar faces. But I keep wondering about that woman—sleek and tawny, sitting in profile, wearing a seriously elegant tiara. Last year, while sitting in the waiting room, buried in a newspaper, I overheard Dr. Peele's office manager telling Dr. Peele's nurse: "The king's daughter is on hold."

My private equipment shares a discerning caretaker with a handful of world-famous celebs and at least one exotic princess. Or maybe even a queen. For some reason, I find that comforting.

"You were asking about twins."

"What I really want to know is—when I deliver, does my husband have to be present? I know everyone's doing it but I don't think I can handle it."

"Have you discussed it with him?"

I'm afraid to! "Well, I have reason to believe . . ." How to explain this to Dr. Peele? "I think he expects to be included at every stage."

"But you're not pregnant and you're talking about going on the Pill. It seems that the cart and horse are out of sequence."

"It might seem that way but they're not. This is my sequence! I never understood why birth control was called family planning. When I was a teenager, I thought it was just a silly euphemism for not getting pregnant. Now I get it. So I'm planning my pregnancy."

"So you want to plan your pregnancy and you plan to start by not getting pregnant."

"That's right," I said. "I can't plan properly if my brain is fogged with the fear of conception. I want to do everything right. And I want to find out more about my husband before I try to conceive. Not his—I'm not worried about his ability to get me pregnant." (Intuition tells me that's a no-brainer.) "I think he wants to . . . watch me give birth! Can I tell you something? I have *never* been an exhibitionist."

"Actually," Dr. Peele said, "we do not encourage that here. You can comfortably tell your husband we don't urge him to be present. When the time comes."

The Imperial We of an ob-gyn who runs her medical boutique with an iron fist.

"Really? You don't?"

"No. But when a couple insists, we suggest that the father . . ."

"Stay at the north end?"

"Correct. But your husband expresses a desire to participate?"

"I know it's weird but there are some things I would rather not discuss with him. Yet."

"This is not usually the father's initiative. Most men do not insist on being in the delivery room—"

"I think that's changing, Dr. Peele. My husband is already much too involved with my pregnancy and as you said yourself I'm not even pregnant. Sometimes I think, if things were reversed, and *he* could get pregnant . . ." Now I had her attention. "Do you see what I'm getting at?"

"I'm beginning to."

I left her office with a prescription and a sample. In a lighter mood. Until my phone rang, flashing Unavailable ID.

"What's the deal?" Jasmine said. "I just spoke to Allison."

"Did she tell you?"

"About what? Listen, if she's about to ruin her life, she's being very cagey about it. Or she's in denial. She's telling me nothing. And frankly, I don't think she has a *clue* why I called her. She sounds very serene. It's weird."

"Well, Allie *would* be the last person to realize it if she does ruin her life. This is a path she can't return from. Once she goes on television—"

"Television? Is she nuts? If her customers see her on TV, they'll run for the hills."

"There's still time to talk her out of it."

"And what about the domino effect? Lunacy by association. They might think *you're* part of this political freak show. Or me. You know how these guys are. They want everything discreet!"

And what if Matt sees Allie on TV? He'll recognize her, I'm

sure. How will I explain my friendship with an out-and-proud prostitute? Pretend I didn't know? Act really shocked? Do I also have to act horrified and appalled? Or would that be overdoing it. Perhaps normal prurient curiosity is more convincing.

When I got home, I tucked my medical booty—pills and prescription—into the pocket of a winter coat. I checked the Call History record on my cell phone and erased all the incriminating numbers. I turned on my French conversation tape—I like to have that running when Matt comes home from work, a subtle reminder of what I'm really supposed to be doing all day. Then I changed into a pair of jeans, to marinate the Cornish game hens.

•◆• MONDAY, 4/16/01 •◆•

Today, a last-minute call from Milt, badly in need of a session.

"What a weekend! My stepson got arrested and my wife started blaming *me* for letting him use the car. I was a witness at my own crucifixion." He sighed. "But you can make it all better. Are you free at two-thirty?"

"I have to check with Charmaine," I warned him. "She's, you know, entertaining today. How's three-thirty?"

After negotiating with both, I managed to squeeze Milton into Charmaine's afternoon while she was getting her highlights repaired. It's not my style to rush—especially with Milt—but he was turned on when I told him: "We *must* be out of here before Charmaine's hot date arrives."

"God forbid that I should run into some other horndog with impeccable taste," Milt told me.

After my weird afternoon in the interrogation camp training center, Milt's straightforward appetite—his overly friendly 69-ing, followed by energetic (for me) fucking, capped off with an extended blow job—was a welcome relief. Despite the hard work.

"And why *did* you let him have the keys to the car?"

Milt was lying on his back, recovering from his orgasm, while I wrapped a hot cloth around his cock.

"Thanks. I had no idea he was high! And I'm not sure what he was on. Now he's playing his mother off against me and hitting us up for money." But Milt smiled happily. "What's one weekend in sleepless hell if the reward I get for my suffering is a blow job from you?" He looked at his watch. "Charmaine's hot date must be getting warmer."

After Milt was gone, I rushed around the apartment removing all traces of our session. My cell phone was ringing but I ignored it. With Allie and Jasmine waiting for me at Caffe Bianco, and Charmaine's date expected in less than thirty, I barely had time to make the bedroom look pristine and take a shower.

When I arrived at Bianco, Allie was nursing an eggnog.

"Where's Jasmine?" I looked around the bar. "Are you okay?"

"She's coming right back. I really think Jasmine needs to form a truly intimate relationship. She's just so meddlesome. I told her about NY1 and she asked me for the names of all the TV producers I'm talking to! Of course, I didn't give them to her! There's a huge empty space in her life and she wants to fill it by controlling my—"

"All the TV producers?" I felt a little faint. "How many are you talking to?"

"Oh, just three or four. I have a really important opportunity coming up. I know you don't agree with my plans, but you're open to dialogue and I value that. I can't even talk to her! She's trying to control my life!"

"But why do you want to be on TV? Don't you think you can accomplish . . . whatever you're trying to accomplish . . . by staying away from the cameras?"

"Can I tell you something?" Allison leaned toward me. "Please don't repeat this to Jasmine because she won't understand. I need to increase my Google presence."

"Your . . . what?"

"If you go to Google and type in my name, well, first of all, it's a very common name, but if you add NYCOT or sex work as a search term"—Allie was frowning unhappily—"there's only a few listings. I Googled myself the other night and it was kind of sad."

"Who are you comparing yourself to? A zealot like Roxana?"

"No. Not Roxana. Lucho has hundreds of Google listings. And so does his ex-wife."

Christ. His & Hers Googling.

"You can't imagine how it feels! Sometimes I wonder if she—" Allie slugged some more eggnog. "Anyway, I have to develop my Google presence. By doing more media. I figured *that* out. And speaking engagements. I want to be Lucho's peer, his equal. I think that's why they lasted so long, even though now, of course, they're just friends. They teach in the same department."

Allie waved at the waiter and indicated another rum eggnog.

"When is your period due?" I asked her. "This guy's in love with you. He's crazy about you! You're feeling way more insecure than you should."

Jasmine appeared, brandishing her cell phone, but Allie was too absorbed in New Boyfriend Angst to see her. Poor Allie. The excitement of his infatuation has worn off a little and, for the first time, she's realizing that being loved by Lucho also means being able to have your heart broken. By Lucho. But he hasn't broken her heart yet! She's overreacting.

"He took me to a party last week and I met three of his exes!"

"Three exes at one party!" Jasmine said. "This guy's a serial husband!"

"Only one ex was a wife. But his ex-ex-girlfriend lives in the same building!"

"As his ex-wife?"

"No. The same building as *Lucho*. Can you believe it? I just found out! The other night!"

"How does he behave when he's with you?" I asked.

"He was all over me!" Allie looked like she was about to cry. "But the minute he turned his back, his ex-girlfriend said something mean to me. And when I tried to say hello to his ex-wife, she wouldn't even look at me. It was awful!"

"You have got to get a grip," Jasmine said. "A firm grip. What did this ex-girlfriend say to you? And more to the point, what did *you* say back?"

"Nothing! She said 'I've heard that Lucho's combining research with pleasure these days.'"

Jasmine was apoplectic.

"She said *what*? And you said *nothing*?"

"Like I'm just research! Or pleasure! Not that there's anything wrong with pleasure," she added, "but she was so mean! What could I say? And why didn't he warn me! That—that *bastard*."

"And you didn't say *anything*? You let that bitch have the last word? What is wrong with you!"

"Stop yelling at me! You're as bad as those women at that party."

"Calm down," Jasmine said, opening her tote bag. "Here."

She handed Allie a packet of tissues. "His ex-girlfriend was mean because she knows he's in love with you. She's just trying to fuck with your self-confidence. What does she look like? Come on, be honest."

"She's just okay," Allie sniffled. "She's not ugly and she's not gorgeous. But she has a small waist and—and she has way more Google hits than I do. But not as many as his ex-wife. Or him. He has more than all of us put together. She was one of his students and now she's an assistant professor."

"Google hits." Jasmine looked, for once, overwhelmed. *"Google hits.* Is that what it's come to? Are you sitting up at all hours Googling this guy's exes? All three of them? You're suffering from romantic nausea. If you're going to go out there and be a member of this—this Council of Trollops and tell people about it, you have to be prepared. If you let some snippy West Side professor insult you at a party, you're letting down the side."

"I feel—" Allie blew her nose. "They made me feel like a"— she was trying not to cry—"like a talking dog! But I'm going to have my revenge!"

"By going on TV and getting lots of Google hits?" I asked. "Don't you think—"

"Yes!" Now she sat up, still teary eyed but emboldened. "I don't want to let the side down and I don't want to let Lucho down."

"Does he have any idea what a witch his ex-girlfriend is?" Jasmine asked.

"I didn't discuss it with him."

"Good move," Jasmine said. "I bet he *helped* her get a lot of those Google hits. Think about it. She has *him* to thank for her career and her—whatever-she-does-to-end-up-on-Google. But you can be Google material on your own. Which puts you in another league. Because you're not one of his campus groupies. In fact, if you had any sense, you would realize that he's *your* groupie."

"Don't be silly. He's my boyfriend. Not a groupie."

"Look, in any couple where one person has a bit of a following or a leadership gig, this is always an issue. And you're certainly not *his* groupie—you barely know anything about him!"

"That's not true!"

"He knows a lot more about you than you do about him. All these exes came as a shock to you. If you were a groupie, you'd know all their names and where they work before you ever *met* him. So don't kid yourself. I think I'll have a Cobb salad." She shoved a menu in front of Allie. "Why don't you have something to eat? You look pale."

When I left Caffe Bianco to meet Matt for dinner, they were still debating the finer points of fandom, groupiedom, and Google rankings. In the cab, on the way to the restaurant, I found my cell phone and remembered the missed call when I was rushing to clean up after Milt. I pressed Talk.

"Where are you?" Miranda asked.

"I'm in a cab."

"Maybe you should call when you get home."

"I'm going to Pastis. We have time to talk! Did you hear from Christopher?"

"Yeah, we had dinner at Barolo the other night. Are you alone?"

"Yes! What's wrong?"

"Grandmummy died. They're flying her home, they can't do it right away because they have to order a zinc-lined coffin. But the funeral's next week. If she arrives in time. Well, she was so out of it, you know. She wasn't well, and she wasn't all there. But . . ."

"Should I come over? Are you okay?"

"I'm fine. Go to Pastis. I'm a big girl, Nancy!"

"Maybe you should come have dinner with us."

"Thanks but I want to be alone. And I have to start packing. I'm going to help my dad with the funeral. I don't know where everybody's going to stay. He needs my help. My mother hasn't been feeling well."

It feels strange to have no grandparents. Miranda has one left—on her mother's side—but this is it for me.

"If you change your mind," I said, "just come to the restaurant. You shouldn't be alone."

"I *have* to be alone," she said. "I'm leaving for Trinidad tomorrow night. And I have no clean laundry!"

As the cab entered Central Park, I felt it: my bloodstream was crying out for a drink. I remember mourning the death of my father's mother five years ago, on my living room couch, while tippling ice cold vodka shots. I was single, alone—and free to indulge my grief. Now I fear being tripped up by such emotions. If I drink too much, I might speak too freely about any number of things. I have to keep it together this time.

Death and the Laytons

A voice mail from Mother: "Your grandmother is being flown out of Manchester at the end of the week. We might have to change at Heathrow. Miranda tells me you plan to use air miles. Can you really do that? At such short notice?"

My American Airlines mileage has piled up over the years. When I married Matt, I had no savings, so I think of my AA miles as my dowry. All 147,000 of them! Having miles isn't the same thing as having money in the bank, but it shows that I have the *ability* to save. Or the potential. And I like being able to tell both Mother and Husband that I'm buying my own ticket to Grandmummy's funeral.

In Trinidad, a Layton funeral is a newsworthy event. Laytons are often in the news, especially these days, and not just for weddings and funerals. Last year, Miranda's father, Uncle Gregory, sued his youngest brother, Anthony, for embezzling money from the family business. Uncle Anthony created a scandal by going to the tabloid press, accusing another uncle of insurance fraud, then countersuing Uncle Gregory for slander. Grandmummy has been, as Miranda puts it, "so out of it" for almost two years, that she was never aware of her sons quarreling. *In public.* Over the business her late husband built for their benefit. And the vindictive headlines rage on, with various aunts, great-aunts, uncles, and cousins taking sides.

My three aunts have a tendency to fall into line with Uncle Gregory. My mother, the youngest of the nine Layton siblings, is torn between her childhood affection for Uncle Anthony—he's a year older than she is—and her loyalty to the family cause. For her, Uncle Gregory, right or wrong, embodies the family position simply because he's the eldest. Aunt Vivian, my mother's eldest sister, gets along so well with Kasturi (Gregory's wife) that it's inconceivable for her to support Anthony. Besides, Kasturi lets Aunt Vivian spend three months of the year at their condo in Vancouver. But there are, here and there, dissenting Laytons who mutter about hidden agendas and Uncle Gregory's drinking.

As for my grandmother's side of the family, they've been more skeptical. Grandmummy's brother, my great-uncle Edwin, sees the scandal as a typical example of Layton hubris spinning dangerously out of control on all sides, and likes to position himself as my grandmother's emissary.

The Chans, my father's family, are not high profile. Their funerals and financial disputes don't make the news. During childhood visits to Port of Spain, I went to the house in Woodbrook for lunch with my father's family, or I spent an afternoon looking at old pictures with a great-aunt and a second cousin. But I always returned to the Layton fold at the end of the day. I stayed with one of my mother's three sisters or with Uncle Gregory and Aunt Kasturi. I can remember when Miranda was "the baby" in a household filled with six older boys. Her eldest brother was preparing to leave Trinidad for college when she, the only daughter, was learning how to walk.

In Uncle Gregory's household the days were bustling, eventful, emotional. People seemed to be constantly going somewhere, making plans. There were visitors, car trips, errands, deliveries. The house where my father had grown up had a very different feeling. Life was in a holding pattern. What's the hurry? The women, my father's aunts and cousins, owned the house and outnumbered the men. It was quiet. Very quiet.

I was always, somehow, a Layton, even if I carried my father's name. The Chans never had a well-known patriarch that I can recall. Chans are individuals. Like my father, Egbert Chan. Laytons, however, are always Laytons. One is either a child of Arthur M. Layton (my mother's stern, ambitious dad who got his start brokering condensed milk) or a grandchild. I can only remember talking to him once. He had fifty-one grandchildren. As the first child of his youngest daughter, I didn't loom large. When we met, I was six and he was ancient, trying to sleep in after a long flight to Ottawa. Our conversation was brief.

"Child, hand me the pastilles, I left them on the dresser." Amid the clutter, I found a small tin of black currant pastilles and delivered it to his bedside. "I think your mother is calling you."

It seemed strange to me for a grown-up to be lying in bed consuming sweets. My mother had impressed upon me that a sweet tooth is both childish and regrettable. But I knew I was the granddaughter of an important man and was often reminded of it.

To this day, my father finds it amusing to call himself "a remote satellite of the Laytons"—though never in front of my stepmother. Had he grown up somewhere else, he would have forgotten the Laytons after my mother left him. But he grew up on the same island, in the same town, as my mother and her siblings, so denying his satellite status would be like denying the existence of home. He still visits Uncle Gregory once a year and knows more Laytonian history than my mother.

The strangest burden of Laytonhood is the emotional investment my mother has in being pure Chinese, even though her Chinese family has an English surname. My father's the usual Trinidad mixture but he somehow ended up with a Chinese name. Due to my mother's genetic pedigree and my father's name, I can pass for Chinese. Unless you look closely. And know what to look for.

My telltale pubic hair is curly and thick when permitted to flourish, a non-Chinese feature that sets me apart.

• ◆ • FRIDAY, 4/20/01. FLIGHT 1386 EN ROUTE TO PORT OF SPAIN • ◆ •

The safest place to be is the cabin of a plane during a nonstop six-hour flight. Well, hairdressers will tell you that, as did Lorenzo when I popped in for my prefuneral highlights. "You will have six hours of dry windless paradise," he predicted. "And then it's a battle." He tucked a can of spray into my handbag. "Use it just before you deplane. I know about Trinidad," he said. "Like a steam bath."

Lorenzo has traveled to every region of the globe and possesses encyclopedic knowledge of each climate's effect on shoulder-length hair.

"But I can't get a nonstop flight. I connect at Miami."

"Oh, Miami's just right for your kind of hair. The airport, I mean." While wrapping a sheet of foil around a small piece of my hair, he glanced down at the newspaper in my lap. "The mayor's love life is getting on my nerves. I knew he was mixed up in his psyche when he announced a so-called Northern Italian chef at Gracie Mansion." Lorenzo grew up in Milan. "Personally," he added, "I prefer the food of the south. How about you?"

Lorenzo was right about my layover. No trace of humidity. Yet. And what an extravaganza of service Miami Airport is! Manicures and hair care at Angelo's, Caribbean cooking on Concourse D, a sushi bar that serves proper cocktails, and a hotel restaurant you can visit without ever leaving the airport. As I headed for the gate, I felt like a kid who doesn't want to leave the amusement park. Why is JFK such a drab ordeal by comparison?

At Miami, I had to flee from La Caretta (Concourse D's main attraction) because I was tempted to purchase a whole bag of fragrant empanadas for the plane ride. There's no point arriving in a bloated state, reeking of gluttony. Especially since Miranda has arranged for her brother to pick me up. I wonder if Dennis remembers kissing me—my first French kiss—that summer when I was twelve and he was fifteen. Just in case he does, I want to be crisp, fresh, completely pulled together when I arrive. No pigging out on the plane!

So I headed for the bar instead and found myself sitting next to a silver-haired man wearing an elegant pin-striped suit. We exchanged destinations.

"Trinidad. Have you been?"

"Buenos Aires," he said with a courtly smile. "Not yet," he added.

He looked like the sort of guy who might sometimes pass through New York. Should I give him my number? But when he discovered that I was married, he looked so wistful, disappointed, and rich that I wanted to kick myself. Perhaps . . . *but I don't do that anymore.* Bar hustling is not an option at my age!

My first trick, at fourteen, was a salesman I picked up in a hotel bar but my customers today think I was "always" a private call girl. I keep that a secret from most of the girls, too.

There is a time and a place for everything. Now is certainly not the time to reactivate a phase of my career I've spent years denying. But I can't help feeling that this might have been the place!

•◆• SUNDAY, 4/22/01. THE UPSIDE-DOWN HILTON •◆•

From my balcony on "three"—floor numbers are reversed here—I can see the top of an oil rig in the Gulf of Paria. A group of strapping males, clad in bright pink and lime green, running around on the Savannah kicking a ball. Yesterday, I watched them doing their warm-ups—but the midmorning heat sent me right back to my air-conditioned room. It's hard to believe, but the place where I was born is totally incompatible with my body. Not to mention my hair. The temperature is only bearable at night, and the moisture is punishing.

There's no chain on my door (which makes me nervous) but security guards are everywhere. In New York, I dodge the hotel security. For a hooker, they're potentially hazardous. But here? I find them totally reassuring. Crucial.

Driving into town on Friday night, my cousin Dennis told me about his misadventure in a shopping mall.

"I was picking up some groceries and they came in waving cutlasses. They told everyone to get on the floor. Lie still."

"Oh my god. What do you do when somebody's waving a cutlass at you?"

"You get on the floor and wait for them to leave. It's happening every day. Schoolchildren carrying cutlasses. Kidnapping and murder. But you'll be safe at the Hilton."

Despite all the crime, I *do* feel safe. Eight hours away from my double life, I find there's a lot less to keep track of. In New York, I'm juggling all those names and places, not to mention people. When I come here, I'm just another Layton among Laytons. I don't have to invent, reinvent, or explain myself. There are two kinds of Laytons: those, like Dennis, who are content to be just that, to remain in Trinidad where they can be too easily defined; and the rest of us who are content to become just that, but only when we return for a visit.

Not until I had emptied my suitcase and undressed for bed did I remember to ask myself whether Dennis remembers our kiss.

Perhaps the memory of his tongue entering my mouth belongs exclusively to me. Perhaps he doesn't run a museum of sexual experience. Doesn't see himself as chief curator of his own sex life. He's part of my collection, an early acquisition. Do museum items get to have their own museums? Should they?

I still remember the new sensation: a tongue in my mouth, a boy's hand on my breast, for the first time. A kiss I had been longing for since I was nine, when I spent the entire summer adoring my cousin Dennis and waiting for him to notice me. At twelve, I had the full breasts and budding pubic hair I had been lacking. The approach, as we rolled around on the narrow couch, tipsy from drinking rum punch, was more pleasurable than the kiss itself. Though we never repeated the experiment, and never stayed in touch over the years, I think of it whenever I see him at a wedding or funeral.

Dennis lives in Valsayn Park with his wife and three sons and works for his father. Of course, I would never embarrass him (or myself!) by bringing all this up. But he was my first oral break-through and I've done so much to so many with this mouth. He deserves a prominent spot in the museum. Doesn't he?

Time to get ready for lunch with Mother! Who doesn't know about my private museum. And never will, I hope.

•◆• LATER •◆•

Miranda looked drawn and frazzled when she picked me up at the hotel in her father's minivan.

"You made the right decision," she said. "Staying here. You would never survive a night in our house."

Twelve cousins from four different countries are sleeping in different parts of the compound, along with various aunts, which makes me feel like a selfish freak. But I can't sleep in a crowd, not even a crowd of relatives. I doubt I could sleep in a room with anyone at this point—Matt being the exception. I enjoyed the solitude of my bed last night. It's been months since I slept alone.

"Well," I told Miranda, "I'm a very selective sleeper."

"I sleep like a log in New York," she sighed. "Here, I get no rest. Your mother's a big help though. She made coffee for every-body this morning. I don't know how she does it."

Mother arrived late last night and fell asleep without even calling. She must be exhausted! Grandmummy died in the front room of my mother's B&B. It was her job to accompany the body from her half-timber guesthouse in the Welsh countryside to Chester, where Grandmummy could be properly embalmed. Then to Manchester Airport and, eventually, Port of Spain.

When we arrived at the compound, Mother was nowhere in sight. Dennis's oldest boy, Alister, was sitting at the dining room table alone, finishing a plate of rice.

•◆•

"She went to Piarco with Daddy to pick up Uncle Sebastian," Alister told us. I found myself staring at a preadolescent ghost of the boy who kissed me more than twenty years ago. Dennis never had such a gangly appearance, though. "And she took one of the phones," microDennis added, but he couldn't remember which one.

"Sebastian?" I thought my brother was flying in from Toronto *last night*. "What happened?"

"Oh!" Miranda called from the kitchen. "He missed his flight. I forgot to tell you!"

My little brother is always running late, holding things up, subjecting us all to his hectic middle-management lifestyle.

Miraculously, as Miranda brought a huge bowl of steaming pilau into the dining room, a number of adult cousins and aunts materialized. They had been lurking in different corners of the house, waiting for someone to make the first move. The dining room was filled with people moving, talking, drinking, and eating, searching for a favorite chicken part or a pig's tail in the pilau. Aunt Vivian was accused of hoarding all the chicken feet.

When my mother finally returned from the airport, lunch was over, the crowd of cousins had moved toward the pool, and the aunts were out doing errands.

"Sebastian missed his flight again!" Mother told me. "Did he call? I've been trying to reach Miranda for an hour! The phone's not working!"

Is this how a mother normally greets her eldest child? My brother can be such a nuisance!

Although she's the ultimate granola mom—can't be bothered with makeup, doesn't tinker with her salt-and-pepper hair—I make an effort to look my best when I see her. Today, she was wearing a loose T-shirt over a faded denim skirt, with light brown Birkenstocks. Despite her own fashion foibles, she appreciates my unrumpled appearance. A shining bourgeois surface deeply reassures her—something my cousins fail to understand. They think their Aunt Helen is some kind of live-and-let-live hippie because she's an atheist. In reality, she was stricter about some things than *their* parents were. Even if I didn't have to go to church.

I could tell that the sight of her only daughter's immaculate hair, ladylike fingernails, and lightly starched summer dress briefly improved her mood. But soon she was hunting down a laptop in the hope of retrieving her absent son's latest excuse.

"This isn't the first flight he's missed," I pointed out. "He routinely misses flights. Maybe something happened at work and he can't come."

A likely story! If that were the case, he would have told us by now.

Mother was pursing her lips.

"But he's a pallbearer," she said.

"Has it occurred to you that Sebastian might not be *pallbearer material*? A pallbearer has to show up at the event!"

My mother scowled. Miranda shot me a distressed beseeching look, and I felt guilty. Trashing my brother's bona fides is sooo not called for at a time like this.

•◆• MONDAY MORNING, 4/23/01 •◆•

A puzzling e-mail from Robert, my strangely reliable half-brother who shares none of Sebastian's bad habits. Though my father's second wife wouldn't see it this way, I can't help thinking of their son as the well-behaved spawn of my parents' divorce. Which is no insult coming from a "child of divorce." It's what connects us, since being raised by different mothers is like being raised in different countries. Still, Robert's more at ease with my mother than I am with his:

> NAN. *Bummer about yr grandmom! Please tell yr mom how truly sorry I was to hear the news. I'll call her soon. Dad told me to give Sebastian $100 so he could deal with a local florist down there and send something in our name. What wuz I thinking! Spoke to his girlfriend last night. Sebastian's FLAKING man. CALL if you wanna know more. Dad has no idea what happened.*

E-mail from Sebastian's girlfriend in Toronto, addressed to Mother—with a cc to me:

> *Dear Helen,*
>
> *I feel terrible having to tell you this but Sebastian wasn't able to fly because he's not feeling well. Don't worry, he's going to be okay, but his doctor advised him not to.*
>
> *Love,*
> *Erica*

I'm sure Sebastian's doctor has advised him "not to" do many things! I don't know what my mother thinks or believes at this point but she's going to be pissed when she sees this.

Followed by another e-mail from Erica, addressed only to me:

Nancy,

He came over this morning and fell asleep in my living room. We were supposed to go to a concert the other night and he forgot! I was waiting for two hours! I told him I would never talk to him again, then he went somewhere and got high for a few days. And showed up at my apartment this morning! I don't know what to do. I can't believe he's missing his grandmother's funeral but he can't travel in this condition. What should I tell your mom? Maybe you can tell her he has a stomach virus? That's what he told them at work. E.

Her follow-up, sent five minutes later, was a definite cry for help.

I'm ready to end this dysfunctional relationship, well, I thought I HAD but he just shows up on my doorstep. I want him to start going to NA meetings and eating properly before we break up for good. Do you think he's ready to face his issues?

As boyfriends go, Sebastian's a Fixer-Upper at best. But I don't know what to tell Erica about my brother's rehab potential. A self-made princess shouldn't presume to give relationship advice to a doormat. You can't outsmart the romantic caste system.

A hooker knows instinctively that there's a female caste system. In business, the caste markings have to do with where you have sex: the front seat of a car or a bedroom on the Upper East Side? But there's another kind of hierarchy that applies to business and romance alike.

Forget geography. The female caste system is really about how men treat you. If you try to befriend a woman from the wrong caste, you'll get burned. Occasionally, a princess loses her footing and allows a man to treat her like a doormat. In that case, another princess can intervene and reprincess the errant one.

But sometimes a dyed-in-the-wool doormat reaches out to a known princess for advice. For the princess, this presents a dangerous temptation. The princess tries to help. She imagines for a brief deluded moment that she's abolishing or subverting the caste system. Doesn't she owe it to the doormat? It's a redistribution of feminine privilege. That's when it all goes wrong because a true doormat doesn't *want* to be upgraded.

Sebastian's previous girlfriend was even more of a doormat than Erica, which made her incredibly vicious. When she tried to enlist my support, I fell for it. Somehow she managed to turn me into the wicked sister-in-law who was preventing Sebastian from marrying her. . . . Never again! Erica will just have to cry on Robert's shoulder and wonder whether I'm reading my mail.

·•· LATER ·•·

After figuring out how to work the hotel voice mail, I retrieved a message from Miranda: "Sebastian's alive. He's still in Toronto."

I called her cell phone, the only safe way to converse when so many aunts are hovering near the landline.

"Did Mother get the e-mail?" I asked.

"I think so. She was talking to his girlfriend. And she heard from Robert. It looks like Dennis will have to substitute."

"I *knew* Sebastian wasn't pallbearer material!"

"Your mum says—" Miranda stopped talking for a minute.

"Well, anyway, if you want to come to the viewing, Dennis is driving over there tomorrow morning. He'll pick you up."

"Is she there right now? Can she hear you?"

"Sort of," Miranda mumbled. "I'm outside now. She wants to borrow my phone. I can't talk long."

"Does she have any idea?"

"I don't think so."

"What did Erica *tell* her?"

Robert can be trusted to cover for Sebastian, but Erica's a different matter.

"Hard to say." She was still mumbling. "I'll see you at the viewing."

Coming to terms with a son who is evolving into a middle-management crackhead: I don't think this is what Mother needs to be doing right now. If we can get through this funeral without any traumatic disclosures, everyone will be better off.

•→• TUESDAY, 4/24/01 •←•

Temperature was oppressive today. As I left the air-conditioned safety of the Hilton, I could feel every inch of my skin wilting from the heat.

When we got to the funeral home, more than twenty Laytons were sprinkled around the room in gossipy clusters. Auntie Viv and her daughter, Claire, were having a tense conversation about lipstick, right in front of my grandmother's coffin.

"It's too much red. It's wrong for her. She would never have worn that!" my older cousin complained.

Claire was holding two radically opposed lipsticks in her hand, a deep red Shiseido and a more youthful coral pink. From

Prescriptives, of course. I really didn't want to go up against Auntie Viv.

"If you don't mind—" Mother's frosty voice interrupted the lipstick conference. "Perhaps Nancy would like to have a moment with her grandmother before you apply the cosmetics. If, indeed, you *must* put lipstick on a dead woman? Some of us think it's quite unnecessary. A little tacky."

Atheists can be so uptight!

"It's only tacky if it's too dark," Claire objected. "This is a nice delicate color," she added, holding up her pale pink lipstick.

My mother, who was sitting in the front row, made an exasperated sound and resumed a conversation with Miranda's mother.

I looked into the open coffin. I wanted to liberate my grandmother from Auntie Viv's rather questionable paint job. What would Grandmummy want, if asked? But Grandmummy's body has become the property of her family—and it's not a question of what color, if any, she would have wanted to wear on her lips. It's a question of which faction among the Layton women has more power. Mother's in a minority here and siding with her is pointless.

Claire was on the other side of the coffin, blotting the lipstick carefully with a tissue.

"Don't remove it all," Aunt Vivian protested.

"I won't," Claire told her mother. "We'll blend the two colors." She opened a small makeup bag and took out a lipstick brush. The gold cross she was wearing around her neck dangled over Grandmummy's middle. "Just bring it down a few shades."

"While retaining the vibrancy," I added: an artful compromise that satisfies my aunt and reduces the garish effect.

My mother's right. There's something slightly *off* about applying lipstick to my grandmother under these circumstances. But Mother is too set in her ways. Disconnected from the norms of vanity, she doesn't realize that putting lipstick on a recently dead matriarch is a profoundly thoughtful gesture.

I sat next to Mother and said, in a low voice, "I know it's kind of tacky, but this is how some people show their affection for the deceased."

Now I had the attention of two mothers, my own and Miranda's.

"Oh? Really? I was there for her when she was alive," my mother pointed out.

"I know. But they don't think they're *imposing* lipstick on Grandmummy. They're identifying with her." Mother was unimpressed. Maybe you have to wear lipstick to understand. "Grooming her grandmother will help Claire to achieve closure. Auntie Viv wants to have some personal contact with Grandmummy before they bury her."

"Your daughter has a point," Aunt Kasturi told my mother. "You spent two years taking care of your mother, so you had the contact."

"Quite so," Mother said. "Vivian took care of her for a grand total of three months."

Suddenly, the room went silent. Uncle Anthony was defiant, self-conscious—and very unexpected. He was wearing a navy suit and a crisp white shirt with a dark tie—the only man in the room wearing a suit. He looked around but didn't greet Dennis or Miranda when he passed them, the children of his enemy brother. He walked up to the coffin. Then he bowed his head and stood for a moment, isolated by the silence, meditating over his mother's body. Aunt Kasturi became very stiff and exchanged an enraged glower with Auntie Viv. Mother gazed off into the distance, and nobody spoke until Uncle Anthony had marched out of the viewing.

"Grandmummy would not like this," said Claire. "The way all you are behaving. He has a right to see his mother."

"Mind your own business," Auntie Viv said sharply. "She would have taken Gregory's side."

"You must forget this lawsuit until the funeral's over," Claire insisted. "She would never take sides like that."

"You don't know what you're talking about," Dennis told her.

Suddenly Miranda collapsed into a chair and started weeping. Her face was buried in her hands.

"Look what you've done!" Aunt Kasturi said. "Give the child some Kleenex." Three people, including Claire, rushed to comply. "And don't meddle in things you don't understand."

Grandmummy would be horrified by all this!

· ✦ · FRIDAY, 4/27/01 · ✦ ·

At yesterday's funeral mass, Miranda snuck away from her brothers and sat next to my mother—her favorite aunt. All the cousins in our generation abstained from taking Communion. Except for Claire.

When you consider the ins/outs, ifs, and buts involved in the Communion process—and the fact that Claire's single, living on Queen Street in the center of Toronto—it's worrying. Does it mean she's been going to Confession? Or not getting laid at all? I could tell, from a quizzical gaze, that Miranda was wondering the same thing. How do you live in the center of a modern city, in walking distance of all the hot new places, and still manage to be eligible for Communion?

Uncle Edwin got up to speak, and these furtive sexual questions left my mind. He's Grandmummy's youngest brother and her favorite because she helped to raise him—and he brought home the ultimate academic trophy, the Island Scholarship.

"It has been said," his voice was in thundering mode, "that this. Is the last time. My sister's children will meet *under* the same roof." He's talking about all the gossip in the *Trinidad Express*. "Let us hope that the papers are wrong about that."

Uncle Anthony was sitting just a few rows behind us, and I spotted him later at Mucurapo Cemetery. But he didn't appear at the postburial gathering.

"It's a shame," Claire said to me. "But you think anybody made an effort to include him?"

"Well, he's not making it easy," I said. "His body language is impossible! My mother said hello at the cemetery but he scurried away before she could even think about inviting him."

"And they were so close as children." Claire was clearly feeling vindicated by Uncle Edwin's lecture. But when she saw Miranda homing in on us, she changed the subject. A tall guy with Viking features, the whitest person in the room, was chatting with Miranda while carrying a plate of bite-size meat pies. "Oh, hello, Ian. Have you met Nancy? She's our cousin." Claire crammed two meat pies into her mouth while Miranda presented our plate bearer: "Ian wrote about Granddaddy in his first book. A study of dualism and consumption in the Caribbean. You must read it! He's an anthropologist. And he's been interviewing my father for . . . what's the new book?"

"Haven't got a title yet but I'm concentrating on the sweet drink industry," Ian said. "And I want to continue my discussion about the transnational family. And creolisation."

"Your first book's about tuberculosis?" I asked.

"Ah. No. It's *Dualism and Mass Consumption in Trinidad*."

He turned to Claire, who was staring down the meat pies. "Have another. You look famished."

"Nancy's here for a few more days," Miranda said. "Claire's leaving next week." She was giving Ian a rundown on all the nonresident Laytons and our departure dates. "I must find a copy of your book so Nancy can read it."

"Where do you teach?" I couldn't help asking.

"Not!" he exclaimed. "I'm allergic to organizations. Only like to study them."

"Independent scholars have to maintain their objectivity," Miranda said.

"There's no such thing," Ian told her. "What we have to maintain is our funding. I'm currently in league with people at the Ford Foundation. Or should that be in liege to? It's rather a fine line."

"Ford?" Claire said. "I used to audit their books." Claire's a chartered accountant. "What do you mean, no such thing? An auditor *has* to be objective."

Later, when Miranda overheard Ian offering me a lift to the hotel, she gave me a worried look.

"Let Dennis take you," she said. "Ian's been drinking all afternoon."

"Oh? And Dennis hasn't?"

"But Dennis has been driving here all his life, he knows his way around."

•❖• SATURDAY, 4/28/01 •❖•

A phone call this morning from Ian. "What about lunch?" he suggested. "My treat. I'd like to interview you for my book. You might be the key to understanding the Laytons."

"But I have no connection to the family business," I told him. "I know nothing about soft drinks, insurance, or plumbing supplies. I don't even share the family religion. My mother's anti-Catholic."

"That's what I'm talking about. I'll book a table downstairs. Unless you'd rather eat by the pool."

"Oh god! Not the pool. It's much too humid. But your timing is excellent."

After seven days of hanging out with relatives, I am definitely in the market for some Layton-free downtime. Though, I guess, given the reason for this lunch, Layton-lite is more like it.

•◆• SATURDAY NIGHT, 4/28/01 •◆•

Lunch wasn't exactly Layton-lite. Ian's been studying my family for almost a year: following Uncle Gregory to the office, interviewing the other uncles, and having the occasional meeting with Anthony. His first question—"Do you mind if I tape this?"—made me fidget with my cutlery.

"You'll take this the wrong way, but I'm averse to recorded conversation," I told him.

"No worries," he said, taking out a small notebook. "The tape was only to protect me in case . . . Shall I trust you not to sue me?"

"Oh, really. We're not *all* lawsuit queens," I protested. "I've never sued anyone in my life! Besides, a true Layton only sues another Layton. Haven't you noticed?"

"Quite so. I understand this isn't the first intra-Layton lawsuit."

"I have no idea why my uncles are behaving this way. It's a turf war, I guess."

"Anthony is continuing an old masculine tradition," Ian said. "It all started when he tried to install his 'outside son' as an heir within the company. Following in the footsteps of many European monarchs. A bastard son was trusted more than a legitimate son, because the illegitimate son of a king had nothing to gain from his father's death. In fact, the bastard son needed his father's support. He wouldn't be daydreaming about regicide in his spare time. He might even take steps to prevent it. So, when your outside cousin appeared on the scene, instead of rejecting him, Anthony embraced him."

For business reasons!

"Have you mentioned this to Uncle Anthony? I guess he'd be flattered," I said. "By the king thing."

"Not yet," Ian said. "He's rather complex."

"Complex? He's just a youngest son with a bad attitude. I have two younger brothers. I know about these things."

"You speak as a sibling and not as a niece." Ian made a quick note, then looked up with an amused half-smile. "And your mother's anti-Catholic?"

"Totally. I never took Communion. Miranda thinks Mother is a free spirit, but she's very mistaken. My mother watched my diet like a hawk. She was a foot soldier in the war on sugar. No, make that a general. I came down here for summer vacation when I was nine and my cousins were drinking soda, eating candy bars—I couldn't believe it! Mother was *obsessed* with our developing teeth. I was never allowed to have soft drinks. Not that I mind. I never had a cavity in my life. I just don't eat enough sugar."

"That's remarkable. You're the only Layton I've met who hasn't got a sweet tooth." He scribbled some more. "So your mother rebelled against sweet drinks *and* religion. Sugar's like a religion, isn't it? I wonder what her relationship with your grandfather was like."

"Not good, I think, but don't quote me on that. He sent her to college in Canada. He didn't approve of my dad but she came back here and married him anyway. My parents left the island shortly after I was born."

"Tell me about your parents."

"I once asked my dad, 'Why do you still have an accent and Mother doesn't? When did she lose her accent?' Do you know what he said? I was floored! 'She always talked like that.' She adopted her transatlantic accent when she was a teenager. So what does that tell you? And she insists that if it weren't for her, you know, *cultural* ambitions, my dad would have stayed right here. For the rest of his life."

"Forgive me, but which Layton sister is your mother? I don't think I've met her."

"The youngest. Helen. But I don't know if sugar's a religion," I said. "Rejecting sweets isn't like rejecting God. It's more like rejecting polyester. Or plastic furniture covers."

But soft drinks were my grandfather's bread and butter. So to speak. In a way, Mother reminds me of the difficult daughter in *Mrs. Warren's Profession*. Kitty Warren's daughter rejects her disreputable mom. But Mrs. Warren's profession made it possible for the daughter to get an education! So she could reject her own mother!

I decided not to go there. Ian might scribble it down and open a total can of worms in his next book by making improper analogies. It's one thing to talk about kings and their illegitimate sons. Another thing to compare Granddaddy with a Shavian madam. I stuck to sugar, instead.

"Mother convinced me that, even if I liked sweets, and what kid doesn't, I was superior to every child whose mother allowed soft drinks and candy in the house."

"Very effective!" I leaned over to look at Ian's notepad. He was drawing a chart with arrows and lines. "Isn't that why British colonialism still matters?" he said. "She internalized the expertise of her colonial rulers and established her own quasi-colonial ideology."

"I don't know if I would take it to those extremes. But Miranda might like your theory." And Mother would not! "The strange thing is, my mother taught me that people who drink soda and eat all these sugar products—these people were tacky and vulgar. Much later I found out my family *sells* these products. I've never told her this, but I feel she hid the truth from me, for as long as she possibly could. About how her family made its money."

"I wonder if your mother has time for a conversation with me."

I borrowed Ian's phone and dialed Miranda. She was surprisingly terse when I told her I was lunching with Ian: "Your mother's upstairs. Should I disturb her?"

"Just let her know I called. I'll try later."

"Well, thanks for *telling* me," she replied.

"Telling you what?"

"About your lunch. With Ian."

And then she hung up.

Yikes. What was *that* about?

Finally tracked my mother down—by calling the landline. Thus avoiding Miranda, who seems to be in a snit.

"Ian Pritchard wants to meet you. He's an anthropologist," I told her.

"He is? He does?" My mother has never heard of him. "What for?"

"He's writing a book about the family. Nobody told you? He was at the funeral and wants to interview you."

"Is he *studying* us?"

"Sort of. Well, yes. I know it sounds weird but he has insights into Uncle Anthony's behavior that—"

"You didn't discuss your uncles' lawsuit with him!"

"Mother, no, I didn't discuss *anything* with him. I just had lunch with him. It's you he wants to interview. Anyway, there's nothing much about Uncle Anthony that he doesn't know already. It's been all over the newspapers, and he's got access to Anthony. He's been living here for a year, following Uncle Gregory to court, to the office, everything."

"Does Gregory know this?"

"Of course! Ian's not a spy, he's an anthropologist. He's already written about Granddaddy in his first book."

"And nobody told me about him. That's very strange."

"Well, *I* just told you. But anyway, if you don't want to meet, I'll just tell him you're too busy." I paused. "He suggested a lunch at the Hilton."

"I don't like the interest he's taking in your uncle's lawsuit."

Which uncle? And which lawsuit? But I didn't press the issue.

"He's very impartial. He sees it as part of the human . . ." I stopped myself from saying "comedy"—the last thing my mother

wants to hear about her brothers—and opted instead for
". . . condition."

Twenty minutes later, Mother called back.

"Are you still awake? I spoke to Gregory about Ian
Pritchard."

"And?"

"Well," she said. "I *suppose* I could meet him. Actually," she
lowered her voice. "I could use a break."

I called Ian.

"My mother's dying to get away from that compound. I think
she'd *love* to talk. But you mustn't tell her anything I said today.
Well, you can tell her I don't have a sweet tooth. And she doesn't
want to discuss The Lawsuits."

"Understood. Shall I meet her in the restaurant at noon? Tomorrow? Perhaps you could join us for dessert, after the interview."

• ◄• SUNDAY MORNING, 4/29/01 •► •

A pile of e-mails from the last few days, including some cryptic
smoke signals from a john.

Re: Noon

*Possible to compare notes at noon? Meeting
downtown until 11. Will call when I leave WTC to
come uptown. Don't call the office today. Something's
up. Not in a good way.*

Darren likes to leave all his messages in code. His next was
suggestive but clever, in a boyish way:

RE: Monday Monday

Tried to call yr cell! My loss. How about Monday
2:30? Will you have access to your storage unit? If
not I arrange a place to put the documents. These
documents NEED yr attention! No kidding! A quick
read-through is all I have time for. But document's
huge. Or will be. Dentist appt later.

And his most recent was indiscreet, yet flattering:

Re: Did you get my message?

There's a window of time on Monday and I really
want to see you! Call me soon, gorgeous. The coast is
now clear. Will your apartment be in use that day?
Tell Charmaine to scram so we can get it on. This is a
priority. E me over the weekend. Have BlackBerry,
will travel.

I didn't want to ruin his mood with heavy details, so typed
back:

Family visit. Sorry to be so out of touch this week.
Will call the minute I'm free! Is that a BlackBerry in
your pocket? R U just happy to hear from me?
Apologies to Mae West.

I changed *free* to *available* and hit Send. I was knocked offline
by a phone call from Mother, full of questions about Ian
Pritchard.

"Is this man going to ask me about Anthony's son?"

"He wants to talk about *you*. He's got all these ideas about the transnational family."

I didn't mention his theory about sugarphobic mothering as a form of colonialism.

"Oh? Well, I'm looking forward to it, I suppose. Miranda's dropping me off. She says he's quite accomplished."

"And I'll join you for coffee after your lunch. Why don't you ask Miranda if she'd like to pop in at the end as well?"

•❖• LATER •❖•

Miranda showed up five minutes after I arrived. She was wearing a saronglike skirt I've never seen before, a pair of perfect Prada sandals, and a top that revealed just a flash of midriff. In deference to her aunt who might say something to her father, she made sure the navel stud was covered.

When she sat near Ian, it was the first time I fully realized how madly she adores him, how badly she wants him to want her. No wonder she was snippy with me the other day! I feel sorry for Chris who could never, in a million years, have this effect on Miranda.

Ian doesn't seem to realize that he should flirt back, if he cares about her feelings. If he has any manners! Men can be such jerks.

Instead, his eyes were trained on my mother in her loose tie-dyed shirt, sipping coffee while he reloaded his tape machine. She turned to look at Miranda.

"My goodness, you look very stylish," Mother said.

Finally, Ian stopped focusing on the Laytons in general in order to give his full attention to one in particular. Miranda's lips parted with raw delight when he gazed with approval at her clingy top and her bare arms. But he still wasn't getting it. I felt a pang of frustration, remembering that summer when I fell for Miranda's older brother—who barely knew I existed because, after all, I was only nine and he was twelve.

When Ian returned to the inevitable subject, Mother told him: "V.S. Naipaul came from a huge family. So there was a Naipaul in every classroom. One of his sisters went to India. . . . She was older than my year. I remember when she returned from her trip and came back to the convent for a visit. Her appearance in sari really caused a stir! I remember how elegant she seemed, though I only got a glimpse. We felt so drab in our shapeless uniforms and she was wearing this beautiful sari! But this was something new. People in saris were mostly market women, food vendors. I wasn't used to meeting ladies in saris. . . . Things changed."

Miranda stared at my mother in awe. You don't expect to hear fashion history about the Naipauls or fashion commentary from my mother. And we've never heard this story. It's amazing what a stranger can bring out in your own mother.

And your cousin, too. Miranda is so ready to bed this man. Is Ian just playing dumb because he doesn't want to seem like a lecher in the presence of her aunt? The age gap's much more than it was with Dennis and me—technically, Miranda could be his daughter.

Suddenly, Miranda's phone was bleating.

"Yes? Oh hello, Matt. Not bad, considering. Actually, she's right here."

As the only Layton who can be bothered with a GSM phone, she has become a call magnet during this trip—but Matt has my room number and knows how to leave a message.

Her slim brown arm extended across the table and brushed Ian's sleeve.

"Honey?" My husband, sounding tense and perplexed. "I need to talk to you."

"Shall I call you later?"

"I found something in the guest bathroom. Under the sink."

Is that possible? But he never goes in there! I said nothing and closed my eyes in horror.

"Are you there?"

"What—what is it?"

"I found almost ten thousand dollars rolled up in an empty tampon box."

For one mad second, I thought about denying it all. It could have been sitting there when we moved in, couldn't it? But he'll never believe that—he'll know it's mine because it was wrapped in rubber bands and stashed in a box with a spare key to my other apartment. And the spare key's on the Tiffany key ring he gave me when we first met!

"You did?" I said weakly.

Miranda looked at me oddly but Mother was completely engrossed in her conversation with Ian.

"Is it yours?" Matt asked.

"Sort of."

"Sort of? What kind of—why was it sitting under the sink?"

But why was he nosing around under the sink? That's not like him at all.

"Can I call you from my room? I'm having lunch with my mother."

"But where did all this money come from? I don't understand."

"I'll discuss it later."

He sighed. Then his voice became much harder.

"I deserve an explanation. If you're in some kind of trouble this could affect me, too."

"I'm not in any kind of trouble!" I squeaked. "Don't be ridiculous." Now my mother was paying close attention. Ian was, too. "This trip has been stressful enough! I can't talk right now."

I passed the phone back to Miranda and stared accusingly at Ian's tape machine.

"*Was that recording?* I have to go upstairs. Something terrible happened. I have to call New York."

But what do I tell Matt? How can I explain the money?

My room phone has been ringing and ringing for the last five minutes. It could be Miranda. It could be Matt.

I'm afraid to answer.

The Rise of the Fallen Woman

God. Well, I *hope* I have this under control but it's hard to tell. My e-mail to Matt was brief:

> *Honey. Please don't call right now. I'm sorry I blew up like that but I'm totally stressed out. Things are not going well with Mother. Sebastian went missing and he was supposed to be a pallbearer. Everybody's upset. I will explain everything when I get home. I'm not feeling well, and it's hard to talk. I guess I'm not used to all this island food!*

Actually, I have a cast-iron stomach, like the rest of my family. There's nothing I can't digest! But Matt lives in a different world. Island Food conjures up a major challenge to his senses, not to mention his Anglo-Saxon digestive tract. I knew intuitively that marrying a WASP was the best option for a girl like me, but wasn't sure why exactly. Now I know.

His response:

But what should I DO with this? Are you crazy?
Under the sink? I can't leave it in the apartment.

My husband deals with huge amounts of money every day, in the abstract, but he rarely handles the stuff—physically—in bulk amounts. We really *do* live in different worlds.

I waited five hours to reply:

> *do what u think best*
>
> *cant stay online right now feeling weak/need to sleep*
>
> *will call xxoo*

Hopefully, the thought of his delicate wife napping at four PM, too weak to punctuate her e-mail due to digestive distress will keep him at bay.

But why was he snooping in the guest bathroom? Did he have a visitor? Was somebody using *our* bathroom? Is he cheating on me??? Would he do that? In our apartment?

•◆• LATER •◆•

Still dodging the phone calls. But checking voice mail.

I've got the Twenty-first Century Vapors.

Back in the good old days, whenever the going got weird, a married lady had a spell of the vapors. When we run out of new ways to have the vapors, we'll know the institution of marriage is really dead.

Fortunately we're not quite there yet.

Pleading discomfort, I delayed my flight for an extra day and spent some quality time with Mother. She seems to believe my explanation—that Matt and I had a misunderstanding about a confused debt collector.

I fantasized about staying at the upside-down Hilton forever but e-mail from Elspeth brought me to my senses:

> *We saw Matt last night and he's not himself! Are you coming to Janet's baby shower? Will you be back in time?*

A baby shower for Elspeth's neighbor. I would *love* to miss that.

But more to the point, I wonder if Matt told Elspeth about the money? Whatever excuse I have for keeping ten grand in a tampon box—whatever story I come up with, will it also have to fly with Elspeth? What does she know and when will I know that she knows it? If she knows about his discovery, she must think my disorder sounds "convenient."

But maybe she's not as tuned in as I fear she is. My sister-in-law's the type of woman who doesn't do vapors. If Elspeth had lived 150 years ago, she wouldn't have bothered with marriage. She would have been a well-born spinster, running a good works project, whizzing around on a bicycle in her divided skirt, rather self-satisfied. Women like that never had the vapors. Today they must "have it all"—or at least have sex which invariably leads to relationships with men which leads to marriage and—

What would a girl like me have been up to? Dying in a hospital ward of syphilis? Surrounded by flowers and grateful suitors?

Only if you were high class. If not, I think syphilis was a lot less romantic.

Thank god for condoms. And other things, like my covert supply of monophasic birth control pills. I took my first pill on Sunday morning. Then emptied the pack into an Advil bottle. But I'll have to find a better way to disguise them because Matt (a) knows what an Advil looks like and (b) might need to take one. And (c) he can't be trusted to stay out of my normal hiding places anymore.

I mean, how did he end up looking through my tampon supply? It doesn't make sense. Unless somebody—someone female— was hanging out. In our apartment. And suddenly asked him for a spare tampon. . . .

It can't be Elspeth. She's breast-feeding! Friend? Ex-girlfriend? You have to be on very intimate terms with a guy to hit him up for a tampon! Personally, I've *never* been that intimate with Matt. Or any guy.

A crazy pickup? Would he do something like that? I don't know who my husband *is* anymore.

Thinking cap is *on*. But the brilliant alibis elude me. Oh my god. I have to find an explanation for this money. Before I land.

•◆• FRIDAY, 5/4/01 •◆•

Last night, I timed my arrival to be home before Matt left the office. My plan was to get back to the apartment, run a bath, unpack, and greet Matt in style. Instead, the flight circled JFK interminably and landed on the runway long after Matt had finished an entire pizza. So much for style. I felt like a limp rag when he greeted me, but was determined to stay on the offensive.

"There's something I would like to discuss," I told him. "If you don't want to, fine. I respect your privacy. I'm not going to ask what you were doing while I was away."

Matt looked surprised.

"Doing? Eighty percent of my compensation is bonus. What do you *think* I've been doing. I'm working on a deal."

"Did you have a visitor?"

"You mean a houseguest?"

"You know what I mean! Don't make me spell it out!"

"Would you calm down? Why don't you spell it out? I have no idea what you mean!"

"Don't I have a right to know who was borrowing my tampons?"

If he says Elspeth, I'll *know* he's lying!

"I guess so. But nobody was borrowing your stuff, honey." He shook his head. "You need to rest. You've been flying all day and you need to rehydrate. Take your shoes off." He propelled me toward the kitchen and poured a glass of water. Then he took my hand. "I'll show you what I was doing."

He pulled me toward the guest bathroom and opened the door. Oh my god. The original sink has been replaced with a gorgeous stand alone model. Wraparound shelving eliminates all privacy, and tampon boxes in three sizes are neatly stored on one wall, along with my thong liners. They were under the old basin for a reason, of course, but I don't want to criticize the new aesthetic. He really put his heart into this renovation! Although I don't think my sanitary supplies—which he was never supposed to see—should be out on display.

"You . . . had this done while I was away?"

"I did it myself."

"You repainted, too? But you couldn't have installed the new sink!"

"Well, I got someone to help with the sink. I did the shelves. And the paint."

"And you picked everything out?"

"Of course!"

"Oh honey. It's gorgeous. I never imagined . . ."

Without saying anything, he reached out to hold me. Tears of relief were flowing down my cheeks.

"I wanted to surprise you," he said gently. "I'm glad you like it."

"I thought—I thought you had one of your ex-girlfriends over for old times' sake and she asked you for a tampon!"

"You *what*? I put your stuff on the tank and a couple of boxes fell when I was moving the old sink! Why would I—" He stopped talking abruptly and held me tighter. "How could you think that?"

"I don't know," I whispered, nestling against his shoulder. Everything was okay again. Sort of. I broke away to blow my nose. "I want to explain about the money," I lied. Well, this might be the best time to do it. "Where did you put it?"

"I got a box at the bank. You can have the key. We have to go in together and put it in both names."

The money I got . . . from all those other men . . . is currently in a box that only my husband has access to! I tried not to show my dismay. I have to get that key from him, but I don't want to seem too eager.

"Did you—did you tell anyone about this?" I tried not to look concerned. I don't want him to lie about whether he blabbed. "It's better for me to know." Confronting this money together— I never planned for this. It was supposed to be my personal treasure. Secret insurance. Having something that nobody knows about makes me feel safe. "Did you tell anyone?"

"Of course not." His hands on my waist felt so firm. "Let's open a bottle of wine." Is he trying to make me more talkative? "You must be starving."

"Not really," I said. "I've been feeling rather delicate," I reminded him. "Can we open the wine in bed?" The best place to execute all your confessions. "I need to lie down."

In the bedroom, I waited, clad in my good girl pajamas, lit by the glow of a lavender-scented candle. He placed a glass of zinfandel next to my side of the bed.

"There's something I never told you." I took a sip. "Please don't be upset with me?" He stroked my hair as I imbibed. "And promise me you won't tell Elspeth about this? You have to keep it between us."

"Okay," he murmured, sliding closer to me. "But I think you worry about Elspeth too much. What does Elspeth have to do with any of this?"

Nothing, I hope!

"She's a prosecutor," I pointed out.

"*Was* a prosecutor. Not anymo—" Suddenly, he pulled away from me. "Did you steal that money?"

"No!" I cried. "I didn't steal it, I—"

Earned it, I almost blurted. But stopped myself in the nick of time.

I grabbed the wineglass and almost upset the contents on my pajama top. He reached out to steady my hand.

"Nancy, listen to me." He held my wrist with one hand and removed my glass with the other. "Don't have anything else to drink. You need to keep your mind clear. Talk to me." I was perspiring with fear and anger. How dare he suggest that I stole my own hard-earned stash! I wanted to scream, *I'm a liar, not a crook.* "Tell me everything."

"Everything?"

"If you're in trouble, I'll make sure you have the best lawyer we can afford. Don't lie to me. And don't worry about my sister. I'll protect you, I promise. But only if you tell me what's going on. I can't help unless you're upfront with me. We're partners—. Honey, please don't cry. You need to talk to me."

"But I'm not in trouble with the law!" I insisted. Only with my husband! "And I can't believe you would accuse me of stealing!"

"Honey, no." He grabbed my shoulders, hard. "That's not true. I didn't accuse you. I said I would be there for you if you did! There's a difference," he added softly. "A big difference."

My heart was beating madly. He would be there for me if—?

"What are you saying? You'd be okay with it if I stole? I don't get it!"

"Look, I'm a banker. Not a prosecutor. My sister's the prosecutor. Was," he corrected himself. "If you've done something, I'll do what I can to keep us both out of trouble. If you need a lawyer—"

"Stop that!" I exclaimed. "I am not a thief, okay? I'm just subletting my apartment!"

He blinked.

"You're what?"

"I—I didn't want you to know. I never gave up my old apartment."

"You didn't?"

"I've got an illegal subletter and that money I saved—she pays cash."

"But why—" He grew quiet and looked utterly deflated. Had he been turned on by the idea of being married to a larcenous rip-off artist? Did I let the air out of that one too quickly? After a few moments of contemplation and some more wine, he said in a flat voice: "Why did you lie about it?"

"I didn't. You never asked."

He nodded slowly. He was looking a little dazed.

"You're right," he said. "It never occurred to me. You didn't lie."

"Are you angry at me? I didn't know how to tell you. I thought—"

"No," he interrupted. "Why should I be angry?"

"I thought you would take it the wrong way. You might resent it."

He sighed.

"You really are crazy. Can I ask what you're charging?"

"Almost . . ." What should I be charging? ". . . nineteen hundred."

"You could get twenty-five hundred for your place! Ask for more!"

"But she gave key money. I don't want to soak this girl! She's a struggling actress!"

He handed me my glass. "Does this mean I can have some wine?"

"We both need it," he said. "'But why are you worried about Elspeth? I won't tell her. You asked me not to. But what do you care if she knows?"

"It's illegal! My name's on two leases. And one's rent stabilized."

"But it's not like you're breaking the law. I mean, you're breaking the law but you're not committing a crime."

"Oh?" My husband's logic feels oddly familiar. "How so?"

"You're not supposed to have a rent-stabilized lease if you don't live there. But you can't go to jail for having two leases.

You can't be prosecuted. You would just have to leave the other apartment. Honey." Holding both of my hands, he looked into my eyes. "Why did you hide this from me?"

"I don't know." This lie felt more true than fake. I really *don't* know why—why I was so shortsighted. Why didn't I think up an airtight story before we married? "I was afraid," I said finally. "I thought you might object and then I wouldn't have this extra income. I didn't want you to take it away from me."

My good girl PJs were no impediment to making up. He started unbuttoning the top.

"Did you—did you mean what you said before?" I asked him. "About . . ." I suddenly felt too shy to say the words.

". . . looking out for you?" He opened the last button and leaned over to kiss my neck. I felt his lips against my earlobe, my pajamas sliding away from my hips. "More than you realize."

•◆• LATER •◆•

At two-thirty this afternoon, I was struck by a terrible realization. I called Charmaine pronto.

"Can I call you back?" she asked.

"No," I told her. "We need to change the top lock. Today. Now. Yesterday. I'm calling the locksmith as soon as we hang up."

"Can't we do it later? I'm getting ready to see someone. I've had a slow week!"

"You don't get it!" I said. "This is urgent. After your guy leaves, we need to change the lock."

"What happened?"

Getting into my recent ordeal would be too embarrassing.

"You have to trust my judgment," I said. "I'm doing this for *us*."

In the aftermath of making up, I forgot to ask Matt what he did with the apartment key. It was hidden under the money. Did he put it in the safe–deposit box with my cash? Accidentally discard it? He never mentioned it, not once. I looked in every conceivable area of the bedroom and bathroom. Calling him in the middle of his day will just draw too much attention to my other apartment. Fine, so now he knows I still have the lease, but I want him to stop thinking about that place. Put it out of his mind. What if he held on to the key? Is it on his key ring? Anything's possible, and I have to—no matter how much I trust him, I have to be sure he doesn't have access to the place where . . . !

"I can't tell you why," I said. "But my conscience won't rest until we change that lock. Somebody else has access to the apartment now—"

"Call the locksmith!" Charmaine said quickly. "I'll cancel my date."

I rushed uptown and met the locksmith in the lobby. As agreed, Charmaine stayed in the bedroom, out of sight. Tony's shop is right around the corner. He's one of those neighborhood guys you can totally count on, but who knows whether he gossips with our super? As soon as he was gone, Charmaine came out of hiding, dressed for her next date.

"Is it okay now? Who got the key? What happened?"

"I can't tell you. Here's your key."

"Why?" There was a new, unexpected sharpness in her voice. "Don't I deserve an explanation? I live here. I turn tricks here! How could you let someone else have the key?"

"Oh, for god's sake. I didn't do anything of the sort. And I can't tell you what happened right now. But I didn't endanger you."

"How long did you wait to tell me about this problem?"

"Ten minutes! I *am* on top of this. Okay?"

"Are you telling me the truth?"

"Why would I lie to you?"

"Because," she said, heading toward the bedroom, "everybody fucking lies to everybody! And I think the least you could do is tell me the truth when we're in this together! My phone was dead, all week, no business. I finally have a good day and you come in here and wreck it—and—and—I'm sick of living with all these lies!"

She slammed the door behind her. I sank onto the couch and waited. I could hear Charmaine blowing her nose. But Charmaine's a loner, she doesn't want me in there playing big sister. She needs to get a grip so she can see her next guy. When she came out, she was calmer.

"I'm sorry," she said. "I freaked out when you told me about the key. I'm glad we changed the locks."

"It was the right thing to do," I insisted. "I can't let my husband have access to this place."

"Your . . . husband?" She looked stricken. "Does he *know*?"

"Of course not! He knows you exist—I had to tell him that, but he doesn't have a clue what you're doing here. And he doesn't know your name. He thinks you're an actress. If you ever meet him, for any reason, that's what you tell him. You're trying to make it as an actress and you work for a catering firm. You're a temp. A waitress. Something actressy."

Wait a minute. *What* did Charmaine say? About living with lies? Aside from all the usual "suspects"—our landlord, the super, and her parents—who else is she lying to? Is she having a love affair? She's a hard one to read, and doesn't ask nosy questions about boyfriends or husbands.

It's unwritten but strictly observed: you can't just ask another girl about her problems with men or her family unless she gives you the signal. Not if you want to do business together and stay on good terms.

•❖• SATURDAY, 5/5/01 •❖•

Matt hasn't said one word about going to the bank together and putting my name on the box, but I haven't said anything either. The less I say, the better, as far as I'm concerned. I'd like him to think it's *his* idea to give me access to my own money. Is this the right strategy? The last few days have been scary enough, and I need to make sure things feel back to normal around here.

Last night, I went through his pockets while he was showering, hoping to find the key to my apartment. The key is useless now but that's not the point: You must never stop trying to understand what makes your husband tick. Never take your husband's psyche for granted. When you think you have him figured out, that's when disaster strikes. . . . Where he put the key will tell me a lot about what he's thinking. So, it's not on his key ring or in his wallet. Maybe it's in the bank vault, after all.

When I heard the shower curtain, I quickly ducked out of the bedroom and got busy in the kitchen. Ball-bearing hooks for the shower curtain: what a brilliant decorating ploy. I chose them for the master bathroom to go with a whimsical terry cloth curtain.

When you move the curtain, the ball-bearings make a loud, smooth rattling sound, audible throughout the apartment. If I'm on my cell phone while he's in the shower, or going through his pockets, I just listen—closely—for the telltale rattle of silver ball-bearings caressing a naked curtain rod. Fortunately, Matt didn't redesign *that* bathroom.

I like to think of myself as a domestic genius. But right now my own money is so near and yet so far from my anxious fingers. And my own efforts to play it cool are truly unnerving. Can I trust my own judgment anymore?

•→• MONDAY, 5/7/01 •→•

Must get organized for my date with "Terry." According to Trish: "It might actually be his place, then again it might not. He always says he's borrowing it from a friend. Don't let that spook you."

•→• LATER •→•

The apartment looks so naturally like an East Side lady's nest, not the home of a guy pretending to be a lesbian. I want to believe him!

"Terry" answered the door wearing a straight black skirt, cream-colored silk blouse, high heels, and no makeup. His face isn't feminine but his smile drew me right in. Terry smiles like a 1960s airline stewardess in a soft porn movie. A charming, seductive expression that made me coo: "You look *gorgeous,*" without a second thought.

"Let's put that over here," he said softly. He led me toward a sofa next to a mirrored wall, and I unpacked my tote bag.

"Ooooh, try this on," Terry insisted, picking up a small hat with a veil. "And this." He chose a string of pink costume pearls. "It's too wild for me, but you're so young and pretty, you *should* wear it. But first . . ." He, or I want to say She, undressed me with polite, nimble fingers, as if we were two girls in a backstage fitting room. "You don't mind if I take off your blouse?"

Terry's hand brushed against my bra—an amazing facsimile of how a straight girl accidentally touches another girl. There was nothing predatory about it, and the sensation it produced was intriguing.

When he had me down to my bra and panties, Terry began to arrange my appearance.

"I like these shoes." Terry picked up a pair of outrageous turquoise heels. "But I think these are more 'you.'" He dangled a pretty sandal with tiny straps and tall slim heels. Then suggested that I change into a lace corset with a push-up bra. When we were done, I looked like an extra in an outtake from an eighties music video—and felt like a titillated six year old at a really wild tea party, no boys allowed. "Wait wait wait." Terry opened my cosmetic case. "Where's your lipstick brush? You have such a beautiful mouth. I want to play with it."

I picked out my shiniest lip gloss and opened my lips while Terry applied the gloss in slow deliberate strokes. A shiver went through my nipples. It's strange because, when a man I'm hot for does something masterful with my lips, I get very aroused. But Terry's so convincing that this felt more like harmless pleasure with a girl. My signals were getting crossed, or merging madly.

Terry stood next to me, in front of the mirror, unbuttoning his silk blouse. He'd waxed his chest for the occasion. As I ran my fingertips over his skin, he asked, "Am I smooth enough for you?"

My fingertips lingered on his nipples.

"You feel perfect," I murmured. "Such pretty breasts!"

Then he asked, "How often do you find yourself attracted to a woman?"

Though Trish told me next to nothing about what to do with Terry, I felt hypnotized and knew exactly how to answer.

In a confiding, thoughtful voice I said, "I really prefer a feminine girl. It's not every day that I can get turned on by a woman."

"Me too!" he said. Now we were sitting at the dining table, in front of his makeup collection.

"In fact," he added, "I prefer a girl who's bisexual because I don't want her getting too possessive."

Terry opened a flat case containing twenty different eye powders.

"That's right," I agreed. "If you sleep with a guy, some women get jealous. But a bisexual girl won't."

Terry giggled.

"But I don't want your boyfriend to know about this!" he said. "It's our secret. I don't like it when a man wants to watch. They ruin everything. They're so rough! And they try to interfere."

"You have to be careful. A lot of bisexual girls will only go with another girl to please a man."

"I know." Terry was enjoying the chance to commiserate with another girl about the Bisexual Woman's Dilemma. S/he leaned toward me, and said, as if we were in a nail salon, dodging eavesdroppers, "We're walking a tightrope. But I feel like I've met a kindred spirit. A girl who understands. I'm still trying to decide whether I'm a lesbian. I'm glad you're bi."

I smiled flirtatiously, and began to examine the lipstick colors.

"I don't wear a lot of makeup," Terry said. "Not in the daytime. Just one light layer of translucent powder. See?" I nodded with approval. "But when I go out, I turn it up just a notch. I only buy MAC and Chanel. And I like La Prairie. How about you?" he asked.

"Chanel doesn't work for girls like me. They have gorgeous colors," I assured him. "But they're not really geared for the exotic woman. And all the MAC users I know are blondes." I didn't bother to add that La Prairie might be considered matronly. "I use a lot of Prescriptives."

"You're so right!" Terry exclaimed. "I never thought of that! Well, you're bringing me up to date. What lovely skin you have."

Terry's skin is pale to the point of pink and his hair's hyper-blonde. It's short for a woman, but not too long by corporate male standards. I was about to ask if he had worked on the color but—just as I would with a girl—I zipped my lip. I don't know "Terry" well enough to question the history of her blondness.

I made up his eyes and lips, but he drew the line at mascara.

"Too tarty looking," he said. "I like soft makeup. . . . Would you like to touch my legs?"

Terry's left calf was extended, and he pointed his foot to show off a patent leather pump.

I placed an admiring hand on his calf and stroked his stocking.

"Your legs are so silky," I told him. "And shapely."

"Fogal!" Terry said. "I only wear the best."

"Oh, but your legs deserve it."

Holding up a very elegant burled-wood hand mirror, Terry assessed our makeup job: "More eyebrows? I think strong eyebrows make such a big difference."

He ran his fingers through his hair and sat up straight, leaning forward to receive some more eye makeup.

"Shall we stay with a natural hairstyle?" I asked. I had a feeling wigs might be a no-no around here but I wasn't sure. "I love the way these colors work with your hair and your eyes."

"Natural," Terry agreed. "I don't want to look obvious. We don't want everyone to *know*, do we?" I wasn't sure what he was getting at but I made an agreeable sound and began to brush his eyebrows. "Do you think I could go to that charity ball at the Pierre and pick up some rich guys? Do you think I have what it takes? I really want to work for you!" Terry said. "All the girls want to work for you!"

Aha. I think I'm supposed to be a madam? And Terry's the new talent?

Terry picked up a patent leather evening bag and approached the apartment door, holding the bag by its handle. While I stood in the doorway, he sashayed into the hall to show off his womanly walk—and he does have a great walk. He went as far as the elevator—right past three other doors that could have opened at any moment—and returned to the apartment, laughing quietly like a naughty girl. My pulse was racing. What if someone opened their door and saw us? Me, dressed in a corset, and a black fishnet veil; Terry in his skirt and blouse. Actually, a casual observer might take Terry for a middle-aged mom. I, however, looked bizarre.

"You definitely have what it takes," I said. "We could get five hundred an hour for you." He was in heaven! "But I need to see you in something more revealing. Because you'll have to deliver in the bedroom, too."

"Oh!" Terry's face lit up. "I will?"

This was Terry's chance to model his lingerie collection and his heels. In keeping with his rejection of all things tarty, Terry's lingerie is silky, loose, expensive, and pretty. In the bedroom, while he tried different outfits, I sat on a chair giving hints and directives.

"Try pulling the top down just a little, with the strap falling off your shoulders. Can I see the back?" He tried on a shimmering blue nightgown that stopped midthigh and looked more like a slip. "That looks wonderful on you. Wear that the first time you see a client and you can't go wrong. It shows off all your best angles, darling."

"There's something I'd like you to do." Terry sat on the edge of the bed, knees together, legs folded sideways, in a coy pose. "If you look in the top drawer of that dresser, there's a special toy we can play with."

When I saw the double dildo, I did a double take.

"Can we use mine? I'll be right back." I returned with a longer slimmer specimen and placed a condom on each end of the dildo, while Terry watched with bright anticipation. "I'm fond of this baby," I purred. "A girl gets attached to her favorite things."

Lying on the king-size bed, Terry was still wearing his heels and his short slip.

"Before we go to the Pierre, I need to get off." He lifted the hem. "Is that okay? Or should I save it for my first customer?"

"But you're such a beautiful girl, it would be a waste not to see your pussy before we get down to business. Anyway," I said, "I need to try you out first. All my girls come with my personal guarantee. That's why I'm the best madam in the business! As a New Girl, I expect you to prove yourself."

I inserted one end of the dildo into my pussy. For obvious reasons, Terry had to improvise but he knew exactly what he was doing, and I was grateful not to be in charge of that particular detail.

While squirming around on my end of the dildo, I stayed upright, so I could whisper sweet nothings: "You gorgeous little slut! I had no idea until you undressed. You are so *hot*."

He gazed up at my face just as a girl might when the right man proclaims his love at the right moment. Then, somewhat over-whelmed by the pressure on my knees and the size of even my dildo, I wriggled onto my back.

One of Terry's hands was between his legs, rubbing against the shiny blue slip. I imagined the sensation—charmeuse silk touching his cock—and couldn't look away. To keep both ends of the dildo in place, I tried different angles and positions, none of which felt sustainable.

"Sabrina! Don't stop! I'm coming for you! I'll do anything for you," Terry moaned. "Now . . . now!"

"You're my favorite slut! Do it for me! Oh . . . yes!"

Shortly after *that,* Terry tried to get my number, but I resisted.

"Call Thalia," I said. "She knows how to reach me."

Trish is possessive. If she hears about a number given to a client, she might stop working with me. And her dates are perfect because they're afternoon outcalls, just what I need: I can't work nights and I don't always have a place where I can see a guy.

"But Thalia won't send the same girl twice," Terry protested. "She won't?"

Come to think of it, whenever I've seen a client of hers more than once, Trish/Thalia's been along for the ride. Like a chaperone. Maybe I shouldn't be such a Goody Two-shoes about my number. But I'm scared of my own shadow now. The more you get away with, the more opportunities there are to outsmart yourself. And I'm still feeling haunted by that close call with Matt. And the money!

·❖· TUESDAY, 5/8/01 ·❖·

Last night, while drifting off to sleep, I found myself thinking about Terry's silk nightie sliding against his cock while he made himself come. That slippery fabric . . . Matt was already fast asleep, snoring faintly. The room was dark and cozy, and Terry's lesbian high jinks seemed far away from the stillness in our bed. But I remembered that shiver of pleasure when he touched my mouth with the lipstick brush and I moved a little closer to Matt, opening my thighs so I could press against his hip.

The first time I encountered a "male lesbian," I was eighteen, and I certainly wasn't turned on by it. In fact, I was grossed out and a little indignant. He wore a silk bathrobe around his chubby middle-aged body. Lying next to me, he was gentle and harmless but I couldn't get past the ick factor. *He's a fat bald-headed man! How can he expect me to treat him like a beautiful woman!* I was such a sexual barbarian then that I had no sympathy for him.

I didn't know how to make him feel like one of the girls. All I knew at that point in my career was straight sex. I had been with a few girls and married couples but that was straight fare compared to what he wanted. I wasn't yet enough of a woman to let him be one too. Did I resent him for wanting something I didn't yet have?

I tried not to show my displeasure, but you can't just go through the motions with a male lesbian, and he flat out told me, "You don't understand my fantasy. You're not into this."

But that was then. Over time, I learned how to play other people's games. I never thought the day would come, though, when a john's perversity would prove so bewitching.

Guys like Terry have this Inner Woman they want to be in touch with. Have I discovered my Inner John, yearning to be embraced by the woman I've become?? Well, I guess I've come a long way. But I may have come too far. Is marriage turning me into a freak?

Finally! Matt wants to meet at the bank during lunch hour. I thought he would never ask. I'll have to force myself *not* to empty the box the minute he leaves. Moderation in all things. I must not appear anxious.

And, this morning at the health food store, I found a husband-proof container for my Pill supply: a small bottle of homeopathic salts prominently labeled Menses Regulator.

I'm a domestic goddess after all.

After Matt kissed me good-bye, I withdrew some hundreds from the box and grabbed a taxi heading north, just in time for my session with Dr. Wendy. I was five minutes late but lateness doesn't qualify as Material unless you're (a) lagging by more than five minutes or (b) one of those habitual therapeutic stragglers.

"When I saw my apartment key sitting right there," I told her. "I wanted . . ."

"You wanted?"

"—to laugh, cry and do a jig. All at once. Except that I don't really know how to do a jig."

"Exuberance is a variation on the theme of courage." Wendy smiled. "You have an impulse to do something unfamiliar. This is very fresh material," she added. "You just came from the bank? Does Matt know you're here?"

"*God* no! I don't want Matt to know I'm in therapy. Listen, I pay for all my beauty needs and my therapy. He's supporting me, but he doesn't pay for therapy. And I don't want him to."

"Do you have any reason to think he would oppose it?"

"I don't want to find out. Look, that's why I'm still hooking. It may seem strange to you, but I don't think this is any of his business, especially if it's on my dime."

"Just for the record," Dr. Wendy said, "nothing you tell me seems 'strange.'"

"Nothing?"

"Can you tell me what you meant just now? Would our sessions feel less private if you were dipping into your household income to pay for them?"

"I don't want to talk about money anymore."

There was an abrupt silence. I waited for Wendy to change the subject. Finally she adjusted her glasses, sat back with her hands in her lap, and announced, with a wry smile: "Sex is easy, money is hard."

"Matt makes a lot of money. He never questions my spending. And we have all these joint accounts."

"That's what I'm curious about. You're not struggling to make ends meet. Are you really seeing clients in order to keep your therapy a secret? Or do you keep this a secret so you'll have a reason—"

"To keep turning tricks?" I felt my temperature rising. "What difference does it make? You wouldn't ask me that if I had a *straight* job. Would you?"

Wendy looked thoughtful, and I felt guilty for introducing such an obvious red herring.

On my way to Zabar's, where Trish was waiting to pick up her cut, I felt calm for the first time in days. I've been on pins and needles ever since I got home from Trinidad, but it's vaguely disappointing to feel safe again.

When I was three, my parents left their apartment in Sandy Hill and moved to a rambling yellow house in Aylmer with a well in the backyard and a huge porch. The well didn't work anymore but I remember being fascinated with its construction. Lots of turning points occurred in our first house.

Mother became an atheist. She stopped taking us to Dr. Coupal, who was Catholic, and found a cheerful no-nonsense G.P. whose religion was unknown.

Sebastian learned to walk.

My father finished grad school and got a job with the Department of Forestry as a computer programmer. He would come home with stacks of colored punch cards that were vibrant and pretty—pink, light green—and also glamorous, because they came from somebody's office. One night I had a dream in which my father took on the mammoth project of counting to a hundred. In my dream, I sat up all night while he counted.

I had my first serious accident in that house while fooling around on some furniture and was taken to an emergency room for stitches. I thought I was lying on a large ironing board, but it must have been an operating table. I don't remember feeling afraid, just disoriented.

But the real turning point for me was an incident that never resulted in a hospital visit. In fact, my parents never knew about it. I was playing in the driveway with a group of kids who had come from next door, and my mother was somewhere in the house out of sight. It was a bright, sunny day, and we all had our tricycles out. We rode around in circles where we could and some of us practiced riding to the end of the driveway.

I got on my tricycle and explored the sloping driveway. The trike was cruising downhill, and I liked it. The pedals started moving faster. Though I felt at home on my tricycle, I lost control of the front wheel. My feet weren't fast enough for the pedals. This was a first for me, but I made a split-second decision as I reached the curb. I grabbed the handle bars tight and refused to fall off. I was not supposed to be at the end of the driveway. I had been told countless times to look out for cars when crossing the street, but I knew that looking was not an option. I couldn't stop.

I sat tight, wheels to the ground, unable to turn my head or slow down or do anything more than feel the incredible speed of the tricycle gliding across the street. I was keenly aware of my limitations and totally in the moment. I knew I had lost control, and I knew it was wrong, but I have never forgotten how exhilarating that brief perilous ride was. Silently anchored to the trike, if I could have put those sensations into mature words, I'd be shrieking: OMG! I AM REALLY GETTING AWAY WITH THIS!

The machine kept going and rode straight into the empty driveway across the street, where I came to a natural stop, because the trike was now facing uphill. The entire adventure couldn't have lasted more than forty seconds but I remember it in slow motion as a watershed event. My first experience of a free ride.

At this point, I had enough sense to get off the tricycle. I had a new respect for its unpredictable powers and now that I could, I hopped off. I wasn't ready to ride across the street again, but I had to get back there before my mother noticed. I walked my tricycle back to the curb, looked around, then walked it back to the top of our driveway. I wondered what the other kids would think of me for losing control of my trike.

There were no screams of dismay, no taunts, and no accolades for what I had just done. The other children continued to go about their business. This is also my first memory of opting for nonchalance. Acting as if. I had escaped injury and, just as importantly, I escaped embarrassment.

My first . . . jig.

This morning, two shaky-sounding voice mails from Allie on my cell, the last one (4:10 AM) even more distressed than the first at 2:31 AM.

"Didn't you read my e-mail? You can call back anytime. My phone is on but maybe I'd better try to get some sleep. Okay, so leave a message if I don't pick up!"

There are times when I feel guilty about refusing to share my home number with my best friend.

And there are times, like this, when I know I've made the right decision.

•✦• LATER •✦•

Catching up on Allie's e-mail. The first one, sent just before midnight, is troubling:

> I need to talk to you about something. I've been
> getting these weird weird e-mails from someone called
> Amy Hatchet. At first I ignored her. Then she sends
> another one a week later. I know it's just e-mail. I
> KNOW sticks and stones are just sticks-n-stones but I
> don't like the way she's talking. Now she writes every
> few days. And she knows too much about me.

Another, sent from a Hotmail address at 1:46 AM:

Subject: MY NEW CONTACT INFO from ALLIE
this is NOT SPAM!

*I am sending this new address to five people total.
You, of course, will always know how to reach me.
What would I do without our friendship?? I also gave
it to Lucho but that's another story. Plus Jasmine and
a few of my better guys. Okay, well maybe EIGHT
people have the new address. Max. Please do not give
it to anyone. I may have to shut down my
Trollop_At_Large account but I'm afraid to do that.
In case Lucho's e-ing me at my old address.*

From Allie's new Hotmail account, at 3:03 AM:

Subject: What I'm talking about!

*Look what she sent me the other day! Is this creepy?
She keeps threatening to Investigate NYCOT.*

*>>Your Trollop Collective is a FRONT for Human
>>Trafficking and the Committee will assist us when
>>we investigate your network of sexual enslavement.
>>What will the good people of Ridgefield,
>>Connecticut say when they find out the girl next
>>door is really a conduit for traffickers from
>>Bangkok. Quit while you're ahead. Or should that
>>be Giving head. Danbury Federal Correctional
>>facility is a nice place to visit. Very close to
>>Ridgefield.*

*Lucho told me not to worry about a crank sending
e-mail to the Colloquium Committee. He was totally*

*reassuring but then he left for Bogotá and now I don't
know how to reach him. I'm afraid to ask other
people on the Committee if they've been getting
e-mail from this person. AND LUCHO HAS BEEN
OUT OF TOUCH FOR ALMOST 36 HOURS . . .
No IM's, no voice mail nothing . . . I fear the worst.*

No wonder Allie was bouncing around her apartment, sleep-less, at four AM. It's not really about the stalker.

It's the first time she's ever had to deal with her new boyfriend . . . *being out of town.*

·•· FRIDAY, LATER ·•·

Just back from an emergency Frappuccino with Allie at the Star-bucks on Thirty-second. Despite the late-afternoon sky turning gray, she was protecting her eyes with huge tortoiseshell sun-glasses.

"For god's sake," I told her, "you have to reorganize your fear, break it down into components. Lucho is one issue and the e-mails are another."

"But it's all happening at once!" she said. "It's not like Lucho to be out of touch. For *two whole days?*"

She readjusted her sunglasses, headband-style, and sipped on a bright green straw that was too tall for her drink. Her eyes were pink and slightly swollen.

"It is very rare for a boyfriend to get kidnapped," I pointed out. "Sometimes it's good to have a little break. He's probably just busy. How often were you guys talking before he went to Bogotá?"

"*Five times a day!*" Allie exclaimed, causing a wide-eyed barista to turn around and stare. "And I have to prepare my speech for the Open Society Institute. Oh!" She looked mortified. "I forgot my flash cards. I wanted to get your feedback."

"It's okay. You'll do the flash cards later. Remember what I said. Components. The flash cards are a separate component."

Allie sighed.

"I guess you're right. Well, I sent Lucho an e-mail from my new Hotmail address but I don't know if he got it." She nibbled on an oatmeal cookie like a frightened protein addict. "I have to keep going into my old e-mail account to see if he wrote. And then I see her name! And those horrible subject headers. Don't ever change e-mail accounts when a guy is out of town."

"Have you tried calling him?"

"His phone doesn't work in Bogotá. I left a voice mail but he won't get it till he comes back."

"So who do you think is sending these creepy messages?"

"I don't know. It could be anyone. She sent it to the Trollop_At_Large address. Everyone has that."

"Well, maybe . . ." I tried to think of a tactful way to say this. "Maybe the activist lifestyle is not suitable for you at this point in your—"

"Don't even *go* there!" Allie said. "I'm on the Colloquium Committee. And I'm the media coordinator for NYCOT. Noi's visa application is in the works. People are *counting* on me. Quitting is not an option! And Noi has a right to come here and speak at Cornell about the struggle in Bangkok. How dare this— this Amy Hatchet try to intimidate—"

"Allie, you are being exposed to all kinds of vindictive, dangerous maniacs because of your involvement with NYCOT. I saw that e-mail, and I don't like the language she's using. Or he. An e-mail address tells you nothing. That could be a guy masquerading as a girl."

"You're right," she said. "Thank god for my doormen!"

"No kidding. But Allie, it could even be Lucho!"

"Lucho! It couldn't be."

"How well do you really know him? How do you know he's in Bogotá? He could be sitting in his apartment on the Upper West Side playing a horrible prank on you! He's just someone you met at a conference! Maybe he's a sadistic weirdo!"

"He's—he's the love of my life! He is not just someone I met! You're getting so jaded, Nancy. Ever since you got married," Allie said. "Have you *ever* had a healthy relationship with a man? Well, maybe I haven't either but at least I'm trying. Just because you lie to Matt all the time doesn't mean the whole world is like that. And," she added, "Lucho's the first sex partner I've had who doesn't have to stop as soon as I come! I used to think I was too sensitive for prolonged oral sex. But after Lucho makes me come? He just—he refuses to stop, but he's totally gentle and considerate and it's the most intimate fulfilling oral sex I've ever had with another person in my entire life! How can you call Lucho a sadist?"

I was anxious to take our conversation outside, where my friendly neighborhood baristas wouldn't hear anything more. On the sidewalk, I gave Allie my ultimatum.

"Look," I told her. "I can't afford to be hanging out with someone who flaunts every part of her life the way you do. I have too much to lose. Maybe you think I'm jaded, but I have responsibilities. I had a bad scare last week. Matt found out about my other apartment! I have to keep a low profile now, and I can't afford to arouse any suspicions. You leave messages in the middle of the night about this e-mail stalker, and when I try to help, you call me a liar! If you care about your friends, you'd better start thinking about how your actions affect other people. What do you think will happen if you're investigated?" I asked her. "Your friends will be, too!"

But I don't think Allie, for all her activist cred, has any idea how true that might be. Or what would happen to my marriage if I got swept up in something like that.

•◆• FRIDAY MIGHTNIGHT •◆•

A startling phone call from Miranda, who just got back last night.

"You won't believe what happened after you left," she told me.

Neither would you, I wanted to say but didn't. Even if I spilled all the beans to her, Miranda would have trouble believing the truth about my life.

"Well," she said, "Sebastian's girlfriend called your mother and told her about his crack habit."

"Omigosh. And nobody told me?"

"But you already knew."

"I mean . . . nobody told me that Mother—never mind," I said. "Is she upset?"

"She was shocked at first. But he's in rehab now, so I guess it was okay to tell her? She's flying home tonight. I'm sure you'll hear from her."

Why I Am Not a Crackhead

•◆• SATURDAY, 5/12/01 •◆•

So the cat's officially out of the bag. Sebastian is misty about whether he still has a job. Erica says he does and I want to believe her. Well, my brother has survived one corporate regime change after another. When the entire department gets tossed, he's the one they keep. He may have his job figured out, assuming they don't know his true whereabouts.

Apparently, Sebastian has checked himself into a residential rehab in Whitby, Ontario—but had the good manners to wait until after the funeral before revealing his crack habit to Mother. There is something to be said for being a *diplomatic* crackhead. Robert broke the news to Dad, who is being incredibly philosophical about the whole thing—while my stepmother, who has never had a good word to say about my father's older kids, is in "I told you so" mode.

Mother's last e-mail, sent from the computer room of her B&B, was more upbeat than expected:

> *Sebastian is feeling better though he says the food is rather bland. Erica assures me that Renascent House is secular and Sebastian hasn't been fired. So it's not all bad. Dodie's youngest went to a Protestant recovery center last fall—remember the one with all the rings in her nose? She came out sounding like a charismatic preacher. Terrible. Dodie is wondering where she went wrong as a parent. By the way, Dodie thinks I should turn my computer room into an Internet café. She would invest in some new equipment, advertise the café in her bookstore and share the proceeds. The B&B guests are always needing to use my computer which I find to be an imposition. Why not charge them for it? And get some new equipment in the process. What do you think?*

Dodie is a Birkenstocked pottery teacher who runs a used bookstore in the same village, my mom's best friend and a fellow atheist. Neither Dodie nor Mother is actually *from* Wales but both are avid supporters of Welsh Nationalism. Now they also have in common a grown-up child in recovery.

Mother doesn't realize that her well-groomed Upper East Side daughter has also done the drug that currently plagues Sebastian. Unlike Sebastian, I stopped because I was afraid it might turn my hair prematurely gray. Doesn't Mother wonder why her eldest child hasn't a single gray hair, while my younger brother's hair turns gray before our eyes? But she's been in denial about Sebastian's lifestyle for many years. And mine, too, come to think of it, despite the fact that I ran away from home when I was fourteen.

Being the sensible precocious one, I outgrew cocaine before it could affect my looks. I guess that's one benefit of being a first-born girl, an older sister, with an inflated sense of responsibility.

When I arrived in New York, I was almost seventeen, and "crack" hadn't been invented yet. It started out as "freebase," and the freebasing elites were making headlines by setting themselves on fire. In the early eighties, smokable cocaine was an expensive hobby, a privileged addiction. Freebase wasn't a drug for schoolteachers or salaried folk. Most freebase users were small business owners with lots of cash flowing through their hands.

Like Larry.

I met Larry while working for Jeannie's Dream Dates. Larry, a recently divorced textile wholesaler, lived in a Second Avenue highrise near the Fifty-ninth Street Bridge. Freebasing as an evening ritual racked up many hours on the escort service clock, and Larry was more than willing to pay by the hour. He prepared the stuff himself from a recipe involving Drano, baking soda, tin foil, and, of course, cocaine. He was a freebase connoisseur. Are there any connoisseurs of that drug anymore? It's so much easier to skip that phase and become a crackhead.

I watched him cut a lemon in half and, with an old-fashioned Pyrex juicer, remove all its liquid. Then he added water to the lemon juice and poured this into a glass water pipe. For lighting the pipe, some people preferred a blowtorch, but Larry had his own method. He took a long piece of loose cotton wool, and looped it around the head of a metal device normally used for cleaning a flute.

"Where did you get *that*?" I asked him. "Are you a musician?"

"My brother teaches at Juilliard Prep," he said. "I stole it from him."

When you hear about a coke addict stealing from his family, you imagine money. But people steal the strangest things. I felt rather sorry for his brother, who must have been upset when his cleaning rod went missing. Like sex organs, woodwind instruments need prompt, frequent, and very detailed cleaning. But an addict doesn't care if his actions could be harmful to a musical instrument.

Larry dipped his large metallic homemade Q-tip into a bowl of 180-proof rum. Then he lit the cotton wool with a Bic lighter.

When I inhaled the lemon-scented smoke into my lungs, it was delicious—lemon juice foils the vile taste of the smoke. When I exhaled through my nose, I knew I had found my favorite drug. An exquisite giddy rush filled my head. I announced to my free-basing mentor: "Wow! This is better than an orgasm!"

Any drug that makes sexual pleasure seem puny is a drug that needs watching. But what did Larry care? He was already on that track himself, delighted to have the phone number of a pretty girl who was willing to freebase. Until now, I had been faithful to the escort service, afraid to give out my number. But exchanging numbers with him that night felt absolutely right.

A few nights later, Larry invited another couple to smoke freebase with us. We sat at the dining room table, taking turns with the pipe. When it was my turn, Larry said, "She's got *great lungs*."

The other couple observed while I inhaled.

"Fantastic lungs."

"Amazing."

This was how freebasing conversations went.

I couldn't tell whether they were married, dating, or something more basic. In the haze of freebase euphoria, I wondered if the other girl was a pro.

Then I worried about whether they were swingers. Coke makes you so paranoid!

Did Larry expect me to have sex with them? Was he going to pay extra for this? Did I have to go down on a strange girl? Because I sure wasn't going to hop into bed with them unless—. What was I thinking? Sex was totally beside the point.

After they left, I attempted to give Larry a blow job but he wasn't really up to it. He was, however, up for doing more freebase. I left after four AM with $1,500 in my pocket and slept for a day. When I woke up, I was still hung over so I didn't answer my phone until I was able to work again. In the eighties, it didn't matter what time you woke up, you'd still make money.

My brother never got paid for doing freebase. By the time Sebastian discovered the stuff, it was no longer an elite way to get high. Freebase got downsized into crack.

Crack is thought of as a street drug. That's what Mother believes because she gets all her drug lore from the papers. Actually, crack is freebase padded out with loathsome filler material, repackaged for the middle class.

On a junior exec salary, you can satisfy a crack yearning fairly often. As long as you don't do it every week, you can be a part-time crackhead or even a frequent user for quite a few years before it catches up with you. In the days of freebase, though, the road from initiation to addiction to bankruptcy was a matter of months, not years.

Within weeks of our first meeting, Larry had begun to deteriorate. One night, he placed a chair against the door of his apartment in order to feel more secure. For some reason, that didn't bother me, since he allowed me to remove the chair when it was time for me to leave.

But one night, he tried to talk me into taking a check because he didn't have enough cash to pay for my time. Like most underage hookers, I didn't have a checking account. I was still living in a residential hotel, doing everything on a cash basis. When I balked, he offered to pay with cocaine. That was tempting, but it wasn't kosher. Okay, so I didn't have a bank account yet but I understood that a true professional gets paid in cash, not drugs. At heart, I was always a real hooker. Never a "coke whore."

When I saw the clock silently indicating the end of my first hour, I took out my beeper. I feigned a message from the escort service.

"I have to call them," I said. "Or they'll think I'm working on the side."

This phony logic sounded good enough for Larry who was getting ready to light another pipe.

After a briefly faked phone call, I told him, "I have to go. They'll be upset with me if I don't."

Larry was in the process of exhaling. The freebase was losing its power to enchant. He found it much easier to converse in the middle of a hit than he would have a month ago.

"Can you come back later?" he asked.

"Absolutely," I lied. "I'll call you."

"Have one more hit?"

"Um . . . okay. Sure. Why not?"

He had paid for my first hour and the pipe did seem very appealing. He called my beeper so many times after I left that night that I actually felt sorry for him, but I ignored his calls.

A few weeks later, I began hearing stories about Larry. He called the escort service, requested a two-hour date with one of the newer girls, then refused to answer his intercom. Freebasing paranoia made it harder and harder for him to remove that chair from his side of the door. Soon he was blacklisted for not paying on the occasions when he *did* come to the door.

I wish I could say that Larry was the first and last person I smoked freebase with. He wasn't. But I started to notice a pattern. Freebasing clients were either addicted or on the way. The high was always starting to lose its glory. They all vainly attempted to recapture that first thrill. They were all paranoid, preoccupied with what lurked outside the apartment door, trying to get in. They heard things. They ran out of cash.

And it was hard for me to perform in bed. After a hit of freebase, the last thing I wanted was a cock in my mouth demanding attention. I just wanted to sit back. Stay high for as long as possible. Which was never very long, unfortunately.

One morning at six AM, *I* started obsessing about what lurked on the other side of the door. I was in a room at the Vista Hotel with two other girls, entertaining a freebase addict from Bergen County. When I pressed my ear to the door of the room, convinced that I heard voices in the hall, the girls gave me a weird look. I stared back at them—confirmed freebasers—and thought: *Omigod, the sun is coming up and these girls aren't pretty anymore. Were they ever? When did this happen to them? Overnight?* It was insane. The three of us, coked to the gills at dawn, passing judgment *on each other* for letting freebase get the better of us.

Our half-naked customer remained oblivious. He was busy lighting the pipe.

I disappeared into the bathroom, to examine my face in the mirror for signs of wear and tear. So far, my face appeared unscathed by the best (and worst) drug anyone has ever created. How long had those two coke hags been smoking it? Months? More than a year? Yikes. How long would it take before that happened to me?

I had to make a choice. My looks or this drug. It was time to become ladylike! With the money earned from that last night of freebasing, I bought a $100 mud treatment for my entire body, a clarifying mask for my face, and a special serum for putting under my eyes. I spent the next week getting facials, drinking gallons of spring water to cleanse my system, reading genteel sonnets to improve my debased mind. I spent hours at a health food store, poring over the supplements. A lady takes her vitamins and minerals. My bedtime reading changed from poetry to nutrition. I kept the classical station on at all times, partly for the music but mostly for the subdued voices of the program hosts who made me feel instantly respectable.

I went to Bergdorf Goodman and bought my first pair of seriously expensive quilted-suede flats. When I tried them on, I had an epiphany—like when I discovered my favorite drug, but in reverse. My ladylike feet were channeling Audrey Hepburn, not in *Breakfast at Tiffany's* but in one of her sweet frothy comedies, like *Charade*.

Some people need to get scared straight. I was scared pretty—terrified of becoming a coke hag, an aesthetic has-been.

Sometimes—at the nail salon, in a restaurant—my nose picks

up a tantalizing aroma. That hybrid of rum, lemon juice, fire, cocaine. There are a few things that smell like that. I don't know what they are, but I know they're out there. It happened the other day, while I was walking down the street. Mysterious fumes, a briefly delicious memory. And then it was gone.

Crisis Management

Today, a call from Aaron F., one of whimsy's perviest creatures. He runs a hedge fund in Aspen and comes to town about four times a year.

"I'll be checking in late Wednesday," he said. "Can we get together at eight?"

I tried for Thursday morning—impossible—and finally agreed to Wednesday night. I never work at night anymore, but Aaron's a tempting exception: $1,200.

I headed straight to Gristedes to prepare for his arrival, picked up six cans of Reddi-wip, and dropped them off uptown while Charmaine was taking a shower. Then I popped around the corner for plastic drop cloths.

In the hardware store, my phone began chiming. A call from Allie. Tony, our neighborhood locksmith, stood a little too close by for comfort, so I stepped outside to hear her latest tale of woe.

"That stalker sent an e-mail to the chair of the Colloquium Committee. She's using a different name with them, but I'm sure it's the same person. Saying that the Colloquium on Human Rights is endorsing a human rights violation by letting a NYCOT member sit on their committee! And she keeps talking about sex slaves. *International* sex slaves. She accused *me* of being a shill for sex traffickers!"

The door of the hardware store swung open, and I started walking to the corner, away from prying ears.

"I sent you a copy of her e-mail," Allie said. "Did you get it? And the e-mail from the Colloquium Committee! They say she could bring negative attention to the entire conference by going to the media."

"I can't get to my e-mail now, but I don't think you should be sending me these things. You're creating an e-mail *trail*," I said in a low voice. "I don't want to be part of some investigation into a sex slave ring, thank you very much. Even if it's the sex slave ring of a deranged stalker's warped imagination. What with you being the media maven of NYCOT and this maniac—"

"Well, I can't unsend my e-mails! And I think you should read them. I'm preparing a response from NYCOT to the Colloquium Committee. Sex work is not slavery, it's an informal economic activity. There's a big difference. These abolitionists want to put girls like Noi behind sewing machines and make them work for peanuts!"

"You don't have to practice your spiel on me, Allie. I'm not even part of your debate."

"Just because nobody ever made *you* work at a sewing machine. But girls like Noi are fighting to stay out of the garment factories of Asia!"

"And girls like Noi will always find a way to do that," I said. "I think you should disentangle yourself from this mess *yesterday*. It is okay to walk away from a train wreck."

"Well, there's a meeting tonight and I have to go. I can't let this stalker poison everything that I've been working for. And I want to tell my side of the story. In fact," said Allie, "I'm going to use my talk at the Open Society Institute to take her on! I just called the NY1 producer. And if the Colloquium Committee doesn't support me, I'll address these accusations on TV!"

"You'll what? I want you to remove my e-mail from your archives. Erase me from your cell phone. And stop calling me!" I said. "You should be talking to your lawyer. Call Barry Horowitz and make an appointment with him. And tell him what I said. I don't want to see any more e-mail about this stalker!"

"I can't believe that you, of all people, are being so unsupportive. I am under attack! And you're telling me to crawl away and die! After everything we've been through together! Is that all our friendship means to you?"

I was shaking when I returned to the store for my drop cloths.

•◆• LATER •◆•

Finally got up the nerve to read Allie's e-mails.

After a quick perusal of the Sex Slave diatribes, I deleted quickly—as if virtual contact with Allie's current problems might result in a transmittable disease. The stalker claims that the INS "has the authority" to investigate everyone on the Colloquium Committee! Even if that's a wild exaggeration, no wonder they're getting cold feet about Allie's involvement.

One e-mail, sent *before* our blowup, is so anguished that I feel ashamed of myself for telling her not to call me:

> STILL *have not heard from Lucho. I'm beginning to wonder if his ex went with him to Bogotá. She is*

•◆••◆•

*actually FROM Colombia. So this is not just my
imagination. Well I mean, it's not such a crazy thing
to imagine. He always says they are "such good
friends." Is she trying to get back with him? They
knew each other in high school! She can speak to him
in THE LANGUAGE OF HIS CHILDHOOD and I
can't speak a word of Spanish. I keep remembering
what he said before he left. I am the love of his life?!
Why did he say that. If he did go to Bogotá with his
ex, then he said that for a reason. But what reason? I
wish he were here. I still want to believe he's my soul
mate. Even if he's with another woman, this should
not prevent him from e-mailing ME.*

Out of habit, I began a compassionate soothing e-ply but
quickly closed my e-mail window. With any luck, Lucho has con-
tacted her by now. But then again, isn't Lucho partly to blame for
all the recent uproar? He encouraged her to get involved with
that Colloquium Committee in the first place!

•◆• WEDNESDAY, POSTTHERAPY •◆•

Today, I tried to put into words the true reasons for my nagging
shame. Allie and I haven't spoken since Monday afternoon, but
her accusations have been echoing in my head for two days.

"Okay," Wendy said. "What *does* the friendship mean?"

"Allison's like my bad conscience. Around when I started dating Matt, Allie met a guy called Zack who was *also* the love of
her life. Just like Lucho," I said. "Except, Zack hated the fact
that she was hooking, and she quit the business for him! She
joined Prostitutes Anonymous and started telling everybody she
was powerless to control her sexual addictions."

"Everybody?"

"Just her closest friends," I explained. "Not random people on the street! But she stopped hooking. She left New York, and she stopped talking to her friends in the business. Including me."

"I see," said Wendy. "So Allison's an activist with a past."

"Yes. She avoided me for weeks. I accused her of treating me like a leper! When a friend in the Life snubs you, it's worse than being snubbed by someone else," I explained. "And I hadn't done anything to provoke that! She had no reason to snub me."

"From *your* point of view."

"Well, now I want to protect my marriage, and I want to stay friends with her, but I can't stay friends with a call girl who's challenging an obsessed stalker to a fucking media duel! All in the name of hookers' liberation! And I'm wondering what will happen if Matt sees her on TV," I said. "He might recognize her and ask me a lot of questions."

"Sometimes people aren't recognizable because they're out of context," Wendy said. "It depends on the eye of the beholder. And who the beholder is. Allison's not as central in Matt's life as she is in yours."

"But why does she have to go to such extremes?" I wondered. "That summer when she joined Prostitutes Anonymous, it was, like, relentless. She tried to convince me that *I* was a sexaholic! Her 'enabler'! And now she's part of this—this worldwide sex workers' revolution."

"Allison sounds like a truth-seeker. But is that really the issue?" Wendy asked. "How did you respond when she snubbed you?"

"I was *there* for her! I hid her book for her and almost got into a lot of trouble for that."

"Her book?"

"Her client list. She asked me to burn it! But I couldn't destroy something so valuable. And then she asked me to help her sell it. Anyway," I said. "That was then. I was single. I took a lot of risks. I had less to lose. I wouldn't do anything like that now."

"You're taking a risk with your other apartment, though. With your roommate."

"But Charmaine isn't like Allie," I explained. "She grew up in a crummy part of Pittsburgh. I can trust her. She had a terrible experience when she started hooking, and she takes everything very seriously. Her mind is always on her business. Allie had it easy in the beginning, she's had it easy all her life, and that's why she's never been able to concentrate on business. Going on TV is just another distraction so Allie won't have to grow up!"

"We can't control the universe," said Dr. Wendy, "but we can make choices about how we spend our time. If you know when Allison is scheduled to appear, there are many things you could be doing with Matt that will not bring you near a TV."

"That would involve talking to Allie, though. To find out when." I paused and remembered the damning words. "She said something the other day that still bugs me."

I was thinking about Allison's furious retort: *Just because nobody ever made* you *work at a sewing machine!* So? My impoverished ancestors left Asia before the factories were built. Allie doesn't get it. I have no interest in helping her solve the problems my ancestors escaped from! They indentured themselves so I wouldn't have to worry about such things.

"Something you haven't mentioned?" Wendy asked.

"Well, not explicitly." I groped for the right phrase. "Am I too, um, self-centered?"

Yikes. Just realized. I forgot to pick up the Styrofoam plates for my appointment with Aaron. His *real* wish is to be surprised by a cream-pie-wielding bitch who viciously "pies" him and, many cream pies later, takes pity on him. A hooker carrying that many pies into the Peninsula would be very noticeable. Instead, we craft ersatz pies on the spot out of Styrofoam plates and Reddi-wip. I wish I could say I thought of this myself, but it's Aaron's idea. Styrofoam plates make for Safer Pie Throwing because paper plates have sharp edges. It's my job to create the cream pies while he waits, in his Speedos, on the plastic drop cloths. And it's my job to supply the materials.

Back to Gristedes for plates . . .

•◆• THURSDAY MORNING •◆•

Last night was both delicate and messy. Delicate because Matt was home while I was out working—a role reversal that makes me quite nervous. Messy because of the whipped cream.

Under my navy suit, I wore a white lace body suit and pale pink stockings to complement the abundance of cream. I carried some $29 open-toed shoes with pink ankle straps and white heels in my tote bag. Good shoes would be a mistake! And pastel scenery seemed to fit the situation.

Aaron ducked as I threw the first cream pie in the general direction of his face. After the fifth creamy assault, Aaron gasped and clutched at his brow.

"You hit me in the eye," he said in a sulky voice.

"Oh no." I rushed over to the drop cloth, where I knelt in a pile of cream. "Did I hurt you? I'm sorry."

After some anxious fussing on my end, he snickered with satisfaction.

"Fooled you, didn't I?"

"Oh for christ's sake," I muttered, returning to my pie-throwing duties.

Men!

After the tossing was over and the teasing had begun, my shoes and feet were covered in canned cream. I stood amid the wreckage with my legs on either side of Aaron's face, providing a flash of pussy while he gazed thighward, a stunned defeated look in his big brown eyes.

He persuaded me to bring my pussy closer for a more intimate peek. We had gone through four cans of Reddi-wip, and I was more worried than usual about getting it in my hair, but it was time to start writhing around on the plastic sheet. I hate rushing with a good client like Aaron, but I wasn't in a position to dawdle.

Matt thinks I'm sampling a new exercise class. And I want to get home earlier than promised. Not later.

Aaron's cock was growing under his tight black Speedos. He pressed against my thigh and I wriggled aggressively, staying as close to his bulging Speedos as possible. My hand slid beneath them to finish the job.

After showering, I stuffed my cream-soaked underthings and shoes into hotel laundry bags along with the rolled up drop cloths. I hailed a cab on Fifth and managed to arrive at Seventy-ninth Street before nine-thirty. Charmaine sat hunched over her computer screen, wearing a towel, her face covered with a white mask. She waved and mumbled. The Biologique Magic Mask pulls your skin so tight it's hard to talk or move your eyelids.

"You should really lie down when you do that mask. That's how you get the best results," I told her.

She made a noise that sounded like "I know." She can't talk under the mask, but she can IM. In fact, she had two different IM windows open and seemed to be going back and forth between them. I caught a glimpse of her user id, FoxxiiCharm and had a feeling she wasn't talking to her mother. Is she IM-ing two different guys at the same time??

I showed her the laundry bag with the drop cloths.

"I don't know if I should toss these in the compactor. The hotel bag's a dead giveaway," I said. "It's just a lot of whipped cream and foam plates, but we can't be too careful."

She nodded vehemently and pointed to a shopping bag in the corner of the room. Then she pointed to the street.

"I guess you're right," I said. "It does look suspicious. And you hear these stories about people being Found Out through their garbage."

I changed quickly into exercise clothes and, when I was out on the sidewalk, headed for a rubbish bin. Looking around, I waited for some pedestrians to pass before disposing of my camouflaged drop cloths.

An emotion close to guilt but even closer to fear gripped my heart as the cab sped toward Thirty-fourth Street. Despite my best efforts, I was, in fact, later than I expected. Of course I have a million alibis. *I was browsing at Barnes & Noble and got totally absorbed in* . . . Suddenly my brain froze and I couldn't think of a single book title. *I was—* What's wrong with me? *I went out for coffee after the class,* is more than plausible. Why am I acting, in my head, like a prisoner who must report her every move? I'm not carrying money—after the fiasco of the tampons, I've been storing money in my other apartment with my other underthings—so even if he searched me, I'd be fine.

But why am I thinking this way? Matt doesn't behave like

that! Still, when you're sneaking around, you have to think that way. Imagine the worst, most intrusive, scenarios. Be prepared. Mentally. Physically. In every way. Never underestimate your spouse.

Or am I just getting spooked because I went through *his* things last week?

I entered my own home a nervous wreck and tried to camouflage *that* as effectively as I had the drop cloths. Matt was lying on the couch reading the latest *Wired*.

"How was the class?" he said. "What's wrong?"

"Nothing." I disappeared into the kitchen for a glass of water. What should I say? When I came out I told him: "It's a very challenging class! It was great . . . until I started talking to one of the other women. We went out for coffee. She told me something really upsetting."

Matt's magazine slid to the floor. He sat up.

"Do you need to talk about it?"

"No!" I said. "I want to forget about it."

"So tell me about the class. What's the idea?"

"Lots of emphasis on strengthening the pelvic floor. It's, you know, something you have to learn about if you're preparing for pregnancy."

I felt my equilibrium returning. Two birds with one stone: the perfect alibi and a positive message about pregnancy that strengthens my marriage and affirms our shared goals.

"Is that like Lamaze?" Matt asked.

He's getting way too comfortable with the idea of discussing my pelvic floor muscles!

"No! This class is only for women. Honey, do you mind if I tell you something?"

I sat down next to my husband and looked into his eyes. I do my best improvisation when there's a crisis. When I'm feeling the heat.

"I love you, but there are things I can't share with you," I said. "Maybe I'm a little old-fashioned," I explained. "The pelvic floor muscles are essential to, um, female health, but it's so unromantic. Not a topic for mixed company. If you see what I mean."

•◆• THURSDAY AFTERNOON •◆•

A harrowing voice mail. Delivered at noon.

"*How* could he *do this* to me? When I *most needed him*!"

Omigosh. Did Lucho break up with Allie in e-mail? Remarry his first wife? What exactly has he done? I'm afraid to find out.

Allison's raw distress was so horrifying that I erased her voice mail. I have no choice but to call her back. Even if I *am* trying to avoid her.

•◆• LATER •◆•

It was hard to get through to Allie. Her landline was going straight to voice mail. Her cell phone was behaving oddly. I checked my e-mail, and found no follow-up to her voice mail. Just some nervous nattering about her Open Society Institute panel: at two AM last night, Allie was arguing with herself about

> *sex workers' alliance? or prostitutes' coalition? What*
> *do you think? The OSI panel starts at 3:00 tomorrow.*
> *Call my cell if you want to be in the audience!*

That was her last e-mail.

Around three o'clock my cell phone rang. Allie's voice sounded small and faint.

"Where are you?" I asked.

"In bed," she sobbed. "I'm in bed. I took some Tylenols so I could sleep."

"How many?"

"Two. They're extra-strength."

"Oh." *Thank god!* "I thought your talk was supposed to be—"

"He abandoned me!" she exclaimed. "When I needed him! How could he do that?"

"What did he say?"

"Nothing!" she wailed.

"I don't understand."

"Of course you don't! You'll never understand! You'll never understand what it is to be abandoned like this because you've never given your heart completely to—" She started to sob hysterically.

"That's not what I mean! I don't understand *what happened.* What about your panel?" I asked.

"I can't go through with it! They'll just have to go ahead without me."

"I'd better come over," I said.

"You'd better not!" Allie screamed. "Not if you're going to sit here and pass judgment on my personal life and say I told you so! Because I don't want to hear it today!"

"Have you eaten anything?"

She blew her nose.

"Not really," she said. "I have a terrible craving for ice cream."

When I arrived at Allie's building with two cartons of ice cream, the doorman waved me through. Her apartment door was slightly ajar and the entire place was dark. Curtains were tightly drawn in the living room, and I had trouble finding the light. I stored the ice cream in the freezer and tiptoed into the bedroom, where Allie was sleeping with a big blue ice mask on her eyes. She was lying under a comforter that was pulled up to her chin. Only her long shiny hair, her nose, and the blue mask peeked out. With her arms hidden from view, she looked like a shell-shocked mummy. But, just as I turned to leave the room, she asked, "Did you get the ice cream? I can just have it out of the container."

There was a time when I might have gone along with that. Now that I'm running an actual household with another adult, it's out of the question. I found a bowl in Allie's kitchen large enough to contain an entire carton and presented two flavors with a paper napkin tucked into the underplate.

As she tried to console herself with rum raisin and chocolate mint, Allie described her ordeal.

"He hasn't written to me in a week! Last night, I got a nasty e-mail from that stalker. She says, 'You think you're Lucho's girlfriend but you're fooling yourself.' This morning, I tried not to read any more of her e-mails. I looked at the e-mail from the Colloquium Committee. And I looked in all my accounts for an e-mail from Lucho." Allie put down her spoon. "It was the last straw!"

The straw that broke Allie's heart.

"He nominated me for that committee, and then he left me to fend for myself," she said, in a quiet voice. "I cried all morning. I called Roxana. She thinks I have the flu. She's going to replace me on the OSI panel."

Allie looked away, slightly embarrassed, and said, "I just don't have the heart to do it alone."

Alone! I felt a twinge of guilt.

"But I thought the girls in NYCOT were rooting for you," I said. "Roxana's totally behind you on this. Isn't she?"

"Yes," she grabbed a tissue. "But it's not the same. I'm not like Roxana. She's happy as long as she has her friends in NYCOT. She doesn't need to be in love. Lucho made me feel brave. He—he—" She was tearing up again. "He meant so much to me! I can't explain it."

"You don't have to," I said.

"I *liked* having a man in my life!" Allie said. "I don't want to hide everything I do! I don't want to spend all my nights alone like Jasmine! I don't want to spend my entire life hanging out with—with a bunch of other women all the time, like Roxana! With Lucho gone, I feel empty. And afraid. People are attacking me, and I don't have what it takes to be out there anymore. I thought we were going to be an avant-garde power couple," she said.

After a brief silence, she added: "I guess I'll keep going to NYCOT meetings but I don't want to be out front anymore. I'm going to hand in my resignation tomorrow."

When I left Allie's apartment, it was almost six. She had finished both cartons of ice cream and was getting ready to sleep again. It's a relief to know she's not going on TV. And now I can stop avoiding her. But something doesn't add up. Doesn't feel right. And I can't put my finger on it.

Misconceptions

This morning, I rose early and prepared a decadent breakfast while Matt slept in. Italian sausages, scrambled eggs with crème fraiche, broiled tomatoes topped with bread crumbs. I filled two small ramekins with cultured butter to complement my only concession to virtue: seven-grain toast.

Matt stumbled into the kitchen with a dreamy smile on his face. He found me warming plates and kissed the back of my neck while I poured him a cup of coffee.

"I love the way you look in an apron," he said. "Especially when you wear those shorts."

His hand cupped my right breast gently for a second. As he wandered back to the bedroom, I felt a sharp desire stirring beneath my shorts. Then a terrible pang, closer to my breast.

What about Allie? Is she sleeping off the Tylenol PMs? Crying her eyes out?

Did Lucho understand that he was playing with Allison's heart? Leading her on? I can't bring myself to say this to Allie, but it's obvious to any sensible person that he's visiting his family in Bogotá—and daily contact with homegrown reality has turned "the love of his life" into a fling. An adventure.

As I sat down to share an intimate meal with my husband the morning after making up with my best friend, I felt queasy.

"These are just right," Matt said, cutting into a juicy fennel sausage. "You never overcook anything!" He gave me a curious look. "Why aren't you eating, honey?"

I picked at my food, trying to swallow a piece of toast, and discovered that, while I can fake many things, it's hard to fake an appetite.

Last night's vague doubts resurfaced. Now highly magnified. Horribly clear. As I sit across from my adoring husband, Allison's alone. And not by choice. Feeling—how did she put it? "Empty. And afraid." Disillusioned.

Am I turning into a foul-weather girlfriend? That might be okay, if I were also manless. But I'm not. There is something indecent and even downright creepy about this. No matter how I try to dance around it, Allie's romantic misfortune is . . . the basis for our reconciliation.

Some women disappear from your life when you're happy about a man, only to reappear when you're demoralized and licking your wounds. Please tell me I'm not turning into a break-up vulture!

And if I don't eat something, Matt will be completely weirded out.

"I have to confess," I said playfully. "I couldn't stop myself from nibbling. Cooking in the morning makes me ravenous."

After breakfast, I logged on. Whatever is wrong or right about this friendship, I do have to check in on her. I began composing a friendly note, mindful of not sounding like a foul-weather friend.

Are you okay?

... sounds condescending. Like you're rubbing it in. Could be taken to mean: "Is your bleeding wounded shattered heart surviving okay? I'm taking five minutes off from the sweetest guy in the world while he makes dinner reservations for JUST THE TWO OF US."

How are you?

A little formal, considering that Allie and I performed oral sex on the same guy—at the same time—not that long ago. Quite a few times, actually, in the course of our friendship.

What's going on??

Collegial. Good. I risk sounding breezy, but that's better than sounding like a smug sympathetic married friend.

> *I have some errands, your part of town, Sunday or*
> *Monday. I would love to meet up for lunch or coffee.*
> *Take care, N.*

•◆• LATER •◆•

Time flies when you're on the Pill. Just realized: today is Day 21! So it's finally safe to fuck without a condom. Or so I keep telling myself.

But I can't get my brain wrapped around it. Nor my thighs, which are quite well trained. Hardwired to unlock for a lubricated condom, they stay firmly shut when there isn't one. It's second nature by now.

On Thursday night, when Matt tried (again!) to get inside without a condom, I was almost flattered. But still, I held out for what I wanted. I'm such a pro that I can negotiate for condoms without getting turned off—and being turned on never affects my decision. This *can* be a useful trait, but now it prevents me from taking the plunge.

I need to at least create the illusion of reproductive intent, but can't bring myself to go there! Even though I've been on the Pill for twenty-one days. Even though Matt's my lawfully wedded husband—not some guy with an assumed nickname passing through my apartment in the middle of the day calling me Sabrina. Or Suzy.

I know more about Matt than I do about most men. I have his social security number. I know exactly what he earns. I've met his family. We share an ATM password. He had an annual checkup two months ago. I know because I made the appointment for him. And I love him! Most women would say this is reason enough to start fucking without a condom. Why can't I just get with my own program? The one I so carefully erected?

Jasmine was right. There's no point arguing with Matt about babies and condoms. A secret arms supply is sometimes the only option. The Cold War might be over but its techniques will never disappear.

So now I'm a well-defended Cold Warrior contemplating detente, but I still feel safer with a condom. I superstitiously wonder if Matt's unabashed desire to impregnate is stronger than the medical technology I'm using on the sly.

But that's crazy! The Pill works—when you take it. And I'm taking it religiously. At nine-thirty on the dot every morning.

I can't relate to girls who do their clients with condoms and their boyfriends without. I've spent so many years not being one of those girls that the whole idea of becoming one—even a respectable married version—goes against the grain.

That's the problem with basing your self-image on what you *don't* do.

•◆• SUNDAY, 5/20/01 •◆•

Brunch with Allie at Demarchelier. She didn't mention Lucho until our food arrived. And even then, not by name.

"I'm still mourning the relationship," she admitted. "But I don't think grief is always a negative. It can be a growth opportunity."

"Most definitely," I agreed.

When a boyfriend loses his identifying qualities—when you're no longer discussing *him* and you're getting over The Relationship by dealing with larger issues like attachment, human suffering, and personal growth—then you're starting to mend.

Allie examined her new nail polish. Like me, she's the type to get everything done with a vengeance when things have gone wrong with a man. Her long hair, short nails, and pale skin glowed with maintenance. But there was a subdued look in her eyes.

"I told Roxana I need a break from all this public speaking. She's thinking about taking over for me on the Colloquium Committee." She sighed. "And I'm helping NYCOT plan the Regional Summit but now I'm staying behind the scenes. I don't want to get in the news. I'm not cut out to be a public figure."

She stared wistfully into her soup, then looked up. "Why don't you come to the NYCOT Regional Summit? We're renting a space at True, downtown. Don't worry," she added, sensing my concern, "there won't be any TV cameras allowed. We don't want to scare off the girls who are still working."

I've been adamant about avoiding NYCOT events ever since I got married, but it's hard to do "adamant" when your best friend turns to you for emotional first aid, makes all these concessions to your value system, and sips her Chardonnay with the air of a traumatized kitten.

"I'll think about it," I told her.

When I left Demarchelier, my phone was vibrating. Milton, returning my call.

"To what do I owe the honor?" he asked.

"How about a little party with Allison?" I suggested. "It's a great excuse to get her into bed. And," I giggled, "she just got back from L.A. two days ago. She's looking *very* good. We just had lunch."

"How's four o'clock?" he said. "Tomorrow. I'll bring some Cristal to celebrate her return. You just had lunch? Who did what for dessert?"

"Well, there wasn't time," I said. "I have to go and meet my . . . fiancé. But I'll check with Allison about tomorrow. Dessert's always tastier when you have to wait a day!"

"Your fiancé doesn't know what he's got," Milt chuckled. "Do you organize threesomes for him too?"

"You must be kidding!"

If only we could be as objective about boyfriends and husbands as we are about customers. Milt needs a "threebie" once every eight weeks. It's not absolutely essential but he does enjoy two girls. Without that triangular zing in his life, he would get restless.

A threesome with Milt, accompanied by good champagne, will take Allie's mind off romance and help her to keep things in perspective.

I know now that I've been avoiding Allie in too many ways, ever since she started planning that television breakout. Paranoid about introducing her to my johns! Milton sees her two or three times a year when we have a threeway, and I know he'd be mortified if he caught sight of Allie on TV. Telling the world she's a hooker! He's got a lot to lose and can't afford to risk indiscretion. Thank god Allie has come to her senses.

•→• MONDAY, 5/21/01 •→•

As soon as Matt left for work, I called Allison, worried she might be having a relapse.

"I told Milton you just got back from two weeks in L.A. He's very hot to see you. Don't forget to call me Suzy. I have an extra strap-on here."

"I hope I can get into the right frame of mind," she sighed. "I've had two cups of coffee and I feel catatonic. But I'm rereading this great book, *How to Survive the Loss of a Love*."

One of the self-help classics. Bereavement's *Joy of Cooking*.

"I think I read that when I was twelve," I said.

"Me too! But it's still relevant," Allie said. "And there are things I didn't understand when I first read it. 'The Healing Process Has Its Progressions and Regressions.'"

"I didn't understand that when I was twelve either."

" 'There Is a Beauty in Sadness.' "

"Isn't there a chapter on pampering yourself?"

"Yes! I need to reread that. 'Sexual Desire May Change,'" Allie intoned. "Oh my god. I haven't been able to have an orgasm for six days. I'm afraid to . . . you know, if I try to get off, I might start thinking about—about *him*. It's too painful! If I think about him, I'll—"

"Listen, we've all been there. Just try to focus on getting ready. If you fall apart, you won't be able to work. Then you'll hate him for messing with your income. And you'll hate yourself even more."

"That's true. And I need to make some money. I just got a huge bill from Barney's."

"But you need to keep having orgasms. Isn't there some guy at the gym you can focus on? You need to keep the oxygen flowing to your skin."

"I know. But there isn't."

"Well, just hang in there," I said. "You can't let Barney's cancel your card! We're talking about your infrastructure. You can't let that fall apart over a relationship."

•✦• LATER •✦•

When Allie arrived—dressed like a girl who had just spent two weeks hanging around Rodeo Drive—Milt uncorked the bubbly. His favorite new discovery—*Strap-On Biker Chicks*—was running silently on the VCR.

Allison smiled winningly at the action and said, "Alexandra Silk's my *fa*vorite! Is she in this?"

Allie makes an effort to remember who's who in porn. I guess it's like memorizing the Major League Baseball players so you can talk sports with your clients.

We sipped Cristal and chatted while four dildoed girls took part in a very energetic (and slightly confusing) daisy chain. Our own plans were less elaborate but there's nothing like a simulated lesbian scene—hardware included—to take a working girl's mind off her boyfriend problems. Allie rose to the occasion.

"This is sooooo inspiring!" she said. "I'm dying to get Suzy naked. Aren't you? Let's take the champagne to bed."

Milt followed us to the bedroom where two strap-ons, hers and hers, were prepped and waiting on a pillow. Allie stripped down to a delicate pink thong—almost the same color as her nipples—then disappeared into the bathroom with her equipment. When she returned, she was wearing the harness over her thong, and I was wearing nothing at all. I got on my knees, placed my mouth on the dildo and pretended to play with my pussy. Milt poured some more champagne for Allie. While I licked the dildo, I could hear their glasses clinking.

"Milt's dick is so big and *hard,*" Allie crooned. "I think you should suck his cock while I fuck you."

"Great idea!" I said.

A condom was waiting under the pillow, but soon it was on Milt's cock and in my mouth. Lying on his back, he gazed at the intersection of my face and his erection. I continued to make slutty eye contact while Allison pretended to fuck me from behind.

Our deal is that no penetration occurs with lazy customers like Milt. With some attentive guys, you can't avoid real penetration, but Milt never seems to get off his back these days. When I felt the lubricated head of the dildo sliding against my opening, I brought my lips down to the base of Milton's cock. I moaned intensely.

"She loves it," Milt gasped. "Ohgodthatfeelsgood. Keep fucking her like that."

"She hasn't been fucked like this in weeks!" Allie exclaimed. "I looooove giving it to her!"

By the time Milt finally came, we had exhausted all the permissible options and he was late for his next appointment.

"What a combination!" he said happily. Allison, straddling his pelvis, reached between her thighs to grab the condom and rolled away from him. "What time is it? But I'm late for a good reason. That was an experience to be savored."

After Milt was gone, the commercially induced gleam faded from Allison's eyes, and she confided: "I almost didn't show up! I put all the souvenirs and presents in a bag and tried to throw it away. Then I started crying." She pulled her new bible out of her Burberry tote and opened it. "But the chapter on getting out of limbo got me out of my apartment."

Key phrases were underlined in red: ". . . slow erosion from below. . . . your better instincts tell you there's little hope . . . get on with the business of surviving, healing . . ."

Business, underlined three times, made me hopeful about Allie's survival.

"I'll see what I can drum up for next week," I promised.

•✦• TUESDAY, 5/22/01 •✦•

This morning while nursing a cup of coffee, I turned on my phone. Three text messages from Allie—"CALL ME" "GOOD NEWS" "SO CALL ME"—left at various hours the night before. I delved into my voice mail and retrieved her message:

"I can't believe it. Ten e-mails from Lucho just arrived! *Tonight.*"

I called her back.

"Ten different e-mails? What does he say?"

"He went to an Internet café last night to look for my e-mail. I had no idea."

"How could that happen?" I asked suspiciously. "What are the dates?"

"From last week! I'll show you."

When I logged on, three FWDs from Allie were sitting in my in box. The first e-mail, explaining his initial lapse, was convincing:

> Connectivity does not come easily, darling Alli. It
> seems the phone system here is really sweating as
> more and more of the population gets online. It may
> take years to stabilize. I am in the Internet café
> reading your charming letters, because it's the only
> way to get a decent connection and my first chance to
> write. I was at a semi-rural and completely unwired
> farmhouse just outside Bogotá with in-laws, nephews,
> etc. Now back in town dealing with my mother's
> imperfect phone lines. I will write again tomorrow.
> Last night I couldn't stop thinking about your sweet
> lips, both pairs!! Nostalgic for the company of your
> tender body . . . L.

The second is in the same vein:

> Dear Allison,
>
> Today I was reading some Neruda. "A single star
> with a far-off scent and a purple center" is the best I
> can do, for translation. "Better than any word is the
> pulse of your scent." How can I not think of you
> when I read such things?

The third was sent to her new Hotmail address last Thursday!

Re: UH OH WHAT SHOULD I TELL HIM? FWD: thinking of you, my love

Good morning, dearest Alli. I am so sorry to be missing the OSI panel today but I have the date circled in my agenda and will be thinking about you at the appointed time! Darling Alli, I admire you enormously for your "chutzpah" to borrow a New York expression. It takes courage to challenge the preconceptions of those stuffy do-gooders who will be sitting in the audience, but you are the perfect candidate for the job. And it doesn't hurt for them to see a gorgeous, luminescent woman speaking on behalf of New York sex workers! Congratulations on your televison debut. Don't forget to ask for a tape!

And please, tell me about the disturbing e-mails. Are they coming from a university address? A free account? I don't like to intrude on your privacy, but I should see them before I comment. They are, in the end, only e-mails.

A worried follow-up from Allison:

Re: Sooooo, Ummm. . . .

How embarrassing! He was getting my messages but I wasn't getting his! After Thursday, he got so antsy because I wasn't writing. His last e-mail is REALLY concerned. I wanted to answer RIGHT AWAY but I've been trying to figure out what to say. He will be

so disappointed if I tell him the truth! Won't he?
What a terrible mix-up! I felt so much better when I
got his mail last night, but I couldn't sleep a wink.
Thank GOD I didn't throw away the souvenirs!

•◆• **LATER** •◆•

Just spoke to Allie, who *still* hasn't written to Lucho: "His last e-mail was frantic! But I don't know what to say to him!"

Because she's too embarrassed to admit the truth, Lucho's paying for a crime he didn't actually commit.

"For god's sake, tell him what you told Roxana."

"Really?"

"And don't embellish," I advised her. "Just tell him you had to miss the event because you weren't feeling well. And now you're finally better. The less you say about not feeling well, the more convincing you'll be. Let his imagination *fester*. Do you want me to write it for you?"

"I can handle my own e-mail!" she said. "But shouldn't I tell him his mail got delayed? For a week?"

"No! That kind of talk opens up your emotional floodgates. You'll end up telling too much. Just keep it short, mysterious, and sweet. But if you don't write soon, he'll start thinking you got run over by a bus."

"Do you really think so?" Allie was intrigued by my theory. "I wonder how *that* would make him feel."

"Let's not put him to the Bus Test just yet. I guarantee that once you've written to him, you'll be able to sleep properly."

What I was thinking last night while Matt was going down on me:

Time to cross the latex threshold. A diplomatic necessity. Further delay could backfire badly and weaken your marriage.

Besides, you're already halfway there. . . . I belong to the subset that uses condoms for commercial blow jobs. But oral sex with a boyfriend or husband is another matter entirely. Nobody even pretends to be rational, much less consistent, about blow jobs and boyfriends. Condoms for unpaid oral sex? Life is too short. Safe sex is a flawed concept if you actually like anything about sex. You have to make exceptions. Who can be bothered with those vanilla-flavored dental dams we've heard so much about—and rarely seen?

You're not exactly violating a sacred temple. My body's more like a boutique with flexible hours. The policies of such a boutique may be subject to change.

It's hard to have an orgasm when shop and temple are competing for mindshare but I forced myself to come, by concentrating on something I'd rather not discuss. Even with myself. So I could be nicely wet the first time he ventures there uncovered.

When Matt reached for the condom drawer, I grabbed his wrist to stop him. He gazed into my eyes for a long moment, as I opened my thighs under his hips.

"Are you sure?" he said.

I pulled him closer with my legs, closed my eyes, and whispered, "Yes. I'm totally sure."

This afternoon, a quickie with Jasmine at the Excelsior. An eccentric-looking redhead with a tiny Maltese dog followed us into the elevator. Too late, we realized she was going to the same floor. Yikes. What if she lives, like, next door to this guy? We waited for her to exit. Jasmine looked relieved when the Maltese owner continued walking—away from the client's apartment.

Thirty minutes later, we were back on the sidewalk.

"I've gotta pick up some custom powder," Jasmine said. "I'm going to Bloomingdale's."

"I could use some cleansing milk."

After equipping ourselves with various staple items—while dodging the perfume touts and skincare hawkers—we stopped upstairs for a snack.

"Well," I told her, "I finally took your advice. I went on the Pill."

"Thank god for that," Jasmine said. "And you didn't tell him?"

"No way! I keep them—here, I'll show you." I produced my homeopathic pill bottle. "I keep them in here."

Jasmine nodded with approval.

"Don't you feel better about yourself now? The future belongs to chicks like us," she said. "We can see a conflict coming and squash it like a bug. Technology is your friend! There's no reason in this day and age for any woman to be arguing with any man about her breeding schedule. It's *your* pussy and your everything-else-that's-in-there. What's wrong?"

"I just feel weird."

"Don't tell me you're having some kind of moral crisis about lying to Matt at *this* stage of the game."

"Not exactly, but"—I lowered my voice—"we finally had sex without a condom!"

"And?" Jasmine asked. "How was it? Are you glad you saved something for marriage?"

"Well . . . a hot time was had but not by all concerned. I mean, it wasn't a *bad* time. But, without the condom? I'm not relaxed. I feel like I'm betraying myself. Back in the day before we all used condoms, I enjoyed it just fine. What happened?"

"Paradigm shift! Sex without condoms-and-lube just seems so fucking inefficient and last century. Or maybe it's a case of 'you can't go home again.' How do you keep 'em down on the farm, after they've—"

"Could you say something a *little* more encouraging? I really miss coming with my husband."

"But you totally made the right decision," Jasmine insisted. "It's just gonna take some getting used to."

•◆• FRIDAY, 5/25/01 •◆•

Jasmine's got a point. It's the paradigm shift. You spend years feeling that you're Not Supposed To Do X. If you do X, it's worse than breaking the rules, you are sleazy and disreputable. Overnight, due to a change in your status, X becomes as normal as washing the dishes. No, X becomes socially obligatory, a sign of true commitment. Your husband expects it of you. So do your in-laws, come to think of it.

X being rubber-free intercourse. Without X, you may obtain a trophy—marry a banker. I used condoms throughout our courtship with no problem. But you have to engage in X if you want the next trophy: a banker's baby. Your husband and his in-laws can't imagine why you'd be reluctant to claim that trophy. It's just . . . inconceivable.

The journey from hooker to wife doesn't require a passport or visa—not if you stay in Manhattan. There are no checkpoints or embassies. It's supposed to be like moving from Ontario to Quebec. Or California to New York. But it's more like living well in a banana republic—then moving to a NATO country. The paradigm shift.

•◆• SUNDAY, 5/27/01 •◆•

This morning, as I lay beneath my husband, hands firmly grasping his buttocks, limbs wrapped tight around his body, I felt an orgasm starting—ours—and was quickly distracted by the end of *his*. Sex in the raw is so much fun for Matt that he simply has no self-control! And when that happens, he thinks I'll be content as long as I have *some* kind of orgasm. Which he's willing to provide, as many times as I want. . . . But so are my customers!

I fell in love with Matt after a full day of work. In fact, I had already come that day.

Having my pussy attended to orally is a perk of my job and sometimes an obligation. Oral sex for me will never be like . . . what Allie says she's been getting from Lucho. It's a surface pleasure, something I can have with a john, and my body never gives itself away when I come during oral sex. I give myself to Matt while fucking, which I can't do with customers, and I fear I won't have another orgasm that way unless he starts wearing condoms again.

There is only one way to reintroduce condoms into our bed. It has to be Matt's idea, not mine.

Hotter Than July

•→• TUESDAY, 5/29/01 •←•

Last night, after Matt came inside of me, I seized the postcoital moment.

When you have an important announcement to make, timing and location are key. Matt, playing gently with the nape of my neck, was relaxed but not sleepy. My body was responding happily to the attention of his fingertips, but my mind was on a mission.

"I've been thinking. . . ." I paused to whet his curiosity and organize my thoughts.

"Honey?" His hand reached down to cup my right buttock and I felt a light pinch. "Thinking about what?"

Snuggling much closer, I was now resting my head on his chest, pressing my nose against dark curly hair. He has just the right amount of chest hair—and I've seen every variety out there. I know what I like.

In a cozy manner, as if I were talking about getting up and making a cup of Ovaltine, I told him: "I think we should raise our children in the Catholic faith."

"In the what?"

He was still holding me but his arms grew stiff. I disentangled myself and sat up.

"As Catholics. What's wrong?" I pulled the sheet up so that my nipples were still visible.

"Your mother's an atheist," he protested. "If you weren't raised Catholic, why would you raise your own children that way?"

"My mother was raised Catholic and she raised us as atheists. She followed her conscience. Why can't I follow mine?" I replied. "I want my children to have an identity."

"You want to label them with a religion before they're old enough to talk?"

"Isn't that what happened to you? You're an Anglican."

"Episcopalian. But I never went to church. Nobody in my family does. Just for special events. Funerals and weddings."

"Well, I'm not suggesting *you* convert. This is about our children."

"And what about you? You're not even Catholic."

"I *am so.* I was baptized. I just didn't go to church or take First Communion. But I'm still a Catholic. I haven't been excommunicated or anything. I can return anytime. That's how it works. It's a very accepting religion."

"Accepting? I don't know about that. Do we have to decide this tonight? It's a huge decision."

"In what sense?"

"I know you have all these Catholic relatives but I don't and I'm not even sure about God. Sometimes I believe and sometimes I don't. I can't tell my kids to follow a strict religion I don't believe in. What happens when they start asking questions? Are you thinking Catholic *school* because that's really insane. There is no way a child of mine—"

"How can you say that? Miranda went to Catholic school and *she's* not insane."

"She did?"

"Holy Name Convent in Port of Spain. I'm sure you know lots of Catholics and you don't even realize it."

"I didn't realize *you* were."

"How could you not? It's hardly a family secret! I've never hidden it from you."

"But you never talked about it."

"So? You have this idea that Catholics have to go around talking up their religion? We're just like everybody else. We're not all fanatics. I can't believe you're so prejudiced!"

"I never thought of Miranda as a Catholic. Or you." Matt looked up and frowned. "This is a very serious decision you're asking me to make. And I am not a prejudiced person. Don't say that."

I'd better not—in case he caves, just to show that he's not.

"What were you planning?" I asked. "On raising them with no religion at all?"

"I never gave it much thought. It's not important to me." He rolled onto his side and reached for the alarm clock. "I really don't like the idea of our kids getting a Catholic education. It just feels wrong."

"But children need a foundation, a system of belief. Are you serious about having kids? Or is this just a whim? It's not just about getting me pregnant—there's an entire lifetime of care and responsibility!"

"I don't know." He closed his eyes, massaged his temples briefly and said, "I really have to think about this, honey."

This morning, I found him in the breakfast nook, sipping coffee, immersed in his *Wall Street Journal*. He looked up from the paper.

"I want to explain something about last night," he began. I was still half-awake, clutching my first cup of the day. It was hard to respond. "I'm glad you take all that stuff seriously. I want you to be the mother of my children. I've known this for a long time." The caffeine was hitting me and he seemed—oh no, to be coming around! "And you're right about children. They need a foundation."

I gulped more coffee and gazed at him with as little expression as I could muster.

"But," he said, "I think you're wrong about the Catholic church and I need to do some soul-searching. Figure out what my true feelings are. It's really bothering me."

Enough to start using condoms again?

·◆· WEDNESDAY, 5/30/01 ·◆·

This morning, a call from Jasmine, warning me about Allison's latest project.

"She's organizing a handbag drive. Well, she called at the right time. I was cleaning out my closets, and I have all this faux alligator. My starter bags. I haven't worn them in years," she boasted. "Now that I can afford the real thing. You *must* have some bags you don't use anymore. Don't you buy a new handbag every three months? I'm taking mine over tonight. You should come!"

"Charmaine won't like it if I go up there to dig around in my closet for old handbags," I said, remembering her outburst when we had to change the locks. But I called anyway to see if I could fit myself into her schedule. Then I called Allie.

"I might have some bags for you," I told her. "But I can't get to them right now. Maybe tomorrow? They're, like, in the back of my closet."

"Oh good!" The music has fully returned to Allie's voice now that she's exchanging e-mail every day with Lucho and getting occasional phone calls. If nothing else, his trip to Bogotá has made it possible for Allie to scale down her communication needs. She has discovered that you can, in fact, get by on one e-mail every twenty-four hours and one phone call every two days, and still feel like a love object. There is no way that intensity—five times a day!—can be sustained as your relationship progresses. "So I'll tell Jasmine to come tomorrow," she said. "The Nevada Three will really appreciate your donation. I just got an e-mail from Renee."

"Nevada Three?" I asked. "Who's, um, Renee?"

"They had their own escort service in Las Vegas," Allie explained. "Nina's still in prison and Barbie's release date is coming up. Renee got out a month ago. After four years! She desperately needs some nice things. All their assets were confiscated by the authorities! Every thing they owned. It's something to do with RICO."

"Are you serious? You're exchanging e-mail with a convicted felon? Do you have any idea—"

"I know what I'm doing," Allie insisted. "You shouldn't call them felons. These girls are victims of a terrible injustice! They were running an escorts' co-op, just the three girls, and the Nevada prosecutors turned it into a racketeering thing. But they were just trying to make a living! And it's not illegal to send handbags to Renee! She served her time. Can you imagine being in jail for four years and you don't have a single handbag to your name? We're helping her to reintegrate!"

It's hard to argue with Allie's logic sometimes.

This afternoon, while Charmaine stepped out for a call at the St. Regis, I did a major excavation of my front closet. When you hold on to the housing from your single years, you never get around to throwing things away. This apartment is my illicit insurance against the ups and downs of marriage. My secret workstation. My uptown attic. How many Manhattanites can lay claim to an attic of their own?

I almost broke two nails, moving a stack of plastic storage bins to reach my inactive handbags: a collection of designer fanny packs, convertible clutches, and some twentieth-century evening bags purchased at the height of the Reagan years. I peeped inside one bin and found a mangled cardboard box filled with clunky earthenware plates from a Pottery Barn sale.

I still wince at the memory of that day, when I had to leave my very first apartment—the first that was really mine—and move to a fading residential hotel where I shared the floor with an impoverished ex-milliner. I had been living in a small modern studio with a view of the Chelsea Hotel's back wall for three weeks—overjoyed to have my own immaculate bathroom, my own tiny kitchen, my own address—when Jeannie's Dream Dates abruptly closed shop. I never got around to unpacking all my stuff; evading the police was too urgent. I left my first apartment without a forwarding address, and my unopened boxes, badly organized, hastily retaped, went quickly into storage along with my furniture. It was a step backward but there was no other option.

My new neighbor at the Allerton Hotel for Women was convinced that people like me were the downfall of Manhattan: society had betrayed her by going hatless, destroying her business, and I—bare-headed—was part of the syndrome. After a few weeks of her ranting, I tried the George Washington Hotel, where I coexisted with some elderly women, a handful of street pimps, and young tourists with backpacks. I stood out in my little suits and almost-ladylike heels, running around at all hours, unable to hide what I was doing. One afternoon, I received a phone call from a friendly voice asking for "Suzy"—the name I was registered under. He suggested that I was the kind of girl who needs a "manager." I yelled back like a juvenile fishwife: "How dare you talk to me like that! You'd better leave me alone! I'll report you to the police!" A completely absurd threat, since I was actually *hiding* from the police, but he never called again.

When I finally got resettled, the cardboard boxes had started to sag a little but they were still doing their job. Over the years, cardboard gave way to square plastic bins with lids. For some reason, I saved one cardboard box—while always tempted to discard its homely contents. My first dishes are nothing to be proud of—they're horrible looking—but I can't bring myself to get rid of them.

As for the box itself, I'm not against cardboard, but it doesn't hold its shape. When I stored everything in cardboard boxes, I always imagined the strategy was short-term. Cardboard stacked upon cardboard, I've learned from those years of storage facilities and cheap hotel rooms, is scary looking. Cardboard symbolizes hope gone rotten. Plastic is the reality principle. Plastic is for people who can manage the past and confine it. Plastic persists. Cardboard is for dreamers, plastic for realists. But cardboard inside of plastic is hope everlasting. Very difficult to throw out.

Due to a last-minute date with Steven, I lost precious time hand washing my delicates and spot-cleaning the carpet. He's supposed to come on my stocking but he was so excited—after so many failed attempts to see me—that his come splattered everywhere, unexpectedly.

I arrived at Allison's apartment much later than planned. Jasmine was already there, hunched over Allie's computer station, glued to the screen.

"She's analyzing the stalker mails!" Allie whispered. "Don't disturb her. She's trying to get inside the mind of the stalker." She grabbed my collection of castoffs and placed my two Duane Reade shopping bags in her living room next to a pile of similar donations. "This is great! More than we ever expected. What's wrong?"

I was frantically searching for my phone.

"I haven't erased my Call History in two days!" I said, somewhat stricken. I found the phone in my makeup case and began to eliminate Incoming Calls. "I'm supposed to erase the history every day. What if Matt picks up my phone and sees all these calls coming from the Plaza? God knows what he might think."

The thought that I've been sleeping soundly while my husband could, if he really wanted to, peek at every number I've called in the last forty-eight hours! The perils of advanced-level multitasking! Sometimes, you just lose track, putting your entire structure at risk.

"I can't believe all the precautions you take with Matt!" Allie exclaimed. "And the lies you tell him! I'll *never* have to erase my history for *Lucho.*"

"You might not have to," I said, frowning at Missed Calls, "but maybe you should."

Why do girls who Tell always feel so morally superior? Just because Lucho knows that Allie *works* doesn't mean she's never lied to him! It's a little early for Allie to be preening about their emotional dynamic, but I suppressed this observation and tried to make nice.

"I just made a pot of raspberry leaf," Allie said. "Have a Soy Newton. It's my original recipe."

"No thanks on the soy," I said, accepting a cup of herbal tea.

"Excellent source of plant estrogen!" Jasmine called out. She didn't turn around. "And we all need all the estrogen we can get. Do you know what happens to your supply once you hit thirty?" Allie rolled her eyes. "But," Jasmine added, "I'm not so sure about the plant estrogens. I mean, we're more like horses than plants when you think about it."

She got up from the computer station.

"Speak for yourself!" Allie objected. "I, personally, feel a deep connection to the plant world."

"You would," Jasmine said, examining a Soy Newton. "For those who prefer to *mainline* their hormones, we have to exploit our fellow mammals. The best supplements are made from mares' estrogen. In Europe they prescribe these premenopausal patches when you're thirty-five so you never have to feel the estrogen slipping away. It's one smooth painless joyride from red hot girlhood to enhanced seniority minus the senility."

"I don't want to hear any more about menopause!" Allison covered her ears. "You've been talking about estrogen for the last hour. We're *decades* away from having to deal with this."

Jasmine bit into her Soy Newton and washed it down quickly with some tea.

"You don't just stay feminine, you know." She flicked a crumb from her Jil Sander skirt. A skirt she only wears for outcalls since she prefers, on her own time, to emphasize her fat-free status in sleek pants. "You have to plan for it. Invest in your femininity. Like insulating your windows in September so you can save on your heating bills in January. Okay, so it's still July but if you don't do your homework *now*, you'll be sorry come January. Well," she announced abruptly, "it's obvious who 'Amy Hatchet' is. And she's not on that committee."

"She has to be. How does she know about my relationship with Lucho? And my friendship with Noi? And my hometown? Can you believe she's calling me a sex trafficker?"

"Of course," Jasmine said. "She knows the lingo. She's talking the talk. And she's up on all your issues. And she *knows you*. So who do you *think* it must be!"

"What if it's a guy?" I pointed out. "Isn't stalking more of a guy thing?"

"Yeah, but this e-mailer's got a mean streak. It's some low-down petty-minded chick. And you're both myopic. It's not a guy and she's not what she appears to be. It's someone in NYCOT," she told Allie. "She's jealous of the attention you're getting. It could be Roxana. Weren't you sort of edging her out? Speaking at too many events? I bet *she* wanted to be on that committee all along."

"That's ridiculous," Allie said. "It can't be Roxana. She's my mentor! We had a meeting last night at Judson Church and there was so much solidarity among the members. And so much love in the room! If you had been there, you would understand. Roxana's designing a website for the Nevada Three so people can send money, to help them when they get out. She's a role model."

"Have you consulted Barry Horowitz about this?" I asked. "I know you don't like to hear it, but those girls are convicted felons."

"It's so unfair! They're only felons," Allie told us, "because the licensed brothel owners in the other counties got together with the FBI to make an example of them! They're victims of a patriarchal conspiracy! Against independent escorting!"

"They're victims of *legalization*," Jasmine retorted. "As soon as it's legal in New York State, you'll have the same problem. They'll make it legal to sell your snatch in Rhinebeck. Or Platts-burg! Manhattan will be like Vegas, totally fucking illegal. The licensed whorehouses will have all the unlicensed whores thrown in jail and you'll have a massive uprising of Manhattan girls try-ing to LYNCH the activists who caused all this to happen in the first place."

Unlicensed . . . whores? Snatch?

"Do you have to use that kind of language?" I said.

"Sometimes you have to call a whorehouse a whorehouse," Jasmine said. "But don't worry," she told Allie. "You can hide in my kitchen while I continue turning my tricks. Illegally. The way it's *supposed* to be done."

Allie was close to tears.

"There has to be an alternative to—to all this polarization!" she insisted.

"Cheer up," Jasmine said, with a shrug. "The day of reckon-ing's a long way off. They'll never legalize it here. . . . And I bet the owner of the Midnight Honey Ranch is the chief trouble-maker. Did you see that profile in the *New Yorker*? He's buying up all the mom-and-pop whorehouses, taking over the entire state of Nevada. Calling for a crackdown on the escorts! He's a total megalomaniac. It's not enough to run one place. He wants every pussy in Nevada paying some kind of tax to *him*. That's what happens when men become madams."

The sun never sets on the Midnight's empire!

"Well," Allie suggested, "you should come to the NYCOT Regional Summit on Monday and talk about this. I wish Renee could come but she's out on supervised release. She can't leave Nevada without permission from her probation officer. They won't give her permission to attend a sex worker summit." Allie sighed. "But all the NYCOT members are coming. And some girls from Philly! We'll have performance art, opportunities for serious debate, and a cash bar! We're taking over the space at True for the whole day. It's going to be a very empowering event. We have sex workers coming from all over the Northeast."

"Regional Summit?" Jasmine narrowed her eyes. "I. Am coming. To your so-called summit session," she warned Allie. "And I'll find out who's been sending you these despicable e-mails." I was surprised by her vehemence.

•◆• SATURDAY, 6/2/01 •◆•

Today, a flurry of e-mails from Allie, thanking me profusely for my participation in the handbag drive:

> *I wish it were possible for NYCOT to offer a tax deduction for your contribution but we're still outcasts for now. Our 501c3 status was denied!*

bubbling over with excitement about Lucho's return:

> *I feel like I'm getting ready for our first date ALL OVER AGAIN. Ever since he started e-mailing from*

*the café, I can't seem to stop self-pleasuring. It's the
total opposite of what I went through BEFORE,
when I thought it was over. Lucho writes such
beautiful e-mails . . .*

and agonizing about Jasmine's suspicions:

*I can't help wondering if she's right about that stalker.
The world's a dangerous place. People in the industry
CAN be vindictive. But I don't think it's a NYCOT
member. I think it's someone from Bad Girls Without
Borders. Remember Molly? From Australia? She told
Noi not to trust anyone from NYCOT. She thinks
she's the only blonde in the developed world who
gets along with the Bangkok bar girls. Well she's
WRONG.*

In a follow-up, she writes:

*But maybe it IS Roxana? Jasmine just called. She
thinks Roxana planned to get me so upset that she
would have to replace me on the Open Society panel!
Maybe she didn't really want me to be on TV? But
Roxana's been such a mentor. I don't understand why
she would go to all that trouble to help me and then
go to so much trouble to hurt me. Is that possible?
Jasmine always sees the dark side of people. She says
I'm in denial about Roxana's unconscious potential
for evil. Maybe I shouldn't encourage Jas to come to
our Regional Summit after all. She's really negative!
PS: Can't stop thinking about Lucho! I'm working
really late tonight. Have to! Because Lucho and I are
planning a two-day "honeymoon" . . . Just picked up*

some cranberry capsules, extra lube, and a box of his favorite condoms.

E-mail from Darren confirming our Wednesday appointment in his usual boyish code:

> *So look, I have those new documents. I want you to go over them twice. By yourself. I'll bring two pencils! You know how to keep things nice-n-sharp.*

And a voice mail from Jasmine, one of the first to arrive at the all-day NYCOT Summit—whether Allie really thinks it's a good idea or not: "I'm here. And I'm getting a definite vibe about that stalker bitch. Got it narrowed down to three people. Where the hell are YOU? Allison keeps asking me if you're coming."

Can I get out of this? I wish I hadn't agreed to attend but it gives Allie credibility with her activist friends if she can get some authentic "sex worker" friends to show up for a NYCOT event. Hopefully, Jasmine won't start speechifying about her apocalyptic visions of legalization.

When I arrived at True and saw the commotion outside, I was tempted to run away. A slim tattoo-covered girl, very drunk, in tank top, red jeans, and denim mules was weaving at the entrance.

"You can't treat me like this!" she yelled. "I'm a prostitute!"

She was arguing with a tall brunette who was wearing . . . a pair of expansive white fairy wings and a very exaggerated Jackie O. hairdo. Her Adam's apple was almost as big as her hair.

"You're disturbing the entire room," said the winged NYCOT member, in a sweet dignified boom. "Nobody is questioning your sex worker credentials but you are too intoxicated to participate in this event. Please go home and lie down, Courtney. I'll help you to a cab."

Her hand reached out to prevent Courtney from lurching to the sidewalk.

"Get your fucking paws off me, you fucking freak! Just because you're a facilitator doesn't give you the right to molest me."

"Oh for god's sake!" the facilitator sighed. "Find your own way to a cab then! Suit yourself!"

She opened the door to the bar and withdrew from the sidewalk in a huff.

Allison came out, holding a clipboard. "Courtney!" she pleaded. "You have to go home and take a nap! It's for your own good." To me, she said, "We've been looking for you! Did you get Jasmine's call?"

"Everybody's talking about what's good for me," Courtney replied in a slurred voice. "What are you, the government?" She wandered, unevenly, down Twenty-third Street while Allison gazed after her, blinking nervously.

"I don't know what to do," Allie said. "I think she was mixing her substances."

A handsome guy wearing overall shorts, no shirt, and a straw hat hurried through the door in pursuit of Courtney. When he caught up with the wayward substance-mixer, he took her arm. Amazingly, she didn't fight him off. It was Peter Pan and Wendy on a good day. He put one muscular arm around her shoulders and she began to collapse on him, while he patted her head.

Allie seemed to find that reassuring.

"Who is *that*?" I asked.

"Oh that's her roommate. Danny's the only person she listens to. He's like her big sister—I mean, brother. He's been in more than forty X-rated videos and he has a huge escort ad in *HX*. Full page! *And* he's the founding editor of *Rentboy.*"

"And what does *she* do? Please don't tell me that misfit is actually turning tricks!"

"Oh . . ." Allie gave me a tragic look. "She does a little bit of everything. I'm worried about her substance abuse. But she has every right to be a sex worker! NYCOT's position on—"

"NYCOT's defending *her* right to work? That's insane! She's a complete menace to the industry! A girl that wasted can't be using condoms."

"Well, she *says* she does. She was scheduled to do a one-woman dialogue—it's really brilliant! We have to find someone to replace her now."

Inside the bar, our fairy-winged facilitator was in a huddle with Gretchen, Roxana . . . and Jasmine.

"I was hurt when she called me a freak but I don't take it personally," said the facilitator. "I know it's the alcohol talking. Or the Midol. Whatever she's on, she shouldn't drink on top of it!"

"I'll talk to Courtney about it at the next meeting," Roxana told her. "Name-calling is not permitted at NYCOT events. That's grounds for ejection right there. . . . NAN-cy! So glad you could come!"

Allison beamed with pride. I felt like her catch of the day.

"We really need Nancy's perspective around here," Roxana added.

I've never been able to figure out what that perspective is supposed to be. For reasons beyond my control, Roxana thinks I should join NYCOT and never misses an opportunity to remind me. It has something to do with being the token Call Girl of Color. Which is almost as good as being, like Gretchen, the token Street Junkie.

"I'm Veronique." The tall tranny with wings extended her hand to greet me. "I hope you weren't intimidated by Courtney's tantrum. She's one of our younger members, and she's still struggling with—is it cocaine or alcohol? I've never been able to clarify which drug she's addicted to and which one she just likes too much." Veronique sighed. "I'm told there's a difference."

"Too bad," said Jasmine in a suspiciously neutral tone. "They tell me she's a comic genius when she's straight. I was looking forward to her show. Something about . . ."

". . . Boule de Suif and Belle de Jour," Allie burbled. "Boule de Suif gets into a . . ."

". . . catfight over a cab! With the skinny high-class hooker!" said Veronique.

"She has a grant to develop it for Edinburgh Fringe," Roxana explained.

"It's got all the right ingredients," Veronique added. "Class conflict for the Europeans; body image feminism for the Americans . . ."

"Sounds like something a grad-student stripper would do," Jasmine ventured.

"How did you know?" Allie asked. "Courtney's getting her master's in women's studies. And she used to be a peep show dancer!"

"Hooker's intuition," Jasmine said, downing the last of her martini. Gretchen cast a dubious smirk in Allie's direction and walked away, while Jasmine turned on her stool to study

Gretchen's movements. She gave me a meaningful look and muttered in my ear: "Gretchen's very quiet today. And she's no fan of Allison's."

Suddenly, Roxana took the stage. "I'd like to welcome our next panel," she announced. "Will 'D.O.T.: Discourse On Trafficking' please come to the front! As we all know, this is a difficult and troubled area. Our first speaker—" The panelists were milling around behind her, playing musical chairs. A girl in a garish red wig waved energetically at Allie, who waved back. "—Foxy Macbeth is here under deep cover. Foxy, as some of you know, published her thesis under a different name, of course, in the *New Internationalist*."

Jasmine bristled and leaned toward me. "That's another one of my suspects. She's a teaching assistant at Cornell! Isn't that where Allison's . . . Colloquium Committee is? And she won't tell me whether she's ever been a hooker! Says she works in a dungeon. Does that look like dungeon material to you?"

Foxy greeted her audience. She seems too girlish and small for domination but then, so do I. If I can do the occasional domme session, maybe she's a part-timer. But she could easily fit that body into a Barely Legal ad!

"My original title was 'The White Slavery Narrative as Female Courtship Ritual or Marital Aspirations of Eastern European Émigrés in the Twenty-first Century.' " Foxy spoke into a microphone. "I was under a lot of pressure to alter the title. In my study of happily married ex-prostitutes from three Eastern European countries, I discovered that their new husbands, under the new statute, could actually be defined as sex traffickers. More surprising was my discovery that they had met their husbands while working as escorts. These men are completely unaware of their own status as traffickers and see themselves, instead, as gallant saviors." The room tittered and a few people at the bar began scribbling on notepads. "At four escort agencies in the New York metropolitan area, the American-born escorts were in favor of deporting their Russian co-workers or, as a second best solution, marrying them off to affluent men who would prevent them from working. When I presented these findings to the Human Rights Working Group in Geneva . . ."

Danny strolled back into the bar, having tucked in his roommate, and sat next to me, compulsively checking his cell phone.

After Foxy and her friends had spoken, four girls in tiny shorts and black bras took over. The Triple-X Cheerleaders waved their pom-poms, leapt in the air, and yelled about their plight—wiggling energetically at strategic moments. Protest poetry by hot-looking twenty-year-old control freaks. Who resent being subjected to catcalls when they're not on call.

"Har-aaaaassss-MENT!" they chanted, jutting out their barely covered rears. "When I'm not working, don't be jerking! It's my day OFF, bro! Not a free PEEP show!"

Danny leaned over and asked, "Do girls really hate getting cruised? For me, it's an affirmation of my earning potential. Even when the gawkers aren't buying. But I'm beginning to get that there's a gender gap."

This must be the opportunity for serious debate that Allie was talking about?

"Gender shmender," Jasmine told him. "It's a *generation* gap. No sensible chick over twenty-five objects to being seen as a viable piece of ass. Those junior feminazis will be singing a different tune when the guys on the street stop whistling at them. That, or they're in the wrong business."

"And what about you?" Danny asked. "You must be Nancy. I've heard so much about you!"

"You, um, you have? From who?"

"Roxana." He glanced at the rings on my left hand. "We're starting a discussion group for married hookers. Roxana sees you as the catalyst. We're thinking: weekly support group with a monthly newsletter."

A monthly newsletter? I should have known it was crazy to attend this thing!

A pretty girl walked by wearing a T-shirt that read: "Nobody Knows I'm A Stripper." Her jeans were so low in the back that I could see a pair of white cotton panties sticking out of her waistband. I had the urge to run over and tuck them in. "That's the last straw!" I moaned. "Butt cleavage! Half these girls were born after I started hooking!"

I excused myself while Danny and Jasmine chatted about their looks, the fading youth of others—and the social value of wolf whistles. Allie was standing near the door, monitoring the new arrivals.

"How dare you tell Roxana about my husband?" I hissed at her.

"I've never discussed Matt with anyone!" Allie protested.

"Then why is Courtney's roommate pestering me about a support group for married hookers?"

"Well, you certainly need one!" Allie said. "Why are you leaving so early?"

"I'm making poached poussins for dinner. It's very time-consuming. And I don't need a support group," I told her. "I need to pick up the Pinot Grigio vinegar for the dipping sauce."

This morning, I persuaded Charmaine to let me have the apartment for two hours while Darren dropped by for his extralong session. Sometimes, Darren is the quickest of quickies. Occasionally, when he lands a big commission, he likes to celebrate by going twice. If I ruled the world, he would just come over on two separate days in the same week. But Darren likes to overload his senses.

After giving him an extravagantly slutty blow job, I sprinkled talc on his body and tickled him all over, very lightly, with a large pink feather, paying special attention to the crook of each elbow, his groin area, and his feet. In the other room, my compilation tape—designed especially for two-hour calls—played at a low but audible volume. (When it reaches the end of "Fantasy for a Gentleman" and segues into Oscar Peterson's "Nice Work," I know it's been exactly one hour and ten minutes.) I turned him over and slowly tickled his back with the feather, feeling very much like a smart chef who knows exactly how many times her bird needs to rotate before he's done. After drifting off slightly, Darren was ready for seconds.

During our second act, I spent more time on my back, legs apart. I encouraged him to eat me, then to fuck me in his favorite awkward position. At the right moment, I let out a stream of dirty expletives in a sweet childish voice. He groaned long and loud as he came—just when Sinatra was launching into some forbidden Kipling: "And there ain't no Ten Commandments, And a cat can raise a thirst!"

A totally productive morning. I felt smug when I arrived for therapy ten minutes early with the morning's take jammed into the pocket of my jeans. Ready to report success on so many fronts.

Dr. Wendy was impressed to hear that Matt and I are back to using condoms.

"We started three days ago," I told her. "And I feel like we're dating again! I've been noticing something about married sex. When you're having sex to make babies—it's not a hobby anymore, it's a business transaction."

"How so?"

"Well, if the sex isn't great, if it doesn't last long enough, whatever happens, you can just measure the encounter in terms of conception. So, if he comes too soon, that's okay! Because your chances of conception are good so that's, like, the pay-off."

"I never thought of it that way."

"As soon as you stop using birth control, there's a shift. If the sex is relevant to creating your potential baby, it's valid. When you're dating and using birth control, the sex has to be *hot* to be valid. This . . . child-centered sex . . . I don't think it's for me."

"Did you share this discovery with Matt?"

"Not exactly. Now that we're arguing about religion and he's having some kind of deep crisis about whether he's a bigot, we're having hot sex again. When he thought he was producing the next generation, I felt like our sex life was on our To Do list. This is much better."

"Arguing about religion." Wendy adjusted her glasses. "Is that something you'd like to discuss today?"

I walked her through the underlying logic of my having played the Catholic card on my agnostically Protestant spouse. Who now feels compelled to use condoms.

"Well," she said with a dry smile. "Even I didn't realize the extent of your self-identification as a Catholic. So his surprise is not surprising."

"I intended to get that reaction," I confessed. "But I was surprised when I succeeded. I thought maybe he'd go along with it and be too agreeable. And my plan would backfire."

Fortunately, it didn't.

"He's taking this matter seriously?"

"Very. And being quite stubborn. But he's lasting longer. I find the combination more than attractive."

"Are you still taking the Pill?" Wendy asked. "Have you considered telling him?"

"If Matt thinks *I'm* reluctant to have babies, that'll just confuse him! A husband should be in charge of the major decisions," I told her. "I know that's really old school and kind of not what my mom and all her granola friends think, but look at them! They're all divorced. Their marriages didn't last! They were always demanding equal time, complaining about having to take some man's name. I'm for letting my husband have his way, and he's happier for it." I paused. "Even if he's a little tormented about my Catholicism."

My mother says adopting a husband's name "renders a woman invisible" and I hope she's right! When your name's on two leases—and one is rent-stabilized—invisibility's a *goal*. Not to mention all my other reasons for becoming Nancy M____ without the cumbersome hyphen. And since I'm always changing my first name, why not my last name, just this once?

•✦• FRIDAY, 6/8/01 •✦•

Today, as I was leaving Pilates, my phone rang.

"I need your advice," Allie said in a breathless voice. "I just got the strangest e-mail from Noi in Bangkok."

"What's it say?"

"It's about her passport! And I can't find Barry Horowitz! I've been calling him for the last hour!"

"Maybe we'd better talk about this in person," I said warily.

"I'm putting on my sneakers! Where are you?"

She met me at the corner of Seventy-ninth and First and we headed for Agata & Valentina's coffee bar. Allie was carrying a bundle of printouts in a Burberry tote bag.

"Just when I thought it was safe to concentrate on business again," she sighed. "I get hit with all these curve balls and political challenges." She showed me some e-mail from Renee, writing from a friend's place in Nevada:

> *Sleeping on a couch is not what I'm used to but it beats being in jail. I hope to be up and running and wanna be on my own before the end of '01. Also, we need your help with this press conference we're having. Believe it or not, your support for our fight gives me a reason to get up in the A.M. And Barbie is on board . . . Please thank the NYCOT posse for those donations to my wardrobe. I wear a different one each day. AND MUCHAS MUCHAS GRACIAS! For replacing my long lost Magic Wand! You're a thoughtful compassionate lady. Power to the $isters! XXOO*

"Magic Wand?" I asked. "People still use those?"

"When they confiscated her belongings they took away her primary erotic resource. Can you believe it? Talk about cruel and unusual! Oh. Here's the mail Lucho sent to the Colloquium Committee. He's very upset with them for excluding me from their last meeting."

Re: Committee Protocol

Upon my return, I discovered that one member of the Colloquium Committee, who is also our sex industry liaison, was not present at the last meeting. This is a regrettable oversight, and the NYCOT members are angry. Allison is their voice on our committee, very committed to representing her community. She did not find out about the meeting until yesterday—more than an oversight, this is a malicious omission. The chair tells me she was ALSO unaware of the omission. So who is responsible for sending announcements? It is not appropriate to use the BCC function for committee meetings. Please correct this error and let the entire committee know who is invited and who not. The Colloquium Committee must operate in a forthright and transparent manner, especially when dealing with sexual minorities who are very familiar with the politics of exclusion.

"I didn't know Lucho was so chivalrous," I admitted.

"Of course he's chivalrous!" Allie blushed like a schoolgirl, shuffled her printouts nervously, then became more composed. "But look at *this*." She flipped past a nasty message from the stalker and showed me Noi's terse update:

Re: your mail

have new zealand passport!

solidarity for now,
NOI

"How can a person just change passports overnight?" Allie looked puzzled. "She never said anything about this and suddenly she's a citizen of New Zealand instead of Thailand. She wants me to redo all the visa forms!"

"Is it the first time you discussed her nationality?"

"Of course not! She sent all kinds of documentation in April. Now she's asking me to change everything. With no explanation or warning? Is that—is that normal?"

"How do you know it's really from Noi?" I asked.

Allie sipped her espresso.

"I guess I don't. We've never spoken. And when I asked for her number, she said she has no phone for now. So I e-mailed all my numbers and told her she could call collect."

"*All* your numbers? Don't write to her again until you talk to Barry Horowitz," I told her. "And don't talk about this to anyone else."

"What am I going to tell Lucho? What about the Colloquium Committee?"

"Before you say one word to your boyfriend or anyone on that committee, you'd better consult your lawyer."

My Apprenticeships

"By means of an image we are often
able to hold on to our lost belongings."
—*Colette*

•◆• SUNDAY, 6/10/01 •◆•

Have been waiting all day for Matt to go to the gym so I can log
on. Just got a reminder from Miranda about Ian Pritchard's visit
to New York. He's getting some kind of academic award for *Dualism and Mass Consumption in Trinidad:*

> *Don't forget Thursday! Ian's party at Borgia Antico.
> Is Matt coming? I hope so. Have appt with dentist,
> about five blocks south of the French Institute. Want
> to meet up/cab down together?*

Not really! But I don't want to provoke questions about my
alibi, either. My brief e-ply:

> *Bien sur! Let's coordinate by cell.*

Lots of anxious e-mail from Allie this weekend:

> *Noi wrote again and wants to come sooner, stay at*
> *my place! What should I tell her? I still have to talk*
> *to Barry about her visa. Don't worry! I'm sitting tight*
> *til I see Barry but I hate to be unfriendly. Doesn't she*
> *understand that I see guys in my apartment? I can't*
> *really have a houseguest AND make a living. Don't*
> *the girls in Patpong work out of their apartments?*

I typed back quickly:

> *Discuss ZILCH with Noi—especially NOT your*
> *work habits for god's sake.*

While Allison tries to untangle the mystery of Noi's national-ity, the stalker continues to rattle her by cc-ing key members of the Colloquium Committee:

> Re: A SECRETIVE SEX TRAFFICKING MACHINE
> WITH TENTACLES IN EVERY COUNTRY,
> INSIDIOUS RECRUITMENT TECHNIQUES &
>
> *an amoral figurehead who advocates the importation*
> *of Prostituted Exotica from a Bangkok Sleazepit . . .*

And so on and so forth. Insidious recruitment techniques? Now *that* takes me back.

I began hearing about these techniques when I was eleven, vis-iting France with my mother. Madame Ducharne was an unlikely friend for Mother: a beautician with two kids who lived in Notre Dame de Bondeville on the Route de Dieppe. The two mothers met through the French Immersion Network, an agency for pairing Anglophone children with French families. Before dropping me off for the rest of the summer, Mother spent a week with the Ducharnes practicing her language skills.

The Ducharnes lived "above the shop." To enter the salon from inside, you had to pass through the kitchen where Madame cooked all the meals. Monsieur Ducharne, a big beefy man, spent the weekdays in Paris working for the sanitation department and came home on weekends. He spent those two days in a snit, because all of Madame's attention was now given to their four-year-old son—who, in turn, became cranky when forced to share some of that with his father.

Every morning, little Philippe would begin to shriek or moan from his upstairs bedroom while the rest of us were downstairs in the dining room—the only common room in the house—having our breakfast. "MaMAAAN!" he would scream repeatedly and, if it was the weekend, Monsieur would begin mumbling, "Oh la LA la LA" under his breath, steadily growing more incensed until his son was silenced. On weekdays, Monsieur Ducharne's exasperation was not a factor and Philippe was much louder. His twelve-year-old sister, Gabrielle, was as good-natured and self-contained as he was hysterical.

A devoted businesswoman, Madame Ducharne wouldn't have understood Take Your Daughter to Work Day. We children were never permitted in the shop, and there was a separate entrance in the back. Even Philippe stayed away from his mother when she was working. His needy antics were only permitted before the salon opened, perhaps during lunch, then at night after closing time: the antisocial contract writ small.

One morning, I came downstairs for breakfast and found Gabrielle sitting at the table next to a wicker baby carriage.

When I peeked inside, there were two dolls dressed to the nines, in white bonnets and frilly dresses, looking like candidates for a double-baptism. There was even a toy bottle and a rattle. Gabrielle finished her bowl of hot milk, got up, and wheeled the carriage out of the room with a real sense of purpose.

I was dumbfounded. We both had breasts, of almost the same size, and she was older than me. I had not seen anyone my age playing with dolls for many years. It was a stage of life I had forgotten. While it might be acceptable for a twelve-year-old in Ottawa to collect dolls for display, wheeling them around in a pram was unheard of. I wasn't sure I wanted to spend six weeks alone with this family, when my only age-appropriate companion was still dressing and feeding her dolls. It's hopeless when another child is older yet more babyish. At eleven, that's a profound disappointment.

The night before my mother returned to Ottawa, Madame made Coquilles St. Jacques. She always served an appetizer first, followed by a main course. Very different from my mother's style, which was to place everything on the table at the same time. During the cheese course, I overheard the two mothers discussing Modern French Life. My own saw no reason not to translate since I was there, after all, to learn about another culture—its language *and* its ideas.

I still remember Madame explaining to Mother why French families had to be so protective. She would not be sending her own children abroad anytime soon. In Marseilles, she explained, a young girl in a clothing store, trying on a pair of jeans, was likely to be kidnapped by Arabs. Flesh traffickers hid in the dressing rooms. As my mother translated all this for me, I glanced around the table. Gabrielle and Phillipe just kept eating.

Conversations between adults did not appear to interest them. Their father was lost in his own world.

Madame Ducharne believed beyond doubt in the perils of white slavery. My mother attributed this quirk to the fact that Madame had "never really traveled." Before I went to sleep that night, Mother quietly explained that Madame Ducharne had rarely been to Paris, that Rouen was the nearest city and Madame hardly ever went *there*. I was not to condemn or pity her but simply to reflect on my greater fortune, for we were in a different league: world travelers. Mother had a point. Parisians wouldn't believe fantastic stories about dressing room traffickers, nor would people in Ottawa. And god knows, Ottawans do like to travel.

But now I realize that Madame Ducharne was viscerally aware of something my mother wasn't willing to entertain. While there probably weren't any lustful Turks hiding behind false mirrors in the dressing rooms, you might have reason to be grateful if your twelve-year-old daughter still played with dolls. The world was too big. Something—some opportunity or impulse—could steal your daughter away when she outgrew her dolls. And it would *feel* as if she'd been kidnapped by invisible traffickers. If you let your daughter roam free and try on different things at will—not just clothes, but ideas or friends, the way my parents did—she might not stay virginal. She might become profane. A scenario my granola-minded forward-looking mother never considered. Profanity. Chastity. White slavers! Such quaint ideas.

In her suspicious small-town way, Madame was perversely open-minded. She was able to picture her daughter—under the wrong circumstances—ending up as a prostitute. She was more provincial than my mother yet less naive.

Was she trying to warn her about the problems of having a precocious daughter? Or was she just expressing the everyday concerns of Notre Dame de Bondeville—repeating local gossip?

During my six weeks immersion, I spent more time conversing with Madame Ducharne than with Gabrielle. But every evening, just before dinner, I had a thimbleful of something sharp, reddish brown, and alcoholic. Even Philippe was permitted his half-thimble of the mysterious aperitif. Following that, a glass of red wine mixed with water, to go with our meal. This more than made up for the lack of any viable adolescent culture in the Ducharne household.

Just a few years later, I became the embodiment of Madame Ducharne's anxieties. I hadn't been kidnapped but, at fifteen, I was confirming the predictions that plague old-fashioned, carnally obsessed parents. Despite the fact that I ran away from home at fourteen to live with my twenty-something boyfriend, Mother retained her modern innocence. When I wrote and told her I was working as a waitress, she chose to believe me.

Before finding my niche at the Kontinental, a small nightclub just off Oxford Street, my juvenile imagination led me to a Mayfair escort agency. Ultima had a full-page ad in one of the local tourist magazines, which I found encouraging, and their second-floor office across from the Heywood Hill bookstore did not disappoint. I took a minicab every evening to Curzon Street dressed in whatever I thought was appropriate, and sat in a closed waiting room with eight or nine other girls. Customers would visit the reception area outside where they could flip through a photo album of glamorous head shots.

In those days, the pictures were quite genteel—nobody was posing in her underwear the way girls do today. If a chosen escort was in the waiting room, she left the agency with him. If not, she would get a phone call. Sometimes, all the girls in the waiting room were invited to the reception area, one by one. I was the youngest and rarely got picked on these occasions because I had no idea what I was doing—how to dress, how to relate to a customer. My head shot was enticing but, in person, I was too much of a girl. Others had the ability to be both girl and woman simultaneously, and they were the pros. I could afford to flounder and stay off the street—I was living with Ned, my boyfriend in Highgate who paid the rent and turned a blind eye to my nocturnal habits.

One night, as I left the agency to go home, I noticed a small green car parked across the street. It was after midnight and the street was fairly quiet, but I managed to find a cab. As I got into the cab, the green car began moving. When I looked out the back window, the car was right behind us. We turned left, and I looked again. The car was still there. I didn't know how to be an escort but I knew how not to get caught. And all the cabbies knew exactly what a girl like me was doing on Curzon Street in the middle of the night.

"I think that car is following us," I told the driver. He was old enough to be my father. "Can you lose them?"

"Want me to?" he said with great aplomb. "All right. Just wait." He drove down another street at a normal speed, the car continued to follow. Suddenly, we made a perfect breakneck U-turn and we were speeding around another corner. I looked behind me. "Still there?" he asked.

"Gone," I said. "Thank you." When we got to the bottom of Highgate West Hill, I gave him an extra tip.

The next evening, when I showed up at the agency, I was full of my news. Everybody, especially Henry, the owner, laughed at me for thinking I was in a Hollywood movie.

"Lose that car!" Henry kept repeating. "Priceless!"

I insisted that I'd been followed but nobody believed the warning of an awkward wannabe call girl.

Two weeks later, Henry was on the front page of *The Sun,* described as the owner of Ultima Escorts, "a Curzon Street operation catering to wealthy sheiks and other well-connected men." Henry was a good-looking guy of thirty-four with a small mustache and dark hair just below his ears. It was a personal snapshot. Who had given it to them? He was up on charges of living off immoral earnings, facing jail time. I felt sorry for him but began to have more confidence in my future. My frightening "Hollywood fantasy" had turned out to be horribly true, so perhaps I should have more faith in my hopes as well as my fears. I decided to try the hostess clubs.

At the Kontinental, I came into my own. The Kontinental was neither a scary clip joint nor a class act, but the atmosphere was cozy. It was safer than picking up men in hotel bars, more lucrative than trying to work as an escort.

The men here were not as sophisticated as the rich playboys, oil sheiks, and jaded travelers who were drawn to Ultima's Mayfair shtick. These were ordinary English executives who found me both exotic and wholesome. In this slightly seedy downstairs club, I could shine. I now had a customer every night, and all I had to do was show up.

Ultima had been designed for girls who knew how to create atmosphere, size up a punter, set a price. At the Kontinental, those details were taken care of. There was a dress code, so I no longer had to think much about my outfit. Like everybody else, I wore a long dress—sexy on top, demure below the waist—with a pair of heels. I started with one dress, a low-cut wraparound purchased at Top Shop, and bought another—the same dress in a different color—during my second week. I was not the only girl in the club who found that particular Top Shop dress convenient. By the third week, I felt ready for Harrods, where I found something more original. (I still have it, squirreled away at Seventy-ninth Street, in a plastic garment bag!)

The atmosphere was festive but structured. In my flowing polyester, I watched the same floor show six nights a week. There were no grinding lap dancers or flashing pussies. The performers had siliconed breasts—which they displayed at the end of each act—but these were small by today's standards.

My £40 hostess fee—for sitting at a man's table—was arranged by the club. If we left together, it was never discussed with the owners but there was a £100 understanding among the girls. At Ultima, where the rates varied wildly, it was every escort for herself.

The manager was nervous about getting busted for procuring. He made all his money off the champagne and never touched our earnings. Still, each hostess had to fill out a Membership Form to protect him from the law. The Kontinental was supposed to be a "private club" and we, the hostesses, were its only members. Of course, it was the police that really protected him from the police, not this legalistic ritual.

For the first few weeks, I had no idea that the performers were lip synching. And I actually drank the champagne. While it was good champagne, this was not a good idea. Each customer had to purchase two bottles to sit with me, and I lost track of how much I imbibed. I eventually learned to pour champagne discreetly onto the floor, into the strategically placed rubber plants, and to be always knocking my glass over. Whenever possible, I would pour from the bottle with a shaky hand. When we left the club, it was our responsibility to make sure each doorman, coat-check girl, and waitress got tipped. The Kontinental was a cozy personable machine of a clip joint, not one of those vicious enterprises hellbent on scaring the tourists. Our punters were cheerful about paying, not terrified.

I still feel a fondness for that place, whenever I remember the dim pinkish light in that small room, the nightly music that never changed, the layout of the tables. After trying to make it as an escort, after discovering the pitfalls of picking up men in hotel bars and failing to get noticed at the slicker hostess clubs, I at last became a real working girl who had found her calling and her clientele.

Harm Reduction

Yesterday afternoon, on the way to Jasmine's for a quickie, I popped into Seventy-ninth Street. I found Charmaine on the living room floor, sitting next to an open suitcase. Half its contents were on the carpet, the other half tightly folded in her case.

"I always overpack," she said. "But I hate having to shop in Florida. I'll need all the downtime and rest I can get. After my procedure."

"What do you do?" I asked. "After a procedure? Just lie in bed all day popping vitamins?"

"Oh, it depends. This time I'll stay in my room and catch up on my reading." I noticed a manual of some kind tucked into her suitcase but couldn't catch the complete title. Charmaine covered it quickly with a pair of slippers. "Dr. Fielding's doing an endoscopic brow lift. It'll reduce the side effects of the Botox," she said. I tried to detect the side effects without being too obvious. "My forehead's . . . can you tell?" She swept her hair back. "It's a factor for Botox-users. Sometimes, your forehead starts drooping because the muscles aren't working. I'll be less dependent on Botox after the brow lift."

"I don't see any drooping," I assured her.

"Yet!" she laughed. Because of the Botox, Charmaine laughs enigmatically. It's a little spooky! But side effects notwithstanding, forgoing Botox would be, for Charmaine, as reckless as jogging without a bra. Strange to think of myself—a pre-Botox call girl who never had to worry about wrinkles—as the facial equivalent of a braless hippie. Botox makes you see things differently—even if you don't use the stuff yourself!

Jasmine wasn't surprised when I told her about Charmaine's reason for going to Florida.

"I predicted this!" she said. "Didn't I warn her about the dangers of Botox?" What I recall, rather than a helpful warning, is the savaging of Charmaine's entire beauty regimen—but why point that out?

"Nobody listens to me," she added. "Well, that's not *my* problem. Actually," she corrected the record, "Allison called this morning. She needs a sounding board."

"Shouldn't that be her lawyer?"

"Barry's an excellent attorney," Jasmine said. "But he doesn't have my intuitive understanding of the female sex. It's obvious to me that Roxana's a very twisted jealous person," she added, "and she's hoping these e-mails will throw people off the scent. Taking Allison under her wing isn't just a good deed. There's a revenge motive."

"That's crazy! What has Allie ever done to Roxana?"

"From Roxana's point of view? Plenty! Allison's prettier. Younger. And thinner. She's a success in the business. And now she's got a boyfriend. And she's becoming a public figure! Don't you think Roxana hates her? She may be a feminazi but she's still, when you get beneath all those layers of feminazism, a basic primal woman who wants her so-called sisters to fail! So she can play nursemaid."

After our session with Harry, Jasmine checked her voice mail. Two messages from the public figure!

"Allison just got back from Barry's office. I have to find out what's going on." While she dialed Allie's number, she ranted some more about Roxana: ". . . one of those needy mentors who always has to be tutoring another chick. I've seen this with madams. A girl starts out as raw material and outgrows the madam. It's the law of the jungle . . . and the hookers' movement is a jungle! All those egos!"

Some part of me secretly hopes the stalking mails will finally make Allie see the light. Or want to hide from it. But maybe Jasmine's right: Allison—just like Roxana—is a creature of the jungle, unable to suppress her appetite for attention. As I dressed in the bathroom, I heard Jasmine debriefing Allie.

". . . I think Barry's right about the passport. You have to cover your ass. . . . A brow lift? Yeah, I heard. These New Girls! They spend all their money on cosmetic surgery. It's out of control."

A few minutes later, my phone rang. Allie's landline flashed on my Caller ID.

"Have you spoken to Jasmine today?"

"Spoken to her? I'm with her!"

"Oh." An awkward silence. "Never mind." There was a forced chirpiness. "Call me later. When you're alone."

I called Allison from the cab.

"Barry says a New Zealand citizen doesn't have to apply for

a visa," she told me. "I guess that's why Noi's moved her plans ahead? She's arriving in three days! So I don't have to help with her paperwork."

"Well, that's one less thing for you to worry about," I told her.

"And Charmaine's going away for almost two weeks."

"So?"

The cab was turning onto the East River Drive.

"Well, I didn't ask her because it's really *your* apartment. I thought I'd better come to you directly. I think Charmaine would be okay with it but I wouldn't go behind your back."

"Okay with what?" I was truly not getting it.

"Maybe Noi could stay at Seventy-ninth Street for a few days. I can't have her at *my* place because I just got a huge bill from Bloomingdale's! I have to see a lot of guys this week. And maybe next week, too! Since you don't work full-time anymore and Charmaine will be in Florida—."

"Are you nuts?" I felt my blood pressure rising. "And how dare you say I don't work full-time! Did *Barry* suggest this?"

"Um, no! I'm sorry!" Allie squeaked. "And please don't say anything to Jasmine about this!"

When I got back to Thirty-fourth Street, I took two steaks out of the fridge, poured myself a small glass of wine, and threw the latch on the front door. Matt never returns before six but you can't be too cautious when making a personal call. Jasmine picked up on the first ring.

"What's wrong?" she asked. "You sound strange."

I unclenched my teeth and described my brief conversation with Allie.

"Well, you really *don't* work full-time," Jasmine said. "But that's beside the point."

"Beside what point? I was working full-time and supporting

myself when Allison was giving *blow jobs* to high school boys! I have a quota! Does *she* have a quota? You both have a lot of nerve! You have no idea what lengths I go to, to protect my business from this marriage!"

"Would you calm down?" Jasmine yelled back. "You sound totally premenstrual! I'm not the fucking enemy, okay?" After a pause she said, in a calmer voice, "Allison's in over her head. She called me three times today."

"What did she tell you about Noi? About the passport?"

"Barry says it might be a black market deal."

"A black market passport? And she asks me to harbor this girl in my bedroom? So she can pay down her Bloomingdale's card?"

"That's kind of nervy!" Jasmine agreed. "She would never ask *me* to, but she's counting on your codependent friendship. I, on the other hand, have always been good at maintaining my boundaries—"

"If you can please stop blowing your own horn for five minutes, I *had* a codependent relationship with Allie, but I do not as of today. Can you imagine what might happen if Noi gets in trouble while she's staying at my place? My husband's on the partner track. He could lose everything."

"No kidding! You have to protect your man's career. Like a mama lion guarding her cub. Or a pimp looking out for his best bitch! Allison's becoming a liability."

"If you want to call me, leave a message and I'll call you back. I have to keep my distance from Allie. I'm not answering my phone."

"Fine with *me*," she said, "but what about your johns?"

"I'll figure something out," I told her. "Right now I have to marinate the steaks. Matt's coming home in half an hour."

"At least you're not serving tofu kebabs. Allison's been making all these soy-intensive dinners for that boyfriend of hers. The last thing you want to give a guy is *soy estrogen*. She's putting his virility at risk!" Jasmine said. "Allison has zero talent for risk assessment."

•✦• WEDNESDAY, 6/13/01 •✦•

This morning, a totally unexpected request from Matt. I know a lot of married couples do it and swear by it—and apparently feel much closer as a result. Lots of women wish their husbands would suggest it. But it's really, really not my kind of thing.

To be discussed with Dr. Wendy.

•✦• LATER •✦•

When I told Dr. Wendy about Matt's latest request, she excused herself from the running.

"I don't see myself as a couple therapist," she explained. "And even if I did, I'd be the wrong one for you to see. But . . ." She paused to assess my rather tense demeanor. "What did you agree to do?"

"Officially? I'm considering it. But I don't think I can handle therapy twice a week! Of course, I can't tell him that because he doesn't know I'm already *in* therapy!"

"Are you sure?"

"Well, if he knows, he's playing a very deep game! He doesn't seem to have any idea."

"Is there an issue he wants to discuss?"

"He wants to talk about my—about Catholicism," I admitted. It's kind of embarrassing to have created, inadvertently, this new

problem in my marriage. "He's been reading Graham Greene—
The Power and the Glory. He never, in all the time I've known
him, had any desire to read a novel that was published before
1960!"

"Well, you have to accept that your spouse may continue to
grow. His taste in reading is not going to stay the same for the
rest of his life," Wendy pointed out. "I can guarantee that."

"I just found out this morning that he's more than halfway
through. He's reading this behind my back?"

"Isn't that a novel about . . ." Wendy frowned for a second.
Her eyes lit up. "Persecution?"

"Yes! It's kind of scary. He's preoccupied with this whole
question of Catholics being hunted down and silenced. And he
wants us to go to a therapist because his eyes have been opened
by Graham Greene and maybe he *is* prejudiced. But he still
doesn't want us to raise our kids as Catholics. He's not ready to
convert." I paused. "Yet."

In other words, my husband is turning into the sensitive guy
from hell. How could I have brought this on myself?

"What's more," I told her, "he tried to talk to me about my
mother! He's concerned. He thinks I might be reacting against
her issues."

"It would be strange if you weren't," Wendy said. "Most
women do. React to their mothers."

"Exactly! And that's what *she* did—why shouldn't I also?
Why does he want to reverse the normal course of history?"

"Is that what you told him?"

"Of course. But I may have to change my mind about religion
and just let him have his way," I told her. "I'm just not up to an
additional therapy session every week. And with you, at least, I

don't have to lie. If Matt and I start doing therapy together, that's one more person I have to lie to! For an entire hour? At such close quarters? I think that's more than I can deal with right now."

Is this what happens when a working wife tries to play God?

•◆• THURSDAY MORNING, 6/14/01. SEVENTH-NINTH STREET •◆•

Thanks to Charmaine's Botox-induced travel plans, I have the place to myself. With Milt showing up two hours before Ian Pritchard's party, I'm really cutting it close. And I have to pick up Miranda at six because she thinks I'm at the French Institute this afternoon!

My husband has been looking tormented for the last two days. I'm planning my capitulation, my embrace of secular parenting, but can't do it right away. He needs to feel the rising tension in order to appreciate my generous compromise. Meanwhile, he's talking about Red Shirts and the Meaning of Judas, which is driving me mad. I much prefer *Travels with My Aunt*—I have no desire to wallow in Graham Greene's conversion! In fact, converts can be a nuisance and I have to figure out a tactful way to tell him that.

Fortunately, Matt's also working on a deal—very long hours—so accepts the idea that I'm still having serious thoughts about therapy. Very serious thoughts.

•◆• FRIDAY, 6/15/01. THE MORNING AFTER •◆•

When Milt arrived at Seventy-ninth Street, I was wearing my slightly hip and very uptown version of a French maid's outfit: a small blue Fauchon apron, shiny white half-bra (to match the sheen of the apron), and pale blue satin heels. Contrast is king in this business, and this was a definite change of pace after the strap-on session with Allie. Only when I turned around did Milt realize that I was wearing no panties under my apron. Kneeling at the end of my couch, I leaned over, ostensibly to search for a video, and allowed my ass cheeks to open slightly. When I turned around, he was standing very close to me in his suit.

"I feel overdressed!" Milt informed me.

"You're supposed to," I told him. "Get that jacket and tie off. I have plans for you."

"I'm doing my best," he mumbled, as I loosened his tie. I pressed my apron-covered portion against his leg and slid one thigh up the side of his pants. "This outfit is very . . ."

"Chic?" I threw his tie on the sofa.

"That's the word." He placed a firm hand on my right buttock. His palm felt smooth and I was surprised to feel my body reacting to a shadowy hint of a spanking that may or may not have been intended. I pulled away. We are not going *there*. "Can we skip the movie and just climb into the backseat of my car? I promise I won't come in your mouth."

In the bedroom, Milt surprised me. Instead of lying on his back—the default setting for Milt whether he's eating me, getting his cock sucked, or getting laid—he persuaded me to kneel on the bed, displaying the back view of my pussy and the sash of my apron, while he undressed. I opened my legs and began to fuck myself with my fingers.

"Leave your shoes on," he growled. "I wish I had a camera! Your pussy's more interesting than a million videos."

I turned around to play with his cock. When he was ready to fuck me, I moved toward the center of the bed, but Milt tugged at my apron sash and urged me to stay right there. I grabbed a bottle of Astroglide from beneath the pillow and placed a lube-covered hand between my thighs. Milton grabbed the pillow and tucked it beneath my pussy.

"Stay right there!" he insisted, tucking a second pillow beneath me. "Perfect. God, let me just look at that for a minute."

"Fuck me now," I moaned. "My pussy needs it!" And I wanted him to get started before any, er, momentum was lost.

Milt fucked me harder and with more determination than I've come to expect. I was shocked and slightly uncomfortable when he came. I'm used to being on top, controlling the depth and force of his thrusting. Shocked because he's never been able to come this way—standing up? Not bad for a fifty-something!

Despite my businesslike feelings, I'm impressed.

Was that Milt on Viagra? If he's taking and not telling, he's got style. There's nothing more clinical and married-couplish than telling a hooker you popped some Viagra before your appointment. I prefer to think my clever little apron and Pilates-trained ass did the trick. And I think Milt understands that.

I showered and changed as quickly as I could, then grabbed my Bottega satchel: I only carry it when I have to transport textbooks and other French class paraphernalia. When I was safely installed in a big yellow SUV and nearing Fifty-fourth Street, I called Miranda's cell phone.

"Well, it's a good thing the weather's so nice! I've been waiting on this damn corner for—where are you?"

She had no idea I'd been negotiating crosstown traffic. "I'm a block away. And don't ask about my day," I added.

"Okay! I'm on the southeast corner!"

I spotted Miranda squinting at the wrong cab, hit Redial, and stuck my head out the window. She looked up just as her phone began ringing.

"Never mind," I yelled. "That was me. Get in!"

She was chattering happily as she fiddled with her seat belt. "I e-mailed Ian to tell him we're coming. He wrote back! I told him we're arriving before the big mob scene."

"What are you thinking?" I protested. "And why are you throwing yourself at him?"

"He's in town for two days! What do you expect me to do? Wait for him to call?" Miranda opened her messenger bag and pulled out a small compact.

"Give the guy a chance to pursue you," I said. "And let him wonder if you're coming to the party at all. It's a good thing I got delayed. Now you can be appropriately late."

Miranda rolled her eyes. "You and your neocon dating strategies!"

If Miranda knew what my relationship strategies really entail, she'd be . . . surprised? Perhaps disapproving?

"So what ever happened to Chris?" I asked. "Wasn't there a second date in the works?"

"We had a huge argument. About drug sentencing."

"Are you serious?"

"He's an assistant prosecutor! Do you realize, if Sebastian were here instead of Toronto, he could be sitting in a jail cell? Locked up twenty or thirty years? And his girlfriend's vehicle would have been confiscated by now! Their lives would be in tatters."

"Why do you think I never encourage Sebastian to visit me? *Please* tell me you didn't get into all this with Chris!"

"Well, I didn't say it was *your* brother," she reassured me, "but I take these draconian laws personally because they could affect my own family, and I told him so. Too bad he's so right wing! We're compatible in bed and I'd like to . . . one more time, but he's an agent of the state." Thank god Miranda doesn't know anything about my business! "He wants to stay friends," she added, with a cynical smirk.

When we arrived at Borgia Antico, the crowd she was hoping to preempt had already gathered. Now that Ian was lost in the social muddle and impossible to find, Miranda was annoyed with me for making us late.

"Hard to get," I told her, "can be just as effective in reverse. Or in tandem. Right now, you feel like *he's* hard to get but the end result is, *you* are. Anything that delays meeting up with him makes you less available. You can enjoy the outcome of playing hard to get without even trying."

"Your logic really escapes me," Miranda said, "but—drinks first!" She wandered toward a tray of pale pink cocktails and obtained one for me as well. "I wonder what this is?"

"A Ruthless Cosmopolitan," said a man's voice.

Miranda turned around and almost spilled her drink on Ian's blazer. I tried not to spill my own, but the satchel was threatening to slide off my shoulder. My alibi-friendly props felt heavier than usual. Miranda gazed up at Ian with a combination of relish and expectation. This time, he caught the hint and leaned toward her. When his lips met her cheek, she seemed to glow.

"I just found out!" Miranda told him. "Someone I work with is coming tonight. Jane Berry. She remembers you from school. But there's something I, er, want to ask." Ian had one eye on the room. "I really really prefer it if you don't tell Jane that you've written about my family. Our family," she added, moving next to me.

"Oh?" Ian looked at me quizzically. "I won't if you both prefer, but it's hardly a secret—people, places, and things all have names."

I was completely mystified. As Ian turned to greet someone,

Miranda waved at the entrance. "Matt's looking for us! Why can't he see us?"

I felt my phone vibrating in my bag and spied my husband holding his phone to his ear, but my cell phone access was blocked—by the ruthless cosmo in my right hand. When we caught up with him, he looked surprised.

"You made it!" said Miranda. "I saw you coming in but I couldn't catch your eye. It's starting to feel like a pattern!" she added.

Matt grabbed a drink from a passing tray. He placed an arm around my waist and I could tell that he was inhaling my perfume. He pressed a little closer.

"I saw Matt—well, maybe it wasn't. Maybe it was Matt's lookalike," Miranda told us. "But I thought I saw Matt coming out of an apartment building on Wednesday afternoon—and I tried to catch up with him." Matt seemed to be drinking more rapidly than usual. "That wasn't you, was it?"

"Wednesday? I spent the whole day in, uh, meetings. In the office. Couldn't have been me."

"This guy looked just like you but when I tried to get his attention, he started walking very fast. And he almost fell over trying to hail a cab."

"That doesn't sound at all like Matt!" I exclaimed.

"No," Miranda said gaily. "It couldn't be. But you know how sometimes you see a person who just has that—well, there's someone out there who looks *just* like Matt. Come to think of it, everybody knows bankers never get out of the office until midnight!" She patted Matt's shoulder. "You have an evil twin!"

Before I could ask where she had seen my husband's body double, she half-yelped, "Be right back!" and walked briskly toward the circle surrounding Ian. I felt Matt's body relaxing somewhat.

He pressed his lips against my right temple. "I feel like I haven't seen you in three days," he sighed. "You look gorgeous tonight. . . . Let's go to La Goulue. I'll see if I can get us a table."

As my husband negotiated a table for two, I could see Miranda and Ian in animated conversation with a small group. Miranda was shaking hands with a handsome olive-skinned man and . . . it couldn't possibly be!

Allison?

She hadn't noticed me yet. Too busy enjoying her cocktail. If we could just slip out of the room without being waylaid by Miranda, I can avoid Allison. . . . I looked around frantically for an exit. Allie and her companion were very cozy. That must—with his dark eyes and thick wavy hair—be Lucho. Ian and Lucho hugged like long-lost buddies. Omigosh. Is this chronicler of the Layton Saga actually Lucho's friend? A colleague of my former best friend's boyfriend? Allison, chatting to Miranda, was looking *much* too happy, and Miranda was giggling madly like a girl with a new playmate. If I had a fire hose . . . I'd spray them down *right now.*

"An hour?" Matt was saying. "Nothing sooner?"

"Let's just take the reservation and go!" I hissed at him. "If we show up early, we might get lucky!"

"Hold on," he told me. "I'm trying Verbena."

Allison's face lit up as she spotted me across the room. I've been missing her calls for a week, but she seems to have no idea this is intentional. When she waved at me, Miranda turned around. Both girls were now urging me with expansive arm gestures to join the crowd. Did they both realize they were waving at the same person?

I moved closer to my husband, clinging to his jacket sleeve for dear life. Then, fearing that the foursome might be moving toward us, I chose the lesser evil and went over. "I'm just going to talk to some people," I mumbled.

Matt—engrossed in the pursuit of a table—retreated toward the stairs with his phone.

"Poor Matt!" Miranda laughed. "Slaving away in the middle of all this. Nancy's husband is a banker. He gets no rest."

"I am Lucho Rivera," said Allie's date, extending a hand. "Allison has told me so much about you."

"About . . . ? Maybe a different Nancy?" I ventured.

"Maybe so!" He gave a courtly smile. "But whichever Nancy it was—she said charming things. I think," he turned to Allison, "I have trouble keeping all those Nancies in your life entirely straight."

Lucho didn't miss a beat. He's sharper than the average boyfriend—which shouldn't surprise me. But it does.

"It's amazing!" said Allie. "I *never* thought I'd run into you here! Did you get my voice mail?"

"My, ah, voice mail is a mess! I don't know *what's* going on." I was dying to find out how Lucho knows Ian, but questions about that might provoke more of a conversation about *me*. I was eager to avoid that—and to pry Miranda away from Allison, who might, after one more sip, feel empowered enough to share her personal story! What wheels might start churning in Miranda's mind if she discovers that her own cousin is acquainted with . . . a member of the New York Council of Trollops? I'm as attached as she is to my slightly uptight image.

When my bag started buzzing, I looked around for my husband and quickly found my phone.

"Where are you?"

"I got us a table," Matt said.

"Can we add a third?"

"I don't think that's a good idea. Come outside. We're going to La Goulue."

"But Miranda might—hello?"

Matt was gone. Strange! But I wasn't quite ready to join him. When Ian was pulled away by two handlers, I held my breath. I can't leave Miranda in chat mode with Allison!

Much to my relief, Miranda was unwilling to play it cool with Ian. She was here to get into his pants and, when she realized what had happened, she followed him downstairs. Maybe her bohemian dating strategy will actually save my neocon reputation: if she stays focused on her mission for the rest of the evening, she might never talk to Allison again.

"Matt's had a rough day," I told Allie and Lucho. "He just organized a romantic dinner for the two of us. I'd better not dawdle."

"Romance is a priority," Lucho said. His eyes twinkled with intelligent mischief. "Your husband knows what he wants. And should therefore have it."

On the sidewalk, Matt was pacing nervously, talking on his phone. I heard fragments of deal jargon: "Black-Scholes . . . disastrous model . . . and what if they decide to read the thing? We've had ten conversations about this and you're telling me . . ."

Despite his tone, he looked blissful when he saw me approaching. He grabbed my hand and ended his call. In the cab, as we headed uptown, he was eager to hear more about Allie and Lucho.

"Was that Allison's new boyfriend? What does he do? We should have dinner with them sometime."

Later, we sat, knees gently touching, at our favorite corner table, and I didn't have the heart to ask why he was avoiding Miranda. I was too grateful for my own escape.

I couldn't ask but I couldn't help wondering. Much as I want to, I can't deny what I saw with my own eyes and heard with my own ears. Miranda had a near-encounter . . . with Matt's double? There *are* guys who look like my husband, I suppose. But . . . his reaction, his sudden disappearance, just at the moment when all the elements of my life were threatening to become entangled?

Too good to be true.

Last night, for all the wrong reasons, we had what every healthy marriage needs in order to survive. A shared goal. A common purpose. Complementary needs.

What if this is as mutual as it gets?

•◆• SATURDAY, 6/16/01 •◆•

Why did Matt really start using condoms? Was I kidding myself about my own cleverness? Could his renewed commitment to condoms have something to do with . . . that odd business of (perhaps) being spotted by Miranda in the middle of the day?

If so, then what about his sudden interest in Catholic issues? Was that some clever ploy on his part? All this time, when I thought I was operating like a Cold War mole . . . Is Matt capable of doing the same? Could it be that he's beating me at my own game?

There is one solution to being outsmarted. Play dumb. In short, outsmart him right back. But where does that really get me, other than the catbird seat?

Today, a call from Miranda dying to gossip about the party.

"How do you know those friends of Ian?" she asked. "They're a good-looking couple, don't you think?"

"Oh, from around the neighborhood," I said. "I used to go to Allison's gym."

"They're the *last* people I'd expect you to be hanging out with! Lucho's so lefty." Miranda giggled. "And his girlfriend's a hoot! *What* does she do?"

"I always thought Allison was a little deranged. She makes up these bizarre stories. Well, I *think* she makes them up. She's very nice, but I'd keep a healthy distance if I were you."

I felt a tiny prick of remorse over this comment, but the guilt passed: it's not like I'm depriving Allie of a business opportunity.

I was dying to ask Miranda about that strange conversation with Matt. Where exactly was she when she "didn't really" spot Matt? How do I ask? Without sounding like a neoharridan?

In the eyes of the world—well, in the eyes of my cousin—a question like that would weaken my marriage. I can't have people thinking that I doubt my husband's integrity or devotion when we're still newlyweds! And there's nothing more uncool than being labeled as a snoopy wife.

Instead, I asked about Ian's schoolmate, Miranda's boss. The one who's not supposed to know about our family.

"What was all that about not telling Jane Berry? I thought you were quite proud of Ian's research! Don't you want your friends at the museum to know all about it?"

"I am," she said. "But it's complicated. Nobody at work knows about our family. They all think I'm Afro-Caribbean."

"They what? How did they get that idea?"

Miranda so wishes! But it's me who's got the Afro-infusion, somewhere in Dad's lineage. I've always had to keep that quiet on my job but Miranda, who works for a museum, is stretching the truth—way the other direction. Did she make this up to get her job? Or is it a story she invented to go with her Rasta hat?

"Did you, um, say this when you were applying for your job?" I asked.

"Not exactly," she said. "Well, sort of. Anyway, if that's what people think, why not let them?"

New Yorkers of any color don't think "Miranda Layton" sounds Chinese. But Layton comes from a Chinese ancestor, an indentured servant in Guyana trying to simplify his paperwork by adopting his employer's name. And now Miranda's going around telling her New York friends that the Laytons . . . are descended from African slaves?

"Does your mother know about this?" I asked.

"Of course not. You know how she is!"

I do, indeed. Aunt Kasturi, who gave Miranda that brown complexion, would not relate to her daughter's racial ruse. Call it a generational quirk.

The things we manage to hide from our mothers!

·-•· SUNDAY, 6/17/01 ·-•·

This morning, I felt compelled to answer Allie's e-mail before deleting her message from my inbox:

> *Dear Nancy, What's going on with your phone? I've tried to call you to give you an update on Noi's*

situation. It was great seeing you the other night! Too bad we didn't get a chance to hang out with Matt. And your cousin seems really cool! Love, A.

I quickly wrote back:

My cousin's very nice but somewhat unstable. Not someone you should get friendly with. I'll explain later. But I urge you to be cautious around her. Let me know if she tries to contact you.

I should feel guilty, but what else can I do? As for Noi, I'm afraid to ask what the update might be.

•→• SUNDAY NIGHT •→•

Matt is still at the office. This shouldn't bother me since I know that bankers keep strange hours. But . . . is he really working on a deal? Even if he *is,* does that explain his behavior?

Why has he stopped asking me to take a position on therapy? He's no longer pushing me to meet him on his terms, and he acts like he's more committed than ever to preventing a pregnancy.

What's the real reason for Matt's sudden change of mind? For being at the office until ten PM on a weekend? Last night, he was affectionate but rather silent. The quieter he gets, the more tender, like he's trying to compensate for something. Is Matt having an affair with someone who doesn't use condoms? That would *really* piss me off.

Attics and Basements

This morning, I cornered my husband in the breakfast nook while he was pouring a second cup of coffee: "I spoke to Miranda last night." Matt looked wary. "There's a party," I lied, "at her boss's apartment. Tomorrow. She wants us to come."

If he says yes, I can always change *my* mind.

"I may have to work," he said abruptly.

This confirmed my suspicions. He's totally avoiding Miranda.

"Are you still thinking about relationship therapy?"

Matt looked as if he'd seen a ghost.

"Are you?" he asked.

I poured myself a cup of coffee, allowing both topics to hang before us.

"Would you agree to having our children baptized?" I asked him. "The way I was? Then they'll always have the option." Backing down completely would be unnatural. "Maybe Catholic school isn't really the answer," I added.

Matt's arm circled my waist, pulling me close.

"I . . . I was hoping you'd come to this conclusion."

"Why didn't you suggest it, then?"

"Because . . ." he sighed. "I was going to. I should have."

"What's wrong?"

"There's something I have to tell you. If I don't, someone else might. Well, someone has, in a way. Already."

"What are you talking about?" I had to pretend not to know he was talking about Miranda, after bringing up her name to test his reaction. I looked into his eyes and he looked straight into mine for the first time in many days.

"Miranda saw me on Eighty-seventh Street."

Feigning confusion, I asked, "When? What do you mean?" I don't want Matt to think I remember their conversation in so much detail. . . . Hang on a second. Did he just say *Eighty-seventh Street?*

"Last week, I almost ran into Miranda on East Eighty-seventh in the middle of the day. It was really embarrassing. I felt like an idiot."

"You mean when she saw that guy who looked just like—. That was you? But you said—"

"I know what I said. It was me."

"But it couldn't be!"

My entire system is based on the premise that Matt is nowhere *near* the Upper East Side, especially in the afternoon!

"Honey . . ." He cleared his throat. "When we found this apartment, a buddy of mine asked me to do him a favor. It's kind of weird. I should have told you this a long time ago."

"Maybe it's not something I need to know," I said in a shaky voice.

"I don't want us to have secrets." He looked at the microwave clock. "Can we talk about this later? I promise—"

"No!" I was at my wit's end. "Don't tell me anything! Don't promise me anything! What are you talking about?"

"I just want time to sit down and explain—"

"What is there to explain?"

"I never gave up my apartment! When we moved in here, I just kept paying the rent on my old apartment."

"But—but—you never—when I told you—"

"When you told me about your apartment, I wanted to tell you about mine but I felt guilty. Your situation makes a profit."

"You're not subletting? What are you—" I was afraid to ask.

"I can't justify the expense," he said. "It started out as a favor for a buddy. He wanted a place to hang out with . . ." I tried to look uncomprehending. I wanted him to spare me these lurid details, but straight people, when the going gets rough, have a tendency to get graphic. "Gary was seeing—having an affair. She's married, too."

"Gary? That guy from your office? The one who lives in Scarsdale?"

"So does she. They're neighbors."

"I can't believe you're—you're involved in something so tacky!"

"Neither can I." He looked sheepish and ashamed. "I promise I'll never do something like that. But I wanted a bolt hole, a place to be alone. I love you. I'm committed to this relationship, to our life together. But when I was growing up, my dad always had a room in the basement where he could go and bang on a piece of wood or something. When we signed the lease here, I felt my options closing off. Gary was just there at the right time. When you told me about your place . . ."

I suddenly remembered Matt explaining the ins and outs of rent stabilization, how it works and what would really happen if my landlord finds out. He knew way too much about the New York housing laws. Why didn't I guess?

". . . I wanted to tell you about mine but I was afraid you would stop trusting me. I'm not having an affair, Nancy. Please don't look at me like that."

"But what do you do there?"

"I watched the whole World Series last year without ever turning on the set in our apartment. Or having to negotiate with you. Maybe that was a cop-out. I'm sorry. I just wanted a little male space."

But he said he was at the office! How much time does he spend at the office and how much . . . ?

"Last week, Gary's wife found out about the affair. He told her everything. She got hold of the key, went in there, and smashed the TV set. She caused a flood in the bathroom and poured orange juice all over the mattress and the carpet. Then she called the landlord. The day I ran into Miranda, I was up there trying to straighten things out. It's a disgusting mess."

His buddy confessed? These people are such amateurs! I bit my tongue and gave him a numb, shocked how-could-you glare.

"I'm sorry," he told me. "The landlord wants me out of there now. I was hoping I could just close that chapter of my life without you finding out. It's really embarrassing."

"What's going to happen to Gary? And his wife?" I said.

Matt held me tight.

"They're not going to make it. She's talking about a divorce."

"Do you realize what you've done?" I asked. "If you hadn't been so hung up on preserving your male space, he might never—maybe he would have ended his affair! You helped him to prolong it!"

Matt flinched. Held me closer.

"I know. I feel awful."

This afternoon, when I told Jasmine about Matt's other apartment, she was dumbfounded.

"That. Is scary." It takes a lot to stop Jasmine in her tracks. "All this time? You thought he was at the freaking office? And he was coming to the East Side? And you never ran into him!"

We were at Petaluma, waiting for Allison. After much back and forth, I couldn't decline the "normalizing" lunch proposed by Jasmine. She sees herself as a referee for two warring states of mind: paranoia (mine) and irrational exuberance (Allison's).

"This is NOT to be discussed with Allie," I warned her.

"Don't worry," Jasmine said. "My lips are sealed. . . . but haven't you noticed that Allison's a lot saner when *I'm* in the picture?"

Not really, but what's the point of arguing with Jasmine?

"Well," she continued. "Gary's wife sounds like a piece of work! So much for the sanctity of male space. And what about Gary? He endangered your husband's space by confessing to his wife! He's incompetent! The upside is, Matt must be grateful that he's not married to Lady Vengeance."

"He feels terrible. His buddy's marriage is completely ruined. And it's his fault."

"Partly his fault," Jasmine said. "But suburban cheaters are very willful. Gary would have found some other way to screw up his life. And you'd better be careful about going to Seventy-ninth Street. I wonder if Matt's really evacuating the bachelor pad this time. Maybe you should offer to help?"

"He brought home an extra computer last night. He was going there to play computer games! I don't understand. I never gave him any reason to do this. . . . Did I?"

"Well, you're such a model wife. You're always home first. You keep a nice place. You never get sloppy. And you're a great cook! He didn't want to mar your domestic landscape with his imperfections. He's trying to be a sensitive guy," Jasmine said.

"Look. I don't want him on my turf and I need him to leave this area soon, so I can get on with my life. But . . . if he's got some boorish tastes, maybe it's better if he doesn't bring them home. He *says* he was watching the World Series. . . ."

"Could have been Howard Stern! Or cable wrestling."

"Or something much worse." I shuddered.

"Matt's not the kind of guy who expects the mother of his children to watch gonzo DVDs on a Saturday night. He's lucky to have a wife who doesn't ask embarrassing questions and he knows it." Jasmine glanced at the window. "Behold. Her Blondness."

Allie was on the sidewalk, talking on her phone, walking briskly toward the door. She continued her conversation as she approached our table. ". . . I'm looking into airfares this week," she said. "But we still have time." Maneuvering her hips into a chair, she took off her sunglasses. "I wish I could get the producers to fly me down but it's not that kind of show." She snapped her phone shut and grabbed a roll from the basket. "I'm famished!" she exclaimed. "I've been running around all morning. I was at Kinko's before eight so I could see a client at ten, then I had a meeting with Roxana in the Village but the good news is Noi found a place to stay."

"So, ah, where did you put her?" I asked.

"She's in Portland. Working! She changed her mind about coming to New York. She says she'll fly out later for the colloquium but now she wants to concentrate on making money."

"That's quite a transition. From Bangkok to New England—"

"Portland, *Oregon*. She met some exotic dancers in San Francisco who turned her on to a self-help group in Portland. Some of the peep show girls started their own chapter of the Wobblies and they put out a monthly magazine. They gave her a place to stay. I had no idea she was so . . ."

"Resourceful?" Jasmine suggested. "What does Barry think?"

"He says I should let Noi take care of Noi, and focus on the Nevada Three press conference instead." Allie signaled for a menu. "He's advising me on the media participation. We're talking to *60 Minutes*!"

"That's a major network show," I gasped. "You can't . . ."

"It's exactly what we need," Allie said. "They're deeply interested in the patriarchal dimension of the persecution. I spoke to the producer last night. She wants to infiltrate the Midnight Honey Ranch with a hidden camera and get the owner to talk about his collaboration with the FBI."

"Just make sure *you* don't go poking around the Midnight Honey with a hidden camera," Jasmine warned her. "These media types might be setting you up for something ugly."

"Me?" Allison looked surprised. "I can't even *drive*. How would I get there? It's out in the middle of nowhere. I'm staying in Vegas where I can take cabs! Anyway, I'll be too busy organizing the press conference. If I have something to say to the owner of the Midnight Honey, I'll say it in a public forum. This show could be a nationwide teach-in on decriminalized versus licensed prostitution. And *60 Minutes* wants to document Barbie's release. Maybe interview her family . . ."

My phone started chiming in my pocket. Trish, calling from her car.

"Are you alone?"

"No, but it's okay."

"Call me back. It's about Charmaine."

"She's in Florida getting a brow lif—"

Trish ended the call abruptly.

Jasmine was now arguing with Allie about the stalker.

"Well, if it's not Roxana, it's that webmistress in Australia," Jasmine said. "And when she starts dropping nasty comments about your trip to Nevada, you'll finally believe me!"

"Actually," Allie explained, "she . . . the stalker revealed herself. Last week. It's been kind of weird."

"Last week!" Jasmine was miffed. "And you didn't tell me?"

"We weren't sure." Allie looked down at her mozzarella salad. "But Lucho figured out who it was and she finally admitted it. To him, not to me. I guess I should feel sorry for her. It's someone I met once at a party but I don't remember talking to her. She's kind of shy. She's a research assistant for one of his friends on the Colloquium Committee. Lucho says she agreed to seek therapy."

There was a moment of silence during which we nibbled our respective salads, contemplating the dark awful spiral of shyness.

"Why didn't you say anything?" Jasmine demanded. "When did this bitch come clean?"

"The other day. I wasn't ready to talk about it!" Allie sipped her mineral water and looked away from Jasmine. "I'm not sure how I feel about it."

"Is this . . . someone he slept with?" I asked.

"No! But she has a crush on him and she's one of his students, and she came to his building a few times but she stopped a year ago. She's not the only student who acts out this way. He's been harassed before."

"Do you think he encourages it?" I asked.

"I'm not sure." Allie frowned. "He says it's an occupational hazard and he's trying his best to prevent it. Do you think he's *really* trying his best? Or will I always be fighting off these—these—lovesick stalkers and . . ."

"Deranged fans?" Jasmine said. "You have to recognize something. This guy is one of the happening professors. That's why you like him. And he's into you because you've got *your own* following. You're more than a groupie to him. But he's always gonna have some fans around nipping at his heels. You either accept this guy for what he is or you move on."

Allie sighed. "I guess you've hit the nail on the head! I need a glass of wine." She gestured to our waiter. "I've never had a boyfriend with—with real fans and admirers! Women coming out of the woodwork! I'm not saying my other boyfriends were *unattractive* but they resented me for getting too much attention from other men. They weren't like Lucho. I hate to admit this. . . ." She hated it so much that we had to wait for her wine to arrive. "I've always been the one with a following. And I guess my previous boyfriends were all in competition with my following? I just took it for granted. I never had to think about competing with anyone else for a boyfriend's attention! It's kind of humbling," she admitted. "I'm not sure I like it."

"There's a first time for everything," I said.

"But why can't I be like *him*? Lucho's so confident! And generous! He doesn't resent my customers the way my other boyfriends did. And when we go to parties, he's really happy if other men are looking at me! What's wrong with *me*? I don't *like* sharing him with all these fans. I felt sorry for that girl but I wanted to . . ." Allie couldn't bring herself to say it.

"Would you get a grip?" Jasmine exclaimed. "If you didn't want to rip her eyeballs out, you wouldn't be a normal woman.

You have to realize that a cool professor is like a hot stripper. Stalkers are an occupational hazard. But a stripper isn't going to leave her boyfriend for a stalker! Same thing here!"

When Trish got through to me, I was at the cleaner picking up Matt's shirts.

"Have you spoken to Charmaine lately?" Her voice was tense.

"What's wrong?" I said. "Does she owe you money? She's very good about—"

"I can't believe this! Charmaine has all these pictures of Debbie on her website!"

Charmaine has pictures of Trisha's schoolgirlish cousin. On . . .

". . . her what?" It was the last thing I expected to hear. "She has a—?"

"Website! And she put Debbie's picture up!"

"Without her permission?"

"That's not the point. She's taking advantage of Debbie and I don't appreciate it. When you introduced us, you told me Charmaine was discreet!"

"I thought she *was*!" I protested. "I had no idea she was running a website. She never told *me*."

Come to think of it, that *is* rather discreet. But the wrong *kind* of discreet.

"Debbie *lives* here. With my husband and my daughter," Trish said. "If she gets arrested doing outcalls with Charmaine, my whole family could be affected. And if Charmaine doesn't leave Debbie alone, I am throwing Debbie the fuck out of my home. Tonight. I will not stand for this. You can tell Charmaine what I said!"

Before I could respond, she hung up. I stepped outside and tried to call her back. Finally, after many tries, I left a voice mail. As I walked down First Avenue clutching my bundle of shirts, I called Charmaine.

"How's the brow lift going?"

"I'm taking my Vitamin C and—"

"Trish just called me!"

"Um—yeah?"

"Is this true? She says you have a website? And Debbie's working for you?"

"Why is *she* calling *you* about *my*—"

"Listen to me. Do you or don't you have a website?"

"Well, I do, but—"

"Do you realize that Trish is never going to work with me again? She's furious with me for introducing you to Debbie! And I vouched for you! I told her you were discreet! And totally private!"

"I *am* discreet. Look, Debbie and I are both adults. Trish doesn't own Debbie!"

"She feels that you're taking advantage of her cousin—"

"Trish is an overbearing kinky boring pain in the ass who thinks she can run Debbie's life and treat her like a personal sex slave!" Charmaine said. "I've seen her kind before! My relationship with Debbie is totally professional. I take my cut and that's it! I don't try to prevent her from working with other girls and I don't need her for sex—thank you, but I prefer a cock, okay? I'm the best thing that ever happened to that girl! We have a healthy relationship and she's learning how to be independent."

"But you're advertising on the web! You could both get busted!"

"Do you think I want to get busted? Do I look like a moron

to you? If you're so horrified, then tell me how I'm supposed to pay my rent and pay for all my surgery and save for my old age! And if you want to ostracize me from your exclusive little circle, go right ahead. You can pack all my things up and put them in storage. I'll give you my Amex number and you can charge it to me!" she yelled. "I can find somewhere else to live. But tell me this! Have I ever been late with the rent? What about the key money I gave you? Do you think it's contaminated?"

"No," I said. "But Trish is talking about throwing Debbie out of her house! You have to calm her down. It's not fair to Debbie. I wish you would call Trish—"

"Debbie is almost twenty-five! She is not an orphan!"

"She can't stay at our place!" I warned her. "If Trish throws her out—"

"Okay, fine. I'll call them *both*. What do you want me to tell Trish?"

"Tell her you won't be working with Debbie in the future. And don't call Debbie. Wait for her to call you."

"Why should I let—"

"Just listen to me. Trish is acting like a maniac. You never never alienate someone in this business. I'm not saying Trish would ever rat on you. But it's unprofessional to allow another girl to be that pissed off with you. Smooth it out with Trish. Make her feel better. If you don't, you're putting us both at risk. Trish knows too much about me and," I added, "she knows more about you than I did. I want you to keep your distance from Debbie."

"Why are you talking like Debbie's a child? I don't work with minors!"

"How many girls *are* you working with?"

There was an awkward pause.

"Not that many. Maybe three or four."

"So what does that mean? Eight or nine?"

"I'm not running an escort service!" she said. "I'm just trying to make a living!"

Famous last words?

•＋• LATER •＋•

I can't really talk to my shrink about a roommate who's advertising her felonious behavior on the web. That's something for my lawyer to handle. And yet, it's giving me a very personal headache.

No matter what Charmaine says, if she gets busted, the story would be that Charmaine's running an escort service. Out of my apartment. That's where the computer is, where the phone is, and god knows what else. How did she manage to grow this business right under my nose?

Instead, I told Dr. Wendy about my other discovery: Matt's bachelor space and the carnage inflicted by his buddy's enraged wife.

"So Matt has his basement and you have your attic," Wendy mused. "I wonder how many attics and basements there are in Manhattan? I imagine a lot are on the Upper East Side."

"Why?"

"So many small unrenovated buildings geared for single tenants, and the density of dwellings keeps the rent down," she said. Every Manhattanite, even my shrink, has this need to pontificate about local real estate trends. "Marriage is a very delicate and demanding arrangement," she added.

"I had no idea that being a role model for sensitive guys was stressing *my husband* out! I thought that was just his nature.

Does he have to go and hide somewhere to be his true self?" I asked her. "Do I? And what is marriage really about if we're all lying about who we really are?"

"Well," said Dr. Wendy, "there's a naive idea that we have a true self and we're doing something wrong whenever we betray that self. But the true self is a problematic ideal. We don't always know who the true self is. There are people who feel that their truest self is the most uncultivated—the self without manners, airs, or deceptive abilities. But the part of you that hides things from Matt, the self that has a secret history and lets him think you're ovulating when you're really on the Pill—this is also the self that lets a frailer person get on the bus first. Even though you'd like to push her aside and jump the line."

"So lying to my husband is my good deed for the day?"

"It's not a good deed or a bad deed," she told me. "But it's coming from your civil self, a self that knows how to get along with people. If you bluntly told Matt everything you did, maybe you would also tell a friend that she's not as bright as she thinks she is. Or you'd serve yourself first when you have a guest for dinner. This is the same part of yourself that has table manners."

"It's like using the right fork? I guess my mother would approve then! But what if it's more like stealing the silverware?"

"Then, I imagine, your mother wouldn't approve, based on what you've told me about your childhood."

"But I feel like I'm being true to myself when I lie to him!"

"There's also a school of thought that says you can't be your true self unless you're alone."

"Like a monk or a spinster."

"Right. But we're not all cut out for the contemplative lifestyle."

As I left Dr. Wendy's office, I felt impossibly nostalgic, remembering a time when I didn't have a special man in my life. When I lived alone in my hotel room, not dating or in love, just seeing men for money. I was a struggling teenager spending money as fast as I earned it, living from one day to the next. My visits to the better hotels were high points: once, I went to the Skyline Motor Inn and the five-star Pierre on the same day, then turned my last trick for the night at the Holiday Inn. That was a typical work day. Then I became a success, hustling at a more gracious tempo, secretly at home in the city's best hotels. That's when I began to have boyfriends, a social life, a *double* life. There was a kind of purity in my solitary hand-to-mouth existence, but Wendy's right. I'm not cut out for that.

My shrink's comments about the true self dogged me all the way back to Seventy-ninth Street. Is the self just a lot of different aspects, all equally true? Or is there something basic with a lot of add-ons, like the Gucci watch I bought for myself when I was sixteen? It came with a set of colored rings that fit the dial so you could change its color at will. Is the true self the Gucci watch *without* the colored attachments? Is it more truthful to wear all the colors, even the ones you don't like? Or is the true self the watch in your favorite color, and just as easy to like?

Or perhaps, like that Gucci watch, the true self is an outdated, and rather childish, novelty.

Provide, Provide

"Better to go down dignified/With
boughten friendship at your side . . ."
—*Robert Frost*

This afternoon, a call from Liane, crowing about her new cell phone. At seventy-something, she's the last madam in Manhattan to go cellular.

"These things are wonderful! Now I can go for lunch without the slightest trace of guilt. I was the first to have a remote control answering machine when *those* came out. I've been a dawdler about this, haven't I? But now I can't live without it!"

When I first came to New York, call girls had these boxy devices that seemed like the height of advanced technology. You placed the box against a telephone mouthpiece and pushed a black button to pick up your messages from a tape machine. Horribly indiscreet. The device made a whistling sound and was bigger than Liane's new phone.

Touch tone remote was a vast improvement; you could pick up your messages without drawing attention. But answering machines—no matter how advanced—were never a replacement for sitting by the phone. Too many johns just hang up when they don't hear a live voice.

"I have planted a seed," Liane told me. "Remember Bernie and his college student fixation? It's time for him to graduate. As I told him the other day, the college girls are growing up and getting married. I know a very attractive newlywed who likes to play when her husband's away on business!"

"I hope you don't mean *me*. I really don't want . . ."

"Bernie's married, too," she pointed out. "He understands the need for discretion."

"I'm beginning to wonder if my time is just over," I said. "Perhaps you should tell Bernie I've retired."

"Retired? Over? Your time is just beginning. We can reinvent you as a restless young wife. Don't give this up until it gives *you* up!"

"You can't imagine what's going on! With all these websites and New Girls," I said. "Things are changing out here."

"Well, that's probably true," she laughed. "It's 2001, after all. And I'm getting a computer next week. Bernie has promised to plug it in and show me the ropes. Tell me about these websites!"

Bernie's probably buying the computer. No wonder she's eager to supply him with a newlywed!

"All the New Girls are advertising," I told her, "and they see nothing wrong with it! I just found out that someone I know has a website. I'm in a state of shock! You're not going to like what you see when you go online."

"It can't be anything I haven't seen before, dear. I worked for many years. And was a New Girl myself once," Liane said. "At my age, nothing is very shocking. And Bernie would love to spice up your life now that you're so married and respectable. And so easily shocked!"

"Let me think about it," I said. "I'm a little stressed out right now."

I can remember when marriage was something other people did. It seemed so foreign to me. Married people were almost another breed of humanity. Johns, of course, belonged to that breed, especially when I became a private call girl. The men who go to a girl's apartment, the men who call Liane, are usually husbands.

But when I worked for Jeannie's Dream Dates, it was different. I saw married men when I did hotel calls, but met lots of bachelors, widowers, divorced men . . . and married couples. To call an escort service, you had to have your own place, after all. So I met a lot of people who did.

As customers go, the opposite of a married man is a married couple. Married men are easy because they have to get home eventually, and they want to keep the encounter secret. With a married couple, it's different. They *are* home. You're not a secret.

My first "couple call" at the Dorset Hotel was a breeze. I remember tasting K-Y on her pussy while we were 69-ing. Later, another escort told me that they weren't a real couple. The "wife" was a pro! To make the fantasy complete, her "husband" told each escort they were having a major breakthrough in their marriage: it was the first time his wife felt secure enough to let him come inside another woman. A harmless fantasy.

My second couple turned out to be the real thing, in a typical highrise apartment on East Fifty-fourth with lots of floor-to-ceiling mirrors. It was late when I arrived. The lady of the house answered the door in bare feet, wearing a black lace bra and matching panties. She ushered me into the master bedroom, holding a finger to her lips. "Someone's sleeping in the other room," she whispered. She had dark wavy hair, pale skin, and a slender well-managed body. Her face could have looked hard but something gentle in her attitude—toward me—made her pretty. Her husband was waiting on their king-size bed, a trim polite man with a tan and a gold chain around his neck.

I undressed and showered in the master bathroom, twice as concerned about being fresh and clean: as a working girl in bed with a wife, I felt self-conscious.

When I got into bed with them, her husband held back from touching me. I pressed my mouth against different parts of her body and hoped for the best. I was about half her age and very new to my job. Her body felt more foreign than his but I knew instinctively that it was safer to focus on the foreign—ignore the familiar. This session was supposed to be for her, not for him, even if it was officially for both.

I felt like a peeping tom, seeing a real married couple so up close and personal. As I teased her pussy with my tongue, I wasn't sure I could satisfy her but she opened her thighs and seemed to welcome my overtures. I could hear him rolling around on the bed, rummaging in a bedside drawer. He rolled back toward us, holding a small red object the size of a large lipstick. An amyl nitrate inhaler. With a tender murmur, he offered his wife the inhaler.

"Oh, not now!" she sighed, as if they were on a long car trip arguing about directions. Whenever she spoke to her husband, there was a hint of petulance. With me, she was warm and affectionate, and rather concerned for my safety. As I prepared to leave, she reminded me to put the money in a secure place. It was past midnight, after all. She opened the bedroom door quietly. "There's a baby sleeping in the other room," she explained, and she smiled with playful delight because I looked rather shocked.

•❖• FRIDAY, 6/22/01 •❖•

Charmaine was in the bedroom, unpacking, when I arrived at Seventh-ninth Street. She poked her head through the doorway and displayed her tweaked forehead.

"So far so good," I said rather grimly. "Have you spoken to Trish?"

"She won't take my calls," Charmaine said. "Debbie called, though. Trisha may be a bitch but her bark is a lot worse than her bite. Debbie isn't homeless, okay? And I told Debbie to tell Trish I'm out of the picture."

"I keep my *money* here. And you're letting all these strange guys come to my place? That is totally unfair!" I protested.

"Is any of your money missing?" Charmaine asked.

"That's not the point. I deserve to know the risks!"

"I do not have strange guys coming here," Charmaine said quietly. "You don't know anything about how I work if you think I'm going to let some stranger come to this apartment. I *live* here. Do you think I want that?"

"Are you telling me the truth? How long have you been advertising?"

"Almost eight months! And I do know what I'm doing!" The manual I spotted when she was leaving for Florida was now sitting on a pair of jeans: *Java for Dummies*. "I spent a year studying the escort sites. I hired photographers. And you know why I'm investing in my looks? I always felt pretty but I never photographed well. I take my website very seriously. The way you and Trish are carrying on, you'd think I put a hand-painted sign in your window offering discount blow jobs!"

"Nobody is saying anything of the sort! But I've seen some of those websites—"

"Well, *I* do not have one of those websites. Mine is very classy and I don't attract creepy guys. And I screen these guys for weeks before I see them. I turn down a lot of business!"

"You screen for *weeks*? How many weeks?"

No escort service I worked for had that much patience.

"At least ten days. Sometimes two weeks. It depends. And I never introduced Debbie to a guy I hadn't seen before."

"What about the other girls you work with?"

"They're part of the Provider Forum." Charmaine looked exasperated. "It's a website where the guys go to comment on the providers."

"Providers?"

"We call ourselves 'providers'! It's just an expression! We're living in 2001, Nancy! Where have you *been*? Anyway, we all met online and started trading our Bad Date lists. Then we started meeting up around town. On Tuesday nights, a few of us go to Nascimento for drinks. It's a really nice circle of girls. I don't know why you're so hung up about it."

"Do you know anyone who's been arrested?" I asked her. "Not for turning tricks. I'm talking about getting charged with running a business. Every escort service I worked for got closed down by the police. People I worked for went to jail and lost everything they had. I'm not some irrational snob, okay? I have totally earned my hang-ups. And I've been through a lot more than you realize. You shouldn't lie to me about the important things!"

Charmaine sat on the carpet with her back against the bed, staring out of the window, blinking furiously. The sunlight was bouncing off her pale red hair and when she looked back at me, there was a hint of remorse in her eyes. But only a hint.

"I'm sorry, but I didn't lie," she said. "I knew you wouldn't like it, so I didn't tell you about my website. I know how you and Trish work but New York has changed. The private girls are ten years older than me, sometimes more. They don't want to exchange dates with a twenty-two-year-old and I can't build a business on a few referrals from Liane and Trish. I need volume. The girls my age—the girls who want to work with me—all have websites. That's the way it is," she said. "I tried to buy someone's book—a client list? I met a girl who wanted seven thousand for her book, but I don't trust her and her guys are horrible!"

And I know as well as she does that buying or selling a client list can be dicey. God knows, I almost got into a lot of trouble trying to sell Allison's book, two years ago. Am I really in a position to lecture Charmaine about risk management?

"Seven thousand's a lot of money," she said. "I don't want to get ripped off. I'd rather invest in a website and cultivate my own people."

On my way to the nail salon, I heard my phone chiming in my purse.

"Hey!" Allison, calling from *her* cell. "I'm at Zen Palate. With Roxana and Lucho! Want to join? The blueberry tofu cheesecake is yummy."

"I have to be somewhere in five minutes. I can't!"

"Barry Horowitz is negotiating with Fox about an appearance

on *The O'Reilly Factor,* and *60 Minutes* is definitely flying down for our press conference," she said. "I'm going to be on national TV! So is Barbie. Lucho just confirmed the reservation. We got a great deal on the flight *and* the hotel."

"National TV? When?"

Maybe I can make sure Matt is safely occupied, or find some way to scramble the TV signal?

"Welllll, Barbie's getting out of prison September fourth. Just after Labor Day. She's going to spend some quality time with her parents. And then I'll fly in on the tenth. And we do the press conference on the eleventh. We're announcing the birth of Bad Girls Without Borders Nevada and exposing the conspiracy between the FBI and the licensed brothel owners!" she told me. "I don't have air dates yet . . . but Renee's talking to the mayor of Las Vegas. So far he's kind of iffy about attending the press conference. Do you know what he told her? 'I like the girls here too much to see you all legalized!' but he agrees she was a victim of injustice, and he's going to attend our panel discussion on the twelfth at the University of Nevada Women's Studies Department! Lucho says there's hope wherever there's discourse. Are you *sure* you don't want to join us?"

"Very sure," I sighed. "I mean, I would if I could but I just can't."

• ► • MONDAY, 6/25/01 • ◄ •

Last night, Matt brought home a few boxes from his "basement" apartment. I never knew about my husband's comic book collection, a childhood project that apparently continued right through business school. But I should have noticed, when we moved in together, that a number of his favorite things had never made it into our new apartment. Like his battered copy of *Catch-22* and a small collection of colored shot glasses.

This morning, after he left for work, I moved some of his boxes into his closet, cleaned the shot glasses, and found a prominent spot for them on our dresser. Then took a cab to Eighty-seventh Street.

Out of curiosity, I wandered into the vestibule of Matt's old building. His name was still on the buzzer but I spotted some mangled-looking boxes and stray shelves on the sidewalk. Standing closer, I thought I detected a scent of rotten orange juice. The shelving had a familiar look. Then I spied the busted TV set. I think the Upper East Side is mine again, but I'll never be quite so smug about what is or isn't mine. Matt's old apartment is perilously close to Allison's building! And not far from Jasmine's.

I walked down Eighty-seventh Street toward Carl Schurz Park.

Is Allison really going up against . . . the licensed brothel owners of Nevada? On national TV? It's time to face the music, or the lack of music.

Our lives are on different tracks, though Allie's taste in men is improving. She's got what she needs—a boyfriend who can compensate for her shortcomings without trying to change her. Lucho is wiser, more sophisticated—and more in love—than I had expected. But I can't see myself as the female half of a bohemian power couple, the way Allie can. The life she's embarking on with Lucho doesn't include me—or my marriage. I have to wind down our friendship before Allie achieves national prominence as the telegenic poster girl for borderless hookers.

Now is the time to start.

As I reached the Promenade, I considered Charmaine and her website: compared to Allison, she's a beacon of sanity. And has rational goals—saving for her old age, not getting ripped off, and looking as good as she possibly can. Is it time to leave the field to brave new players like Charmaine?

I leaned over the railing, stared down at the East River, and opened my Bottega satchel. I found my ingenious container: my hidden supply of Loestrin masquerading as a homeopathic cure-all. I checked the clock on my cell phone. Time to take my pill. Instead, I unscrewed the top and poured a three-month supply of pills into the river. Then I fastened the top and threw the container into my bag. I felt a sudden pang: should I believe all those stories about manmade estrogen polluting the waterways? Too late.

There are two ways of looking at life.

You can quit while you're ahead: thirty-something passing for twenty-something; never arrested; successfully married. I've gotten away with it for this many years: I can afford to stop.

Or, as Liane says, don't give up this business until it gives *you* up. I've been faithful to the business since my teens. And most of the lies I've told—to my family, to my husband, to countless boyfriends and, on one occasion, the police—have demonstrated unwavering fidelity. To my job.

I've been married to the business for much longer than I've known Matt. A marriage of convenience? Not necessarily.

I strolled back to York Avenue. At Seventy-ninth Street, I wandered into Duane Reade and picked up a small box of condoms, for my appointment with Bernie as a newly minted newlywed.

About the Author

Tracy Quan lives in New York City. Her first novel, *Diary of a Manhattan Call Girl,* was acquired by Revolution Studios for a major motion picture, to be produced by Darren Star, creator of HBO's *Sex and the City.* Her writing has appeared in the *Los Angeles Times Book Review, San Francisco Chronicle, Men's Health, The Philadelphia Inquirer, South China Morning Post, The Globe and Mail,* and many other publications. Visit the author at www.tracyquan.net.

Also by Tracy Quan

Diary of a Manhattan Call Girl
0-609-81010-3
$13.00 paper ($20.00 Canada)

"*Diary of a Manhattan Call Girl* is a nifty trick of a first novel, combining sexual slapstick with luxury-goods, hotel-lobby sociology, exposing female vanity and male self-delusion with equal aplomb."

—James Wolcott,
author of *The Catsitters* and *Attack Poodles and Other Media Mutants*